SECRETS
CAN KILL

ELLEN SHAPIRO

INDIES UNITED PUBLISHING HOUSE, LLC

ISBN13: 978-1-64456-171-3
Library of Congress Control Number:2020943161

INDIES UNITED PUBLISHING HOUSE, LLC
P.O. BOX 3071
QUINCY, IL 62305-3071
www.indiesunited.net

Other Books by the Author

Looking for Laura

For Sam, always in my heart.

CHAPTER 1

I was alone in my office when the call came in. There was silence, and then I heard a woman's voice muffled at the other end of the phone.

"My name is Stephanie Harris. I need to speak with you today. It's urgent," her voice cracking.

The person on the other end of the phone sounded distraught, and I was having a hard time understanding her as she rambled on, choking out her words. I interrupted her. "Ms. Harris, can you come to my office?"

"I could be there at four. Please wait for me," and abruptly hung up.

I wondered what that was all about. It sounded as if she had been crying. I put it out of my mind hoping I'd find out the answers when I met with her.

My name is Tracey Marks and I run an investigation firm. About a year ago my business was on death's door and I was in a panic. I was saved by a gentleman who walked into my office and told me his wife was missing. Though I had no experience with missing person cases, I took the case. It was a gutsy and maybe a dumb thing to do, but fortunately for me it worked out.

Four o'clock came and went and no Ms. Harris. By five-thirty I knew I was stood up, but why? She said she needed to see me right away. Maybe my imagination was getting the best of me but I couldn't shake the feeling that something wasn't right. I left a message on her voicemail just in the off chance something came up or she forgot to call me. I packed everything up and walked outside to the biting, freezing cold. It was the beginning of December. I put up my hood and walked to my apartment on the upper west side, fifteen blocks from my office. Wally, my doorman, greeted me with a big grin.

"Hello Ms. Tracey. I don't see any gloves on your hands. You must be freezing."

"I ran out this morning and left them in my other jacket. You weren't here when I left to remind me," I said with a smile.

Wally has been my doorman since I leased my apartment more than ten years ago. Actually for me, Wally is more than a doorman. I think of him as my guardian angel, always looking after me. Though Wally is probably near seventy, you would never know it, his face as smooth as a baby's. He's big, with a slight paunch around the middle. I waved goodbye as I walked to the elevator.

As I stepped out of the shower my phone beeped. "Hey Susie, what's up?"

"You wanna get some dinner?"

"Sure, I'll meet you at Anton's at seven-thirty. Anton's is a neighborhood Italian restaurant in walking distance for both of us and our favorite place to go. The food is really good, especially their linguini and clams. It's not as noisy as some of the trendier places.

I slipped on a heavy cotton pullover, zipped up my jeans, grabbed my gloves and hooded jacket and walked to Anton's. Susie was already at the bar chatting with John, the bartender. Susie Jacobs has been my best friend since high school. We are completely the opposite in every way. Susie is about 5'2", boyish figure with red curly hair, and a positive, outgoing personality. I on the other hand am 5'8" with straight light brown hair cut to my chin, a bit more curvy than Susie, with a less positive attitude and a bit more reserve. I have to mention Susie is six months older than me, a sore spot with her.

"How's Mark?" I asked as I sat down. I can't believe it's been a year since you guys shacked up and you're still together," I said grinning.

"To tell you the truth I can't believe it myself. I thought we would have killed each other by now. And to answer your question, Mark's good. I left him hunched over his laptop frantically working on a presentation that he's giving tomorrow. A client is interested in buying a company that Mark has been researching."

I ordered a glass of Merlot. As John was putting my wine down we were called to our table.

"How are you ladies doing tonight?" Our favorite waiter Sam asked.

"Starved, as usual," I said. "I'm ready to order my usual linguini and clams and your house salad."

"I'll have the lasagna and your house salad. And another glass of Chianti," Susie said.

"Something weird happened today," I said to Susie. "A woman called me up this morning sounding very distressed. We set up an appointment for four o'clock but she never showed. I left a voice message and haven't heard back. Normally I wouldn't think too much of it but something doesn't add up. She sounded so upset."

"Try her again in the morning. Maybe she just changed her mind or got distracted."

"I guess. How was court today?"

"The judge ruled in my client's favor. Now we have to pray the husband ponies up the alimony and support each month."

"Well we can always hope for the best," trying to sound optimistic. Susie is a matrimonial attorney at a small law firm in Manhattan. I know I can always count on her for advice when I'm stumped on a case.

"How's it going without Carolyn?"

I hired Carolyn last year when business started to pick up. Unfortunately after I trained her, she decided to leave and follow her boyfriend to California.

"It's fairly quiet with Christmas coming in a few weeks, and fortunately the two estate cases she was working on before she left were completed."

"Are you looking to hire someone else?"

"I think I'll wait a while and see how it goes."

After dessert, we called it a night. I thought I would give Ms. Harris a call in the morning

The next day I was up by six and headed out to the gym. I did my usual routine, consisting of weights, sit-ups, push-ups and running on the treadmill. I showered and put on my standard work clothes, jeans, a pullover sweater and short black boots. It makes my life a lot simpler when I don't have to figure out what to wear each day.

On my way to the office I stopped at my favorite place for coffee, the Coffee Pot. Anna handed me my coffee and Banana Nut muffin before I had a chance to open my mouth. If you can't tell, I'm a creature of habit.

"One of these days I'm going to surprise you and order something completely different."

"I can't wait," Anna chuckled.

I walked into my office balancing my coffee, muffin and laptop bag. I called Ms. Harris right away, still no answer. I sat there mulling over what to do. I found an address for her in Scarsdale, New York from an internet website. I headed out to get my car that I keep parked in my building garage. I still had my Beetle even though I could probably afford a bigger car. Getting into parking spots is a lot easier with a small car, especially living in the city, and my patience for finding parking spots is almost non-existent. That's why I try to walk to work most days.

Luckily, there was very little traffic on the way up. As soon as I was on the Bronx River Parkway, the scenery changed. I saw grass with lots of trees even though they were bare. Unfortunately my thoughts were on Ms. Harris and not on the landscape. I couldn't imagine why Ms. Harris never showed for her appointment. There was such urgency in her voice. I hoped nothing happened to her.

Ms. Harris' house was on a beautiful tree lined street with brick colonial homes. When I arrived at her address there were two police cars parked in front. What the hell was going on? I parked down the street and sat in my car wondering what to do. The thoughts running through my head were making my heart beat faster. I got out and slowly walked up to her front door.

CHAPTER 2

There was a police officer standing at the door. "Excuse me," I said. "Can you tell me what happened?"

"I'm sorry miss this is a crime scene. I need you to leave."

"My name is Tracey Marks and I'm a private investigator. Stephanie Harris called me yesterday and we were scheduled to meet, but she never showed. Did something happen to her?"

"Please wait here."

The officer went inside and a few moments later another policeman came out.

"I'm Detective Lucas. Can I help you?"

"I hope so. Ms. Harris called me yesterday. She was very upset and said it was urgent that she meet with me. She was supposed to be at my office at four o'clock yesterday but never showed and she never canceled her appointment. I was worried since I thought it was odd that she never made it to my office and wasn't answering her phone. Has something happened to her?"

"I can't give you any information. What can you tell me about your conversation with Ms. Harris?"

"Unfortunately, not more than I already told you. She seemed agitated and I was having a hard time understanding her."

"So she never disclosed why she wanted to see you?"

"No. She hung up abruptly."

"Can you give this officer your information, and if I have any further questions I'll contact you."

He didn't have to tell me. I knew it was her. Though I never met Ms. Harris, the fact that she reached out to me, I somehow felt responsible to find out why she called.

As I was walking back to my car my thoughts were interrupted by the buzzing of my phone. "Hi Jack."

"You sound like a woman deep in concentration. I like it."

"Flattery will get you, well we'll see where it'll get you," I said smiling. Jack is a private investigator who I met on my missing person case, and is now someone who I'm very fond of. He lives in the Berkshire's, which makes our relationship sort of long distance which is fine with me since I like living alone.

I filled Jack in on my conversation with Ms. Harris and what I found out when I went to her house.

"Poor lady, why do I get the feeling you're going to stick your nose where it doesn't belong."

"I resent that," with no real conviction behind it. "I realize I didn't even know the woman but if you would have heard her on the phone."

"So what's your plan?"

"Well I don't exactly have one, but I thought I would come back to Scarsdale tomorrow and talk to some of the neighbors. The police of course aren't telling me anything. I think she was murdered. If you could have heard her, you would know something was wrong. Since I don't have anything pressing at the moment, I thought I'd do some snooping."

"Keep out of trouble. I'll see you Saturday."

On the drive back my mind drifted to the day Danny almost killed me. Danny injected himself in my life pretending we met by chance. For Danny it was his idea of fun to be my boyfriend knowing I was investigating the disappearance of Laura Matthews, the woman he killed. I'm lucky to be alive. He was not so lucky. He's spending the next twenty years behind bars.

I zipped my car into a spot two blocks from my office, barely wedging my way in. My office is in a brownstone. The first floor has three offices, mine, Max Goldstein, a tax accountant, and the third suite is an insurance company owned by my Cousin Alan. The second floor apartment is rented to a professional couple, the Alvarez'. I poked my head in Cousin Alan's office.

"Hey Margaret, how are the rug rats?" Margaret is Cousin Alan's assistant.

"They're good, though I think Tommy might have an earache, only his third time this year."

"Ugh. Poor guy, is Alan busy?"

"Just go right in."

"Hey," I said opening his door."

"My favorite cousin in the world, how's everything?" Alan said.

"Good. Is Michael sleeping through the night yet?"

"Finally, Patty and I are ecstatic. Why don't you come over Friday night say around seven o'clock. Maybe we'll order in."

"Okay. I'll bring dessert." Alan and Patty are in their forties. They had no plans on having children, but Michael was a very welcome surprise. I'm not sure I have the maternal gene and my biological clock might be ticking.

I walked across to my office. With nothing urgent on my agenda, I caught up with bills and sent out a report and invoice for a background check a client wanted on someone he was going into business with. I called it quits around five and headed home.

In the morning I headed up to Scarsdale. I was hoping to find out something about Stephanie Harris. I was relieved to see there were no police cars in front of her house. I started directly across the street from Harris' house. The first two doors I knocked on nobody answered. The third door was the charm.

An elderly woman maybe around seventy-five opened the door. Her short gray hair was perfectly in place, just like I remember my grandmother's hair when she came back from the hairdresser.

"Can I help you?"

"Yes. My name is Tracey Marks and I was contacted by your neighbor, Stephanie Harris. She made an appointment to talk with me on Monday but never showed." I gave the woman my card.

"Oh, wasn't that horrible. Poor, Stephanie. It's freezing out, would you like to come in?"

I was led into a warm kitchen that probably hadn't been remodeled since the sixties. It had wood cabinets with an aqua stove and countertops to match. The flooring was brown tile and in the middle of the kitchen was a Formica table with red vinyl cushions on the chairs.

"Sit dear. My name is Lottie. I just made some coffee. Can I get you a cup?"

"That would be great, black, no sugar."

"When I was younger I used to drink it that way, but now I like it a little sweeter. So I don't understand, why would Stephanie call you?" as she handed me a cup of coffee.

"I don't know. She sounded very upset. When I stopped by yesterday there were police cars in front of her house."

Before I had a chance to continue, Lottie said. "She was murdered. Do you believe it, right in this lovely neighborhood. They think it was a robbery."

"Really, how do you know that?"

"A police officer stopped by to find out if I saw anything."

"And what did you tell him?"

"I didn't see anything. It was just like on TV. No suspicious cars on the street. Maybe I should have paid more attention."

"You couldn't have known. Was Ms. Harris married?"

"She was divorced, quite a few years now, though I have seen her with one gentleman on several occasions. I hope you don't think I'm one of those elderly nosey neighbors with nothing to do."

"Not at all." Little white lies come with the territory. "Did you ever see them arguing?"

"Not that I remember. Why are you asking these questions?"

"I'm just concerned since she missed her appointment without contacting me."

"Well I guess that is odd. I know her to be a very responsible person. She always came by to ask me if I needed anything from the store. She was such a wonderful neighbor."

"Do you know if Ms. Harris has any children or siblings?"

"Oh yes. She has a lovely daughter, Christine. I believe she lives in Scarsdale, but I'm not positive."

"Is she married?"

"I'm pretty sure she's single. She's only in her twenties."

"Have you lived here long?"

"I've lived in this house for forty years. My husband, George, passed away a few years ago. It's lonely without him. I have friends but it's not the same."

"Oh, one last question, do you happen to know who found

Ms. Harris?"

"It was a friend. I used to see them jogging in the morning."

"Well, I don't want to take up any more of your time. You've been very helpful."

"I do hope they catch that awful person. I'm afraid I might be next."

"Please try not to worry," I said as Lottie walked me to the door.

On the drive back to the office I thought about what Lottie said. The police told her it was a robbery. Right after Stephanie calls me in a panic, her place is robbed. Can it just be a coincidence?

CHAPTER 3

"You're not going to believe this," I said when Susie answered the phone. "The woman I told you about is dead, and the police think it was a robbery."

"Whoa Nellie, slow down and start from the beginning."

I explained to Susie about going up to Scarsdale and speaking to the neighbor.

"Holy crap, you might be right."

"I was thinking..."

"Oh, no, not a good sign."

"Just hold on a second. I thought I would get in contact with the daughter and explain the situation. Maybe she can convince the police it wasn't a robbery."

"That's a good idea. At least that way you've done whatever you could."

"Yeah, but."

"But what?"

"I don't know. It would be great if I could investigate what happened to Stephanie Harris."

"Yes, but you won't get paid for it."

"You're right. If only I would have gone up to see her last night, she might still be alive."

"You don't know that. She may have been killed before she had a chance to talk with you. Speak to the daughter. Maybe she can shed some light on what was going on with her mother recently."

"That was my plan."

"Let me know what she says."

Before heading into the office, I stopped by a coffee shop nearby and picked up a tuna fish sandwich for lunch. Just as I was opening my office door, I heard a familiar voice calling out my name.

"Max, good to see ya, how are you?" Max Goldstein is the tax accountant I mentioned.

"I'm fine Tracey. I've been meaning to talk with you."

"Is everything okay?"

"Wonderful. After talking it over with my wife, I finally decided it's time to retire. My lease is up in June and we've always wanted to travel and see the world before we both got too old to enjoy it."

"I'm happy for you, but it won't be the same. Does Alan know?"

"I told him this morning. I'm meeting a client for lunch so I have to run. Bye."

Max is in his late sixties but has more energy than I do. Between playing tennis, golf and his business, he's like the energizer bunny.

While devouring my tuna sandwich, I looked up Christine Harris on the internet. I think I found the right person but there was no telephone number, just an address. Most people under forty don't usually have a landline, just a cell phone which I then have to track down the number.

I searched in my investigative databases under Christine Harris with the city and state and it had a telephone number listed. Her address was an apartment building in Scarsdale. I called her number and it went straight to voice mail. I left a message explaining who I was and to call me. I realized she might be too upset to contact me right away.

About an hour later, my phone beeped. "Hello."

"Is this Tracey Marks?"

"Yes, can I help you?"

"This is Christine Harris. You left me a voice mail."

"Thank you for calling me back." I wasn't expecting to hear from her so soon. "I'm so sorry about your mother."

"Did you know her?" sniffling as she spoke.

"No, and that's the reason I'm calling. I know this is a terrible time for you, but I was wondering if we could meet. I'm a private investigator and your mom called me the day she died. It's about a conversation I had with her."

"Really, I had no idea. What did she say?"

"It would be better if we spoke in person."

"This is really a bad time but if you can meet me in Scarsdale at the Parkway Cafe in town at five, I can see you for a few minutes. Otherwise the next few days will be very busy."

Christine told me she'd be wearing a blue parka. I made it up there by four-thirty and walked around the town. I couldn't pass up going into the bakery right next to the cafe. I ogled all the great looking pastries, and decided I would return for a miniature chocolate babka for dessert later.

I eyed Christine as soon as I walked into the coffee shop. She was already sitting at a booth. I slid in opposite her. Christine was very attractive with fabulous blond curls down to her shoulders, big blue eyes and a perfectly straight nose. She looked miserable.

"So what's this about?"

The waitress came over and we both ordered coffee.

"Your mother called me on Monday. I was having trouble understanding her. She was very upset and was having a hard time speaking. She asked if she could see me right away and we set up an appointment for four o'clock that afternoon. She never showed. I called and left two messages but never heard back from her. I just had a feeling something wasn't right, so I went up to her house yesterday to find out what happened and that's when I saw the police cars."

"The police think it's a robbery. There was some jewelry missing and the place was turned upside down," Christine said barely audible.

"I'm not so sure it was a robbery. Was there anything going on with your mother? Did she say anything to you?"

"I usually speak to my mother everyday but lately she's ignored my calls and when I did speak to her, she sounded distant. She never told you why she wanted to see you?" as she was wiping away the tears falling down her cheeks.

"No. As I said we were going to speak in person. Was there anyone in her life she was having problems with?"

"Not that I'm aware of. I know she was seeing someone, but she never mentioned anything was wrong.

"Did the police say when she died?"

"Until the autopsy is done they can't be positive, but they thought it may have been sometime Monday afternoon. She was lying there all that time," she said as her voice trailed off. "Oh my God! My poor mother," as her face fell down into her arms.

After a few moments I asked Christine. "Did your mom work?"

"She does, I mean did. I'm sorry I still can't believe she died. She had a web design business with a partner, Jennifer Daniels. But I don't think they were having any issues. I can't believe my mother didn't confide in me. I could have helped her."

"The thing is we don't know what was going on in her life. Maybe she didn't want to burden you. She may have been trying to protect you."

"I'm just having such a hard time understanding any of this. Do you think she called you because she was in danger?"

"I don't know. All I do know is that she was desperate enough to call a private investigator. When is the funeral?"

"Friday. I still can't believe I'm never going to see her again."

When I left Christine, I wasn't sure if I would ever hear from her. I wanted her to hire me to look into her mother's death, but I couldn't tell her that. For all I knew it could have been a robbery, but my gut said no.

CHAPTER 4

When I got home I changed into my running clothes and my new sneakers that flash in the dark and did a three-mile loop around the park. If Stephanie Harris had just come in before she died, I would probably have a retainer in hand and I could investigate her death. Sometimes I wonder about the thoughts that pop into my head.

As I was lying in bed trying to fall asleep I remembered I never went back for the Chocolate Babka. Rats!

The following morning I was in my office by eight-thirty munching on my banana nut muffin. My computer up and ready, I googled Stephanie and her business partner, Jennifer Daniels. I found their business, HarrisDaniels Web Designers, LLC. Their website of course was what I would expect from web designers, montage video with colorful photos dancing all around. My website on the other hand was an embarrassment compared to theirs, pretty straight forward, just the facts ma'am.

I dialed their number, waiting to leave a voice message.

"Hello."

For a moment I was taken by surprise. I wasn't expecting anyone to answer.

"Yes. Hello. I'm looking for Ms. Daniels."

"This is she."

"My name is Tracey Marks and I'm a private investigator. I was contacted by Stephanie Harris before she died."

"I don't understand."

"I believe Stephanie may have been in some sort of trouble."

"Well that's crazy. Are you sure you're talking about my partner?"

"I know this is a difficult time for you, but could we meet? I think it's important."

There was silence at the other end of the phone. "Ms.

Daniels?"

"I'm sorry. Stephanie's death has been such a shock. I'm not thinking straight. Yes of course we can meet. Where are you?"

"I'm in Manhattan, but I can be up to you in an hour."

"There's a coffee place in Bronxville called Slave to the Grind. I can be there by eleven."

"Great. I'll see you soon."

I grabbed a cab and picked up my car from the garage. With my GPS on, I arrived in Bronxville with no problems, but finding a parking spot was a challenge. Just when I was about to go around for the second time, someone pulled out right in front of me. I threw quarters in the meter and walked a half block to the coffee place. It had a few tables in the front and one or two in the back. I spotted Jennifer Daniels sitting at one of the tables in the back. She was easily recognizable from the description she gave me, short black hair, cut very close to her head with wire-rim glasses. I pegged her for about forty-five give a few years in either direction.

"Hi Jennifer, I'm glad you could meet me. I know this must be unimaginable for you."

"I don't think I really believe she's dead. Besides my business partner, she was my best friend. You said she called you?"

"Yes, on Monday. She sounded upset. She was supposed to come in to see me that day, but she never showed. I had a bad feeling since she never returned my phone calls. I went up to her house on Tuesday and the police were there."

"Yes. Her daughter Christine contacted me and said the police think it was a robbery. Poor, Christine."

"It seems like too much of a coincidence, Stephanie calling me and turning up dead the same day. I wonder if there had been other robberies in the neighborhood." I doubted it.

"I can't imagine what she was so upset about. She didn't say anything to me."

"Her daughter told me that her mother had been distant lately which was out of character for her. Was there anything you noticed that was out of the ordinary lately? Obviously she was deeply upset about something since she wanted to talk with a private investigator."

"Well, I'm not sure," wiping away the tears from her eyes.

"Why do you say that?"

"As I said, she was my best friend. I knew something was wrong, but I didn't think it was anything serious. She seemed a little down but when I asked her what was going on, she said nothing she couldn't handle and changed the subject. Do you think someone killed her? But what could've been going on in her life that someone would want to hurt Stephanie? It just doesn't make sense. She was the nicest person..." her voice breaking.

"I know it's hard to imagine. Her daughter mentioned a boyfriend. Do you know if there were any problems?"

"Not that I'm aware of. She really liked Andrew and they seemed to get along well."

"How long were they going out?"

"Almost a year. I thought they might marry eventually."

"Would you happen to know Andrew's last name?"

"It's Carter. Did her daughter hire you to look into what happened to Stephanie?"

"No, I thought I would follow up to satisfy myself that it was a robbery and not foul play. Would you happen to know Andrew's telephone number?"

Jennifer gave me his telephone number and I left her sitting at the table looking lost. I'm not sure if it's a wise thing for me to get involved in something if it wasn't a robbery. But curiosity was getting the best of me.

When I got up the next morning I decided to go to the funeral. I dragged myself out of bed at six-fifteen and did a two-mile run around my neighborhood. When I returned, I showered and fixed myself some breakfast. Well actually I poured some milk into a bowl filled with Cheerios. I stopped at Starbucks before making my way up to Our Lady of Fatima Church in Scarsdale.

The church was packed. I sat in the back hoping to get a glimpse of the mourners as they were leaving the church. The only person who spoke at the service was Christine. As I listened to her speak, I realized tears were trickling down my cheeks. I was back at my mother's funeral, the worst day of my life. Alan and Susie were by my side, but the loneliness I felt as they lowered my mother into the ground had consumed me.

My eyes opened at the sound of a baby crying. Christine was walking out of the church with her father, or so I presumed, by her side. He was very distinguished looking, in his fifties, over six feet tall with a full head of dark brown hair with graying sideburns. Walking next to them was an elderly couple, maybe in their late seventies, early eighties. They were both holding handkerchiefs dabbing their eyes. I wondered if they were Stephanie's parents. It never even dawned on me that Stephanie's parents might still be alive. How horrible for them. I spotted Stephanie's business partner and mouthed hello to her.

I hung outside until the procession got underway. Was I hoping there was someone suspicious hanging around who would confess when I confronted them? Of course! But alas, I don't even think it's that simple in the movies, just in my own imagination.

CHAPTER 5

Friday night I arrived at Cousin Alan's brownstone promptly at seven with an apple pie from my neighborhood bakery. A place I frequent way too often.

I was greeted by Patty and my adorable baby cousin Michael.

I handed Patty the apple pie in exchange for taking Michael. "Well hello there my little man. How are you doing?"

"He's doing just fine, giving us a run for our money."

We went into the living room where I plopped myself down on the floor with Michael. Alan inherited his brownstone from his grandfather who had a seat on the New York Stock Exchange. They renovated a little over a year ago, right around the time Patty unexpectedly found out she was pregnant. Patty is a lawyer advocating for children's rights, and fortunately she had just taken in a partner that made it easier for her to take time off and keep a lighter schedule.

"So, are you ready for college yet?" I asked Michael. "Because I know you're a genius."

"I think you give him way too much credit, though he is showing signs of crawling at a record speed," Patty grinned.

"Did I hear you say my boy is a genius?" Alan said, walking into the room.

"I predict he'll win the Nobel Peace Prize for single handedly bringing about world peace," I said.

"Well for now it's bedtime. The world will have to wait." Alan picked Michael up and carried him off to bed. "And don't talk about anything I should know about until I join you ladies."

"How about a glass of wine," Patty said.

"I would love one, whatever you have open," as I followed Patty into the kitchen.

"I decided to try a new dish instead of ordering in. I hope you like it."

Patty is a great cook. "So I'm a guinea pig?"

"Well, we all are."

"We all are what?" Alan said, joining us in the kitchen.

"You'll find out," Patty said. "Let's eat."

The dining room was modern, with a glass table, high back upholstered chairs and a beige sisal rug under the table.

"This looks great. What is it?" I said.

"It's lamb in a curry sauce with basmati rice. I promise it won't bite. So how is Jack?"

"I love that you don't mince words," Alan said looking at Patty. "But as long as Patty's asking, how are you guys doing?"

"Actually, pretty good. It's nice to be dating someone normal or as normal as a guy could be."

"I resent that," Alan said giving me the evil eye.

"Present company excluded. I like that I can be myself around him."

"Well that's real progress. I'm glad to hear it," Patty said. "How's work?"

"Well that depends." I explained what happened to Stephanie Harris and my subsequent conversations. "This is really good," I said, taking a second helping. "So what's your take on the situation?"

"You may be right," Alan said. "It does seem like too much of a coincidence to be a robbery. Look, I think it's great that you want to do what you think is right by the woman, but this is a big undertaking, and if she was murdered, it could be dangerous."

"So what are you suggesting I do, just leave it alone?"

"Whether it's a robbery or she was killed intentionally, the police are still going to investigate," Alan said.

"That's true, but they probably won't look into her life, not if they think it's a robbery."

"Why don't you wait a week or two and then talk to the daughter again and see what she has to say. Maybe she'll hire you," Patty interjected. "If someone did kill her, it won't really matter whether you wait a little while."

"I guess. The best I can say is I'll think about it. Now, how about dessert?"

On my Uber ride home, I kept thinking about Stephanie

Harris and what I should do about her death. I know the sensible thing would be to wait like Patty and Alan suggested, but from working my last case, I realized how much I relished trying to solve Laura's disappearance. It was so different from the run of the mill cases I normally got involved in. Still, I didn't have a client.

On Saturday I did my morning cleaning ritual of vacuuming, scrubbing the bathroom, wiping down the kitchen and dusting. Though I like a clean apartment, the thought of having to do it every week is not something I look forward to. It goes in the category of working out—neither appeal to me, but a necessary evil.

I was in the middle of drying myself off from my shower when the intercom buzzer rang. I quickly finished drying and wrapped the towel around me as I heard the doorbell.

When I opened the door, Jack smiled and said, "I can't think of a lovelier greeting," as he closed the door behind him wrapping his arms around me, my towel falling to the floor. The next hour or so we tangled with the bedroom sheets.

"Very nice to see you," Jack said as he was holding me close to him, his fingers combing through my hair.

Jack is very easy on the eyes. He's around 6'2", solidly built, his skin the color of cocoa. There is an intelligent look about him. Maybe it had something to do with his wire-rim glasses, and if I didn't mention it, very sexy.

"Likewise, now how about some lunch?"

"Are you making or am I buying?"

"Do I detect some sarcasm in your voice?"

"Would I besmirch your cooking abilities?"

"Yes you would, but I can put together a simple sandwich."

"Yes you can, and I deeply apologize if I have offended you," putting his hands over his heart.

After eating turkey sandwiches and catching up from the week, I poured myself a glass of wine and handed Jack a beer, and we went back into the bedroom. One of the pluses of his absence during the week, I'm always looking forward to our time together.

In the evening we met Susie and Mark for dinner, and on Sunday, Jack and I ventured out into the freezing cold and went to see the Christmas tree at Rockefeller Center. Jack had never been to Rockefeller Center and was enjoying the ice skaters as they circled around the rink, some holding onto the railing, afraid of falling, some gliding around the ice gracefully. I looked at him as his eyes were glued to the rink.

"Have you ever been ice skating?" I asked Jack.

"Once, and that was enough. My ass got a real workout."

It started to snow very lightly as we meandered over to Saks to see their Christmas window display. Each window had a different scene from animated stories, Snow White and the Seven Dwarfs, Rudolph and his Reindeers and a Charlie Brown Christmas.

Afterward we rode the subway to Chinatown for dinner. Since there aren't any decent Chinese restaurants in Stockbridge where Jack lives, he really enjoys having as close to authentic Chinese food as you can get here.

Jack left early Monday morning since he had interviews on a case he was involved with. A trial was coming up soon and he was on a deadline. I walked Jack to his car and gave him a fierce kiss right before he drove off.

I picked up a poppy seed muffin on my way in to the office. As soon as I walked in, I put on the coffee machine. Five minutes later the door opened. It was Christine Harris.

"I hope I'm not intruding."

"No, please come in. Can I get you coffee or tea?" I was overjoyed to see her. You would've thought Leonardo DiCaprio just walked in.

"Coffee is fine, milk, no sugar."

I poured Ms. Harris a cup of coffee and we went into my office.

"Please sit down."

"I'm sorry to come unannounced. I've been so upset and didn't know what to do. When you first told me about my mother I thought you may have been exaggerating the situation, but deep down I knew you weren't. There were too many little signs that I

21

didn't pick up on."

"How could you. Whatever was going on with your mother, I believe she may have been hiding it from you, most likely she didn't want to get you involved."

"I spoke to my father. He thought it was a good idea to hire you since the police have no reason to believe it was anything else but a robbery. As I had mentioned, the place was in shambles and her jewelry was taken."

I could hardly contain myself. "I want you to know that I'm not sure where this is going to lead, but I do know that your mother was frightened of someone or something."

"I have to know why she was killed," as tears were now streaming down her face.

"I'll email you my retainer agreement. Please sign it and send it back with my initial retainer of $5,000. In the meantime, I would like you to put together a list of your mom's friends, boyfriends and anyone else you can think of, including your father. Do you have a recent photo that I can have of your mom? And can I please have her cell phone number so I can find out who she's been in touch with lately?"

After Ms. Harris left, I called the company I use to obtain Stephanie Harris' cell phone records.

I went back into my office and called Susie. "Hey, I have great news."

"I'm excited."

"I was hired by the daughter to look into her mother's death."

"That's fantastic. Why don't we go out for a drink Wednesday and you can tell me everything."

My euphoria was quickly wearing off as I realized I've taken on a case that might be out of my league. Laura's case was different. When her husband hired me, Laura was missing, not dead. I thought all I had to do was track her down. Now I'm hunting for a murderer. I can hear my heart thumping against my chest.

CHAPTER 6

When I calmed myself down, I knew the only way to tackle the problem and my fear was to get into action. I texted Jack about my good fortune, and he texted back with a thumbs up.

As I was ready to call it quits for the day, I noticed an email from Christine Harris. Attached was a short list of people her mother knew: Two friends, her current boyfriend, Andrew Carter and her ex-husband, Philip Harris. It was a start.

I packed everything I was working on into my briefcase and locked up. Snow was coming down in large flakes. I wondered if it was snowing where Jack lives. By the time I put my car safely in the garage, the roads were already slippery.

"Hey Wally, what's the good word?"

"Ms. Tracey. I'm glad to see you have your gloves on today. I wouldn't want you getting sick."

"I made sure I had them since I didn't want any grief from you," I said winking.

"It looks like we're in for a lot of snow. When I was growing up in Alabama snow was something I wished for. I was envious of children I saw on TV playing in the snow."

"I bet you're not so envious now. Well don't stand out in the cold too long," I said.

"Okay boss. Have a nice night."

As soon as I walked into my apartment I went straight to the bathroom, shedding my clothes and took a long, hot shower. Afterward I warmed up leftover Chinese food and ate in bed watching the Bosch series on Amazon. Bosch is a police detective in the Michael Connolly novels, my idea of a wonderful evening. Just as the Assistant Chief of Police's son was murdered, my phone buzzed.

"Hey Jack. Is it snowing in your neck of the woods?"

"It just started but it's coming down pretty heavy. They're predicting around ten inches. Have you come down to earth since you got the case?"

"I've definitely landed. What's the saying, 'be careful what you wish for.' I may have taken on more than I can handle."

"How about hiring a new assistant?"

"If only that would solve the problem, besides I've been thinking."

"Not a good sign. Continue."

"I'm not sure how I really feel about having an assistant. I mean I liked Carolyn and she was a fast learner, but the truth is I would rather have the office all to myself. You know small talk is not one of my strong suits. It felt weird sometimes."

"Believe it or not, I completely understand."

"That's why I let you share my bed. Am I a horrible person?"

"You're just not used to sharing your space with anyone. Being an only child also, it's understandable."

"I'm glad you don't think I'm a complete nut."

"Never. The trial is scheduled for next week so I don't think I'll be able to get down there this weekend. I still have witnesses to prep and I need to locate someone who seems to have left the area."

"I'll survive. It'll give me time to start interviewing people on the case, and since I'm by myself in the office, I'll have to handle whatever else comes in."

"If you need any help just holler."

"Will do. Enjoy the snow," I said.

In some ways Jack and I are alike. We're both independent and neither of us feel the need to talk just to fill in the silences. I turned my attention to the third episode of Bosch and got ready for bed.

When I looked out my bedroom window in the morning the snow was still coming down, but just lightly. I opened up my emails and saw the cell phone records were back. I decided to work on the phone records from home and try to set up some interviews. I meticulously went through every number and looked up who they belonged to. As I was compiling a list of people, I noticed there were two numbers that were probably from burner phones and wouldn't be traceable. I was curious but decided to wait until I set up my interviews.

I called the boyfriend first. "Mr. Carter?"

"Yes."

"My name is Tracey Marks, and I was hired to look into the death of Stephanie Harris. I was told that you and Stephanie were dating. I'm sorry for your loss."

"Can I ask who hired you?"

"Her daughter."

"I see. But aren't the police looking into her death?"

"They are, but I'm investigating a different angle. Do you have time tomorrow?"

"I guess tomorrow will be okay, say around noon. There's a place in White Plains called the Iron Tomato."

"I'll find it."

Before hanging up, I gave Andrew Carter a short description of myself, leaving out how gorgeous I am.

The next call was to Stephanie's ex-husband, Philip Harris. No answer so I left a message.

While I was looking over the cell phone records for the umpteenth time to see if I missed anything, Philip Harris called me back. We set up a time to meet the next day at two o'clock at his office in White Plains.

I tried one of the numbers listed from the burner phone and it was disconnected. The second one, I left my name and telephone number but did not leave a message.

A few minutes later my phone buzzed. "Hello."

"Who is this?

"This is Tracey Marks."

"I don't know a Tracey Marks. You must have the wrong number."

"This number came up regarding Stephanie Harris."

"Never heard of her."

The next thing I heard was a click.

CHAPTER 7

That was definitely weird. I called Jack and explained what happened.

"Well if he was somehow involved in her death, he was certainly going to deny knowing her. Don't call the number again. I know you didn't tell him anything but I'm sure he is figuring it out as we speak."

"You're scaring me."

"That was my intention."

"Is there any way you can trace the number?"

"I don't think so but give it to me anyway. I can ask around but don't get your hopes up. Chances are unless you contact him further, he won't bother you."

"Why don't I feel comforted?"

When I hung up I felt a chill go through my body. I wanted to crawl back into bed and get under the covers. Why was the man at the other end of the phone so hostile? Did he know Stephanie? My mind was swirling with thoughts. I showered and put on my sweats and a sweater over a long sleeve cotton pullover.

I ventured into the kitchen and stared into my refrigerator willing some comfort food would appear. No such luck. Instead I scrambled two eggs and defrosted a sesame bagel. I didn't realize it was almost twelve o'clock. I always thought it would be cool to hire a cook to prepare my meals. I would come home, open the refrigerator and voila, a wonderful home cooked meal would appear, another fantasy of mine.

As I was munching on my bagel I kept thinking about the phone call from the anonymous person. I wondered if he was connected in any way to Stephanie's death, and if so, how was I going to find him? Was I asking for trouble?

I pulled out my corkboard and 5x7 index cards and wrote each person's name that I knew was connected to Stephanie. So far there was very little I knew about her. Hopefully I'll know more after I interview her ex-husband and her boyfriend.

The following morning I was up by seven. I grabbed my gym bag, bundled up and jogged to the gym. I had to be careful since the sidewalks were a little slippery. After my work out, I stopped at a café near my building for breakfast.

"Hi Tracey, sit anywhere you like," Gina said to me.

She brought coffee over as soon as I sat down. "It's freezing out there," I said.

"I haven't seen you for a while. Where you been hiding?"

"I'm trying to eat healthier but for how long can I resist your delicious pancakes and crispy bacon."

"I know what you mean. I'm going on a diet the first of the year. And this time I plan to stick to it. I have to have more will power working here."

"I'd be a horse if I had your job. I'd be eating everything in sight. The only way I can keep my weight down from all the sweets and ice cream I eat is going to the gym and running."

"I wish I had the time to work out."

"Well thanks for breakfast Gina. I'm off to fight crime."

When I got up to White Plains I parked in a lot in back of the Iron Tomato and fed the meter. They were only accepting quarters. Andrew Carter waved to me as I walked in. He got up and shook my hand. I didn't know what I was expecting but he wasn't it. He looked to be ten years younger than Stephanie and kind of disheveled looking. Half his shirt was sticking out of his pants and his hair had that, just got out of bed look. He pushed up his wire-framed glasses from his nose as we spoke. There was a certain charm to him if you could get past the exterior. He was eating lunch.

"So you mentioned you were investigating Stephanie's death," he said as I sat down.

"Yes." I explained my short but upsetting exchange with Stephanie and my conversation with her daughter. He listened intently. "Did she mention anything to you that was bothering her?"

"The past couple of weeks I noticed a change in Stephanie."

"Like what?"

"She was distracted. For example, we were supposed to meet for dinner at seven at a restaurant in Larchmont a few weeks ago, but she never showed. She said she completely forgot which was not like her at all. As a matter of fact she was always on time, never even a minute late. Other times I'd be talking to her and she had that faraway look as if she wasn't even listening. I didn't know what to make of it."

"Did she give a reason for what was going on?"

"Not really. Just that she was distracted with work. I didn't believe her."

"Besides being distracted was there anything else in her behavior that seemed out of character for her?"

"I can't think of anything else, except…"

"Except what?"

"Well once she made a remark in passing that I thought was a little strange."

"What was that?"

"She said something like, the past sometimes has a way of coming back to haunt you."

"That is strange. Did she tell you what she meant by that remark?"

"When I asked her, she just shrugged her shoulders and changed the subject."

"Do you know if the police have any leads?" I asked.

"I haven't spoken to Stephanie's daughter Christine since the funeral." I noticed a hesitation in his voice as he was fiddling with his napkin.

"Is there a problem between you and Christine?"

"I don't think Christine approved of me. For one thing I'm several years younger than Stephanie. I'm also currently between jobs. I know she had voiced her disapproval to her mother."

"What do you do for a living?"

"I'm a teacher or I was a teacher. I went back to school for a masters in languages. I speak several languages fluently and I would like to be a translator. I guess I thought it would be easy to get a job in the field. So far I haven't landed anything."

"By the way, where were you last Monday in the late afternoon?"

"You think I killed her? Are you crazy? I loved her. I have to go."

"Don't go. I'm sorry if I offended you, but I had to ask."

"I have to go anyway. I hope you find out what happened to Stephanie."

I guess I could have been more subtle but I was still surprised at his abrupt exit. Was he hiding something? I went up to the counter and bought a chicken salad sandwich and sat back down. As I was eating, I was going over my conversation with Andrew Carter. Though I never met Stephanie Harris, Andrew seemed like a mismatch, but with love who can tell? He seemed like a nice enough fella, but what do I know? I had dated my stalker who injected himself into my life on the last case I was involved in.

I fed more quarters in the meter and walked over to 175 Main Street. The directory let me know the building was filled with lawyers and Mr. Harris was listed as a Real Estate attorney. I went up to the third floor and introduced myself to the receptionist. She told me to take a seat. Why do all receptionists tell you to take a seat? I think they need a new line.

A few minutes later Mr. Harris presented himself. "Come in Ms. Marks."

The room was stacked with files everywhere. It certainly had a lived in look. There were photos everywhere. "May I take a look?"

"Of course, this is a photo of Stephanie and Christine."

"They look so much alike," I said.

"I know we weren't married anymore but the thought of what happened to her makes me sick. And Christine is devastated. Tell me why you think she wasn't murdered accidentally?"

"Stephanie called me last Monday. She could hardly get the words out. She said she needed to see me right away. We set up an appointment for that afternoon. She never showed. I didn't know what to make of it. Sometimes people have second thoughts. It happens. I called her twice, but both times it went to voice mail. I tried again in the morning but no luck. Though people do change their minds, I couldn't let it go. That's when I went up there and found the police outside Stephanie's house."

"What concerns me is that the police think it was a robbery, and whoever did it might not have expected Stephanie to be home. It's too much of a coincidence. I don't buy it. I think she planned on meeting me with whatever was troubling her, but someone got to her first."

"I just can't imagine what was going on with her that someone would want to kill Stephanie. She was a web designer for God sakes. She was as straight laced as they come," Mr. Harris said.

"Could she have gotten involved in something after you broke up?"

"I really can't imagine."

"What about this guy she was dating?"

"The only thing I know is that Christine had some issues with him but I think she was just concerned for her mother."

"Possibly. What do you know about her past?"

"You mean before we were married?"

"Yes."

"Well, let me see, she grew up in Scarsdale, went to a state college and majored in communications. She tried to make it in broadcasting, but it never happened for her. She did some public relations while we were married. She wrote promotion pieces for companies trying to get business. It was something she could do from home while taking care of Christine. Stephanie wanted to be a hands-on mother. She didn't want anyone else taking care of her."

"Did she date a lot before you were married?"

"I don't know exactly what you mean by a lot, but I guess she had her share. She's very pretty. I mean she was very pretty."

"Why did the marriage end?"

"Is that relevant?"

"Probably not, but you never know."

"I guess the same reason a lot of marriages end. After many years you stop communicating, you take each other for granted. It was amicable and we still talked and of course shared a daughter."

"When I was at the funeral I noticed two elderly people

walking out with you and Christine. Would they happen to be Stephanie's parents?"

"Yes. I'm heartbroken for them."

At some point I would need to talk with them, I thought to myself.

I headed back driving around way too long to find a parking spot. It was four-thirty by the time I walked into my office.

My phone rang. "I'll meet you at the Dublin House at six," Susie said.

"I'm just going to finish up some paperwork. I'll see you then."

Susie was at the bar chatting away with the bartender when I arrived. "Hey, I see you started drinking without me. I'll have a light beer, whatever you have on tap."

"A beer, you never drink beer. What's going on?"

"Nothing, I just thought a change was in order." Susie looked at me suspiciously. "Shall we grab a table?" I said with my beer in hand.

We sat down at one of the wooden tables.

"What can I get you ladies this evening?" Her name tag said Meg.

"Hi Meg, I think we're going to have an order of chicken wings and an order of sweet potato fries," I said.

"And can we also have an order of fried onion rings," Susie chimed in.

"Are you trying to kill me?" I said as Meg walked away.

"Well you don't have to eat them."

"When did you ever know me to have food in front of me and not eat it?"

"You'll live. So what's up with the beer?"

"Nothing, I just thought I would live dangerously."

Susie laughed.

"Are you making fun of me?"

"Kind of, so what's going on with the case?"

I filled her in on my conversations with the boyfriend and the ex-husband.

"So far it doesn't add up to murder."

"Wait, I didn't tell you about the weird conversation I had on the telephone. I called this number listed on Stephanie's cell phone records and the guy who answered said he didn't know her, and abruptly hung up."

"That is strange, any way to trace it?"

"Jack said he'll try and find someone who might be able to, but wasn't optimistic," I said munching on an onion ring.

"Did you speak to the friend who found her?"

"Not yet. She's next on my list. I also need to talk with Stephanie's parents. They might be able to provide more information."

"By the way, there's a fashion exhibit at the MET. I know Mark won't go. Are you up for it?"

"Sure. How about Sunday afternoon? Jack is busy with a trial for the next week or so."

"It's a date. Oh, I didn't tell you the latest." Susie said trying to sound casual.

"Okay, I'm dying to hear it," I said sarcastically.

"Mark proposed," practically shouting the words. I could feel all eyes looking at us.

"And…"

"And what?" Susie said teasingly. You mean what was my answer? YES, I said YES," as she stuck out her left hand.

"How did I miss this beautiful ring?" I said as I gave Susie a big hug.

"I put it on when you went to the ladies' room. I wanted it to be a surprise."

I called Meg over and we ordered more drinks. "Did you set a date?"

"Not yet. It's going to be small. Neither of us wants a big wedding, just close family and friends."

"Sounds perfect."

After finishing up our drinks and talking wedding stuff, we called it a night. On the walk back home I couldn't help but wonder if marriage was in the cards for me. I never felt the least bit jealous when friends I knew from school were getting married and having babies. When my father died suddenly and then my mother, I shied away from relationships with men. Jack is the first man I really opened up to but I still don't know if I could be in it for the long run.

CHAPTER 8

In the morning I ran a three-mile loop around the park. As I was heading back to my building my phone rang. "Hello, is this Tracey Marks?"

"Yes." I said not recognizing the voice. "My name is Mallory Ryan. I'm a friend of Stephanie Harris. I heard you're investigating her death."

"I am. I'm glad you called. Are you the person who found her?"

"Yes, it was horrible. I'll never be able to get that image of her out of my head."

"Can we meet? I would like to ask you some questions."

"I work in the city but we can do it on my lunch break."

"That's perfect. My office is on the West Side. I'll be glad to meet you anywhere that's convenient for you."

Mallory gave me the name of the coffee shop across from where she worked and agreed to meet me at one.

I wanted to call Stephanie's parents, but I was hesitant since they just buried their daughter. I decided to wait another day before calling.

I paid some bills and caught up on administrative stuff before leaving to meet Mallory Ryan. I walked to the coffee shop on Columbus Avenue and 59th Street. I was shown to a booth. A few seconds later Mallory came in and I signaled her over. I recognized her from the white winter coat she said she would be wearing. Mallory was tall with straight red hair that came down to her shoulders. She was very pretty.

"Ms. Marks, glad to meet you. I can't believe any of this. Who would want to hurt Stephanie?"

"Hello ladies, what can I get you?" the waitress asked before I had a chance to answer Mallory.

I ordered a chicken salad sandwich with French fries and

Mallory ordered a turkey club sandwich.

As the waitress was leaving I said, "that's what I hope to find out. Tell me about the morning you found her."

"Stephanie and I usually ran every Monday, Wednesday and Friday morning unless one of us called beforehand to cancel. Most times we met around seven-thirty at the Scarsdale Library and started our run from there. On the day she died, when she didn't show by seven forty-five I called her but it went straight to voice mail. I waited another ten minutes and then went to her house. As I was ringing the doorbell I noticed the door was slightly open. I called out to Stephanie as I slowly pushed the door open. I walked into the living room and saw Stephanie lying on the floor, blood all around her head and started screaming. I ran back outside. I never checked to find out if she was still alive. The next thing I knew, the paramedics and the police were there. I didn't even realize I had called 911."

"How do you know Stephanie?"

"We were roommates in college and friends ever since."

"Did she confide in you?"

"Of course, I believe we shared everything."

I doubt that. No one shares everything.

While Mallory was talking, the waitress set down our food.

After the waitress left, Mallory said, "Stephanie had confided in me about the problems she had in her marriage."

"What sort of problems did she have?"

"I really don't want to say anything bad about her ex. Actually, they had a better relationship after the divorce."

"I'm just trying to learn more about her life."

"He had cheated on her. She said she forgave him since it was supposedly a one-time thing, but I don't think it was ever the same between them."

"What was Stephanie like in college?"

"She was quiet, dated a little but no steady boyfriends. She was definitely not into drugs, not even weed."

"What about before college. Did she talk about her past?"

"Not really. I got the feeling there was something she didn't want to talk about. I asked her if she wanted to try out for a sorority but she said she didn't feel comfortable in groups."

"Was there anything in her behavior that was strange or different lately?"

"Sometimes after our run we would stop in town for coffee. Not more than three weeks ago we were talking and a strange look came over Stephanie's face. I asked her if everything was alright. Just when I thought she was going to tell me something, her phone rang. When she hung up, she said she had to go."

"Did you learn who the call was from?"

"No, but when she got off she seemed rattled. Do you think the call had something to do with what happened to her?"

"I don't know. If you think of anything else please contact me." I paid the bill and we left.

Walking back to the office I thought about the call Stephanie got. Was it somehow connected to her death?

When I woke up Saturday morning the sun was shining but it was bitter cold out. I tried putting the case out of my mind but it wasn't that easy. I thought a movie would be in order to escape from reality. After carefully reviewing all my choices on Netflix, I went with an old thriller, Kiss the Girls, a whodunit mystery with Morgan Freeman and Ashley Judd. It was fast paced and just what the doctor ordered.

On Sunday I met Susie at the MET and saw a fashion exhibit of beautiful dresses mostly from the 1920s and 1930s, very simple and elegant.

While we were having dinner at an Italian Restaurant on Lexington Avenue near 70th Street called Bella Blu, I told Susie about my recent conversation with Mallory.

"Nothing adds up so far. I don't know what to make of what was going on with her."

"Christmas is almost here. What are your plans?" Susie asked, changing the subject.

"Alan and Patty invited me over. I have no idea what Jack is doing."

"You could ask him. Knowing Patty and Alan they would love to have him."

"We'll see."

As we stepped outside the restaurant and said goodbye, snow was starting to lightly fall.

That night as I was getting ready to slip under the covers and enter the world of sleep, my phone buzzed. "Hey Jack, perfect timing. I was just about to go off to sleep land. How are things going?"

"The trial starts on Wednesday so hopefully I'll have everything squared away by then. What have you been up to?"

"Susie and I went to the museum today and then dinner. There was a fashion exhibit at the Metropolitan Museum of Art."

"Did you enjoy the exhibit?"

"I did. I'm glad Susie suggested it since I probably wouldn't have gone by myself. The exhibit was dresses from the 1920s and 30s. They were so simple but so elegant. I could see myself in any one of those dresses."

"You never know, that style may come back. Anything happening with the case?"

"Nothing that adds up to murder from the people I've interviewed so far."

"Way, too early. Keep digging. Go to sleep. I'll talk to you soon."

CHAPTER 9

On the way into work Monday morning I found a parking spot two blocks from the office. I squeezed in between two brand new SUVs. I thought it was a safe bet that they'd be careful getting out of their space.

I went to the deli three blocks from the office and picked up a turkey sandwich for later. Before walking into my office I stuck my head into Alan's office. "Hi Margaret. Is it cold enough for you?"

"Hey there stranger, how's everything?"

"Good. Have any holiday plans?"

"John and I are taking the kids to the Radio City holiday show. The last time I saw the show I had no husband and no kids, the good old days. Nah, only kidding, on most days. Actually this year we're going to John's family so I am free from cooking."

"A Christmas miracle! Is Alan about?"

"Yeah, go right in."

"Are you decent?" I said as I poked my head in.

"Sit. Any further developments since we last spoke?"

I filled Alan in on what had transpired. "By the way did you ask Michael what he wants for Christmas?"

"You're a riot. You can get him a cardboard box and he'd be happy. Maybe Patty has some ideas. Is Jack coming?"

"We haven't talked about the holidays. For all I know he could have family that he wants to spend it with."

"Well you won't know unless you ask?"

"Susie said the same thing."

It had been two weeks since Stephanie died. I was hesitant to call her parents but I needed to speak with them. My hand was shaking as my finger was dialing the numbers on my phone. It rang several times before someone answered.

"Hello." The woman's voice was barely above a whisper.

"Mrs. Howell?"

"Yes."

"My name is Tracey Marks. I was hired by your granddaughter Christine to investigate your daughter's death. I'm so sorry for your loss."

"Thank you," her voice sounding frail. "Christine said you might be calling."

"I know this is a very bad time for you and your husband, but I was wondering if I might talk with both of you sometime later today."

"Would you mind coming around five-thirty? We have some friends who are coming over to be with us during the day."

"Thank you. I'll see you then."

As I was heading up to Scarsdale, I was nervous since I had never interviewed parents who had lost a child, and in this case Stephanie was their only child. Though I really knew nothing about Scarsdale, I knew it was an affluent community and their house did not disappoint me. It was a huge brick colonial. Tall trees lined the property absent of their leaves and blossoms because it was winter. I drove into a circular driveway. They must be fairly wealthy, I thought to myself.

I rang the doorbell and was greeted by the woman I saw at the church service dabbing her eyes.

"Yes, come in dear. My husband will join us in a moment."

Mrs. Howell led me into a sitting room off the kitchen that was furnished with a small brown leather couch and two plaid upholstered chairs. Looking out the window I could see an in-ground pool. I was jealous.

"Please sit," she said pointing to the couch.

"Mrs. Howell, I am so sorry to have to intrude on you and your husband at this time."

"Jerry, this is, I'm sorry I forgot your name," Mrs. Howell said as her husband walked into the room.

Mr. Howell was still a handsome man even though he was probably in his late seventies. He had on a pair of black slacks with a gray shirt and a black wool vest. As he and his wife sat down I noticed his eyes were bloodshot and he looked sad.

"Tracey Marks. I don't know what your granddaughter mentioned to you, but Stephanie had called me and made an appointment to come and see me."

"For what reason did she call you?" Mr. Howell asked.

"I don't know. We never got a chance to speak. She never showed up for her appointment. What I can tell you is that she sounded very upset."

"Oh, my poor Stephanie," Mrs. Howell said wringing the handkerchief she was holding in her hands.

"I don't want to take up too much of your time. I just have a few questions." Not waiting for a response, I jumped right in. "I spoke with Stephanie's friend Mallory and she mentioned a phone call Stephanie received that seemed to trouble her. Did she happen to mention anything was bothering her?"

"No not that I can recall. Did she say anything to you Jerry?" looking at her husband.

"I'm sorry, nothing."

"Did you notice any change in Stephanie recently? Did she seem more distracted or maybe worried about something?" I asked.

"No. I don't think so," Mrs. Howell said shaking her head.

"Can you tell me what Stephanie was like when she was younger?"

"I don't understand why you would need to know that?"

"Please, I know this is difficult for both of you, I'm just trying to find out as much information as I can about her life. It might help me to find out why someone would want to hurt Stephanie." I couldn't bring myself to say the words kill or murder.

"I guess she was a typical teenager. When Stephanie was around sixteen she got involved with a group of kids. They weren't bad kids. I think Stephanie liked being part of a group since she never had many friends."

"Why do you think that was?"

"Stephanie was always a shy child. She didn't make friends easily. Somehow she got involved with this group for a while. I believe it was in her junior year."

"Did they do drugs?"

"Nothing serious," Mrs. Howell said. "I once found pot. I believe that's what they called it back then, under some clothes in her dresser drawer. I can't be sure if she did anything more serious. If I remember correctly, there may have been a falling out with someone in the group because Stephanie stopped hanging around with them. As a matter of fact she kind of stayed to herself after that. I never asked what happened. Maybe I should have," she said looking sad.

"Do you remember any of their names?"

"I still don't understand what all this has to do with anything now."

"I don't know if it does."

"There was one girl who came around to the house sometimes. Let me think a minute. Jerry, do you remember her name?"

"I don't remember. It was so long ago. I'm sorry I can't be of more help," he said holding back tears.

"That's okay," not wanting them to feel bad. "Where did Stephanie go to high school?"

"She went to a private school, Hudson Prep."

"Thank you. If you think of anyone's name from back then please contact me."

I left disappointed that both Mr. and Mrs. Howell did not remember any of Stephanie's friends from high school. I knew this was probably a stretch but I couldn't help feeling that maybe Stephanie's death had something to do with her past but could it be way back from high school? Stephanie's remark to her boyfriend about the past coming back to haunt her seemed so odd.

On the drive back I was racking my brains thinking how I could find out who Stephanie was friends with in her junior year. Hopefully something will jog my mind.

I picked up some Thai food for dinner and stopped at the Corner Sweet Shoppe for my ice cream fix.

"Tracey, nice to see you. I've concocted a new flavor. Would you like to try it?"

"Interesting" I said as I licked the plastic spoon. "It tastes like a combination of coffee and Kailua."

"Your taste buds are very sharp. I'll fix you up a pint of pistachio."

Mr. Hayes and I have a running routine which involves me sampling the flavor of the day, while we both know I'm going to buy either the pistachio or the deep chocolate, sometimes both.

"How are you doing?" Mr. Hayes asked as he was filling up the container with my pistachio ice cream.

"Frustrated, working on a case but not getting too far."

"You're the best detective I know, so cheer up."

"I'm the only PI you know, but thanks for the vote of confidence."

CHAPTER 10

As I was putting the key in my apartment door, my phone rang.

"Hey, I'm just getting home. I'll call you back in two minutes," I said to Susie.

I changed into my sweats and heated up the shrimp and broccoli I bought from the Chinese takeout.

"I was wondering how it went with the parents," Susie said when I called her back.

"I guess as well as can be expected." I gave Susie a rundown of my conversation with the Howell's. "Nothing seems to make any sense. Let's go on the assumption it wasn't a robbery. I've spoken to everyone close to her. It doesn't appear that anything was currently going on in her life that would get her killed. Could it be something from her past, maybe from her days in high school?"

"Anything's possible. You really don't know much about her. Keep all options open."

"Right now I have to figure out a way to track down the names of the kids she hung around with at Hudson Prep. Wait, it just dawned on me, what about Stephanie's high school yearbook," I said.

"That's a great idea. Now you just have to think of a way to get a hold of one."

"I'm assuming the school would have an old yearbook."

"That's a thought."

After hanging up I took my shrimp and broccoli out of the oven and contemplated how to get Stephanie's yearbook. While eating I wondered whether Stephanie's house was still a crime scene. It shouldn't be since it's been more than two weeks. Maybe Stephanie had a copy of her yearbook somewhere in the house.

I woke up bright and early the next day raring to go. When I stepped out of my building the bitter cold air hit me right in the face. I did three miles around my neighborhood streets. When I returned, Wally was at his post.

"Hi Wally, hope you have your long johns on today." I swear Wally must have a heater somewhere stashed under his clothes. He never seems to be cold. That or he wouldn't let on if he was.

"Hello Ms. Tracey. How was your run?"

"Cold. I'm looking forward to a steaming cup of coffee. I'll see you later. Stay warm"

After a long hot shower and coffee, I called Christine. "Ms. Harris, it's Tracey Marks. I hope it's not too early?"

"No not at all. I'm going back to work today though I don't know if I'm up to it yet."

"Where do you work?"

"At Wells Fargo in their Marketing Department."

"I was wondering if we could meet at your mom's house this morning before you go into work. And can you bring the key to the house? I'll explain when I see you. I can be there in an hour."

"Alright, I'll see you then."

I made a mad dash to my car and made it to Scarsdale in forty minutes. Christine was waiting in her car. I tapped on her window. "Hi." I quickly explained my conversation with her grandparents, and that I was hoping to find her mother's high school yearbook.

"The thought of going in there is too upsetting. I'm not sure how I'll ever face walking in there again. Here's the key. It's an extra so you can hold on to it."

"Thanks. Do you know if the police took the computer and her cell phone?"

"They did, but they returned them both."

"I'd like to go through her emails. Do you happen to know her password?"

Christine gave me her mom's password and left. As I entered the house I got the jitters. On the living room floor were the remnants of what transpired. It was hard to look away. Apparently Christine hadn't hired a cleaning service yet.

I saw Stephanie's phone and computer on the console table. After looking through the texts on her phone I didn't find anything suspicious. I turned on the computer. It hummed to life. Going through her emails nothing jumped out at me. A threatening email would be nice.

Next I went upstairs to her office. I opened up the desk drawers, not really knowing what I was looking for and finding nothing that would help solve her murder. I sat there thinking where Stephanie might have her yearbook, if she had it.

I walked into her bedroom and looked in her nightstand and dresser drawers. I didn't see anything that could help with the case. I opened up her closet doors and stood on my tippy toes to see what was on the top shelf but it was too high. I grabbed what I was hoping would be a sturdy chair from the corner. When I looked there was nothing but more clothes.

In the bathroom I opened the medicine cabinet and found a prescription for Lexipro. I googled it and found out it was for anxiety. I made a note of the doctor's name and the date of the prescription. I wondered if Stephanie suffered from anxiety or was it something recent that caused it. I filed it away to ask her daughter.

Downstairs there was a door off the kitchen that led to the basement. There were boxes that thank heavens were marked. I have to say Stephanie was very neat and orderly. There was one box labeled, early years. In the box were trophies she won for soccer, but no yearbook. I moved some of the boxes and I noticed one that wasn't marked. I opened it and under a pile of old clothes was her high school yearbook. I gave out a shout of joy.

I locked up, went back to my car and drove straight to the office. When I got in I googled the telephone number for Dr. Rubin Schwartz in White Plains and left a message with his receptionist.

Around three o'clock Dr. Schwartz called me back.

"I appreciate you returning my phone call. I was hired to look into the death of one of your patients, Stephanie Harris," I said to Dr. Schwartz.

"Yes, I read about her death in the paper. I was sorry to hear about it. How can I help you?"

"I found a bottle of Lexipro in Stephanie's house. Can you tell me why she was taking it?"

"That would be unethical. I'm sorry."

"Is there anything you can tell me? The reason I'm asking is that I wanted to know if her anxiety had something to do with what was going on in her life recently or was it a long term situation."

"Why is that important?"

"Well, if she just started taking Lexipro, it might tell me that her stress was due to something going on in her life right before she died."

"I'd like to help but unfortunately I could lose my license."

"It's not like I'm asking whether she was on anything. That's already been established. I just want to know if she's been taking it long or short term."

"I still can't answer you."

"Well thank you." I hung up.

It didn't make sense to me. If she's dead what would be the harm? They need to change those rules. I was completely frustrated.

I turned my attention to making coffee. At least my coffee maker wasn't giving me any problems.

I decided to call the Howell's. Now that I had the yearbook, I was hoping they could identify any of the kids Stephanie hung around with.

"Hello," Mr. Howell answered.

"Mr. Howell, this is Tracey Marks. I'm so sorry to bother you again but I was able to find Stephanie's high school yearbook. Would it be possible to stop by sometime tomorrow so that you and Mrs. Howell could look through it and see if you recognize any friends from the group Stephanie hung out with?"

I heard some talking in the background, and then Mr. Howell told me to come by tomorrow at eleven a.m.

The next day I was sitting in the Howell's living room on the couch. As Mrs. Howell went through the pages, I was trying to sit still silently praying she would recognize someone.

"My eyes are not like they once were," she said. "The photos are kind of small."

"I know. Just do the best you can."

"This one, she looks familiar. I think she's the one that came over to the house a few times."

"Are you sure?"

"Not one hundred percent, but pretty sure."

That was the only photo Mrs. Howell was able to pick out, but it was something. Her name was Maddie Jensen. "Thank you. This is a big help."

On the way out Mr. Howell said to me. "Please find out what happened to our little girl."

"I will," hoping I wouldn't regret those words.

CHAPTER 11

Back at my office I sat at my desk, turned on my computer and googled Maddie Jensen. There was an article from thirty years ago that Maddie Jensen had committed suicide.

"No way," I said out loud. Could this be the same person? I pulled up the article. It didn't give a reason for her suicide. It listed her parents' names and a little bio, where she grew up, what high school she attended and the name of the funeral parlor. I had the right person.

I searched through my database and found a telephone number for a Lois Jensen in Scarsdale.

Okay, so what do I say as I picked up my cell phone? It was ringing. "Hello is this Mrs. Jensen?"

"Yes," she answered with pause.

"My name is Tracey Marks. I'm not sure if you heard but Stephanie Harris was murdered. You may know her under the last name of Howell."

"Yes, the poor thing. But why are you calling me?"

"I'm investigating her death, and I was told by her parents that Stephanie and Maddie had been friends in high school."

"They were friends for a while."

"I'm sorry to impose like this but would it be possible if I could come by and talk with you? I'm trying to find out more information about that period in Stephanie's life."

"Well I'm not sure I can be of much help but I guess it would be alright. Can you come tomorrow, say around ten a.m.?"

"Thank you so much. I'll see you then."

"Hey Susie, it's me. Call me back."

Not two seconds later, Susie called. "Hi, I was just hanging up from a client when you called. What's going on?"

I explained what I found out about Maddie Jensen. "This is getting very weird. It must be just a coincidence. Maddie's suicide and Stephanie's death can't be related."

"No clue. Just follow wherever it leads."

"I will. If it doesn't pan out, nothing ventured, nothing gained. The police are probably looking into her current life. Maybe they're still going under the assumption it's just a robbery that went wrong.

"Okay, but still keep all options on the table."

I had two cases that I had pushed aside to work on Stephanie's investigation, one was a background check on an individual and their business, and the other was to locate someone for a court proceeding. Since I had some free time on my hands, I figured this was a good time to work on them.

The next day I headed up to Scarsdale after stopping at Starbucks for a coffee and a blueberry muffin. I was a bit nervous knowing the subject of her daughter's suicide would come up.

Mrs. Jensen lived in an apartment building on Garth Road in Scarsdale. She buzzed me in and I took the elevator to the 6th floor. She was waiting for me by her door.

"This is a beautiful building," I said walking into her apartment.

"It was built before WWII. It has a lot of charm."

We sat in a very spacious living room with hardwood floors and an oriental rug between two light gray sofas with needlepoint pillows as accents. There was an upright piano against one of the walls. We sat opposite each other. Mrs. Jensen looked like she was in her seventies, though when I looked her up on the internet it listed she was sixty-eight. Maybe the death of her daughter took a toll on her.

"How can I help you?"

"I'm looking into Stephanie's death and I'm trying to gather as much information as I can on her. You told me that Stephanie and Maddie were friends."

"They were but it was so long ago." Mrs. Jensen looked like she was about to cry.

"Did Stephanie ever come to your house?"

"Yes, many times. From what I can remember for a while they were inseparable."

"Do you know what happened between them?"

"I don't. They were teenagers. Who knows why they weren't friends anymore. I try not to think about that time. My husband never got over her death. He was never the same. Two years after Maddie died, he had a fatal heart attack. We lived in a beautiful house but when they were both gone, I sold it. Too many bad memories."

"I'm so sorry for everything you've been through. Did you ever find out why it happened?"

"I didn't," she said as tears trickled down her cheeks. "Maddie got involved with a group of kids in high school. That's when she met Stephanie. From what I remember Stephanie was a sweet kid, just like my Maddie. It seemed like overnight Maddie changed. She wouldn't listen to Frank or me. Whenever I would try to question her about where she was going or what she was doing, she would be evasive. I thought she was just being a rebellious teenager. I even thought she had gotten involved with drugs. My husband and I wondered if we made a wrong choice sending her to a private school. When she was in her senior year she became withdrawn. She stopped hanging around with those kids. Stephanie stopped coming over. When I tried talking to her to find out what was wrong, I couldn't get anything out of her. When she went to college we thought things would get better."

"Did Maddie get any counseling?"

"No. I begged her to go but she wouldn't. She said things were fine; she didn't need to talk with anyone."

"Would you happen to remember the names of any of the other kids in the group?"

"I'm sorry I don't. What is this all about? What does my daughter's suicide have to do with Stephanie?"

"It probably has no connection. I'm just exploring all possibilities. It appears that Stephanie also became withdrawn in her senior year. Can you think of anyone who might know the names of these other kids?"

"That was a long time ago. I wish I could be of more help." She looked so sad.

"Well if you happen to remember anything, please call me."

On the ride back all I could think about was Maddie's suicide and Stephanie's murder and how or if they were connected. I wondered if any of Stephanie's friends from high school showed up at her funeral. A lightbulb went off. The guest book! I'm brilliant.

At the office I called Christine. "Christine, it's Tracey. Do you happen to know if your grandparents have the guestbook from the funeral?"

"I actually have it. Why?"

"I was wondering if there were any names on there that you or your parents didn't recognize. Maybe they were friends from high school or college."

"Is that important?"

"It may be. Can you look through the names and the ones you don't recognize ask your parents about? I'd like to have a list of those people."

"Okay. I'll try to get it to you by tomorrow."

"By the way, have you spoken to the police on your mother's case recently?"

"No, but I'll call and find if there are any updates."

"One other thing, I found a prescription for Lexipro in your mother's medicine cabinet. It's for anxiety. Did you know she was taking it?"

"I had no idea. She never mentioned it."

"Thanks," I said as I hung up. It seemed like Stephanie had a lot of secrets. Did one of those secrets get her killed?

CHAPTER 12

The sky was dark and the clouds were ready to burst when I looked out my bedroom window the following morning. Maybe it was an omen of the day to come. I contemplated getting out of my warm bed when I heard my phone buzzing. "Hey sleepyhead, rise and shine," Jack said.

"How did you know I was still in bed?"

"I can tell by your voice when you said hello. How's everything?"

"Okay, though the case is getting to me." I explained to Jack what was going on.

"It takes time. You have to learn to be more patient or these cases will eat you alive."

"I know, but it's hard. Were you able to find out anything about the burner phone?"

"I think that's a dead end unfortunately," Jack said.

"That's a bummer. I was hoping it could be a lead."

"Listen, Christmas is coming up and I was wondering how you plan to spend the holidays?" Jack asked.

"I really haven't given it much thought. I'm not really that big on the whole merry holiday season."

"I'm dating Miss Scrooge."

"Ho ho ho, very funny. It's just that since my mother died, Christmas doesn't have much joy for me. It's just another day. What are you doing?"

"I'm not big on Christmas either but I do have some holiday spirit. I usually spend Christmas Eve with my friends Marty and Jen. I thought we might be able to spend Christmas Day together."

"Well I do believe you were invited to Alan and Patty's. I actually think Patty prefers your company to mine."

"Do I detect a note of jealousy in your voice? Though I seriously doubt that, but with your Christmas attitude who can blame Patty," he said, as I pictured the wide grin on his face. "Would you like to come up here this weekend?"

"I think I can manage that even after all the cruel things you said about me."

"Get out of bed. See you soon."

I put on the coffee maker and showered. I decided to work from home this morning. After breakfast I took out my 3'x4' corkboard. I added the names of the people who I spoke with recently on my 5x7 cards and tacked them to the board I had standing against the back of my couch. Can Stephanie's death really be from something that happened over thirty years ago? I still had no idea and until I find someone from her high school years, I have nowhere to go.

I decided to take the day off on Friday and head up to Jack's late Friday afternoon. I still hadn't heard back from Christine. Jack lives in Lee, Massachusetts, a very charming small town in the Berkshire's.

By the time I got off the Taconic Parkway it was dark. I was riding on a two-lane road with no cars in sight. Out of nowhere there was a car that was practically up my rear. I slowed down hoping it would pass me since there were no cars coming from the other direction. What the hell, the car was not letting up. I put my foot on the gas, my heart going a mile a minute. There was no place to turn off and I couldn't stop. I kept speeding up but my little Beetle was no match for the other car. I started sweating, gripping the steering wheel for dear life. There was a loud thud as he drove right into the back of my car. I was panicking, not knowing what to do. I floored the car, praying for a miracle. But he kept coming at me really fast. The next thing I knew my car was reeling out of control, veering off the road heading straight towards a tree.

CHAPTER 13

Squeezing the wheel so tight my body was jolted from the force of the impact. I braced myself for the crash, my mind blanking when suddenly the car came to a stop missing the tree by inches. I felt like I couldn't breathe and was going to pass out. I was shaking all over. I just sat there trying to calm myself. It felt like time was standing still. I reached for my cell phone lying on the passenger side of the floor. My hands were trembling as I called Jack.

I was talking so fast Jack had to stop me in mid-sentence.

"Can you see the other car?"

"I don't think he stopped."

"Are you hurt?" his voice filled with worry.

"No, I don't think so, just shaken up."

"I'm going to call the police and an ambulance."

"No ambulance, I'm okay."

"Do you have any idea where you are?"

"The road you turn on after you get off the Taconic."

"Stay inside your car and don't move at all. I'll find you. I'm going to call the police and then call you right back."

"Okay, hurry."

It seemed like hours before I finally saw Jack's car pull off the road.

He opened my car door, bent down and kissed me gently on the lips.

"Okay, tell me what happened."

I explained everything I knew. Unfortunately it wasn't very much since it was dark and I never saw the license plate number or who was driving the car.

"Can you describe the car?"

"I can't. I was too busy trying to get away. Jack, this person was probably tailing me ever since I left New York. For all I know he's been tailing me for days. I know it has to do with Stephanie's murder." I could hear the sirens in the background.

The police came. Thankfully it wasn't anyone from my previous case. My track record with the police here does not bode well for me. My last case happened to be in the Stockbridge area, and I was read the riot act by the police officer in charge for interfering with his murder investigation.

I told these officers as much as I knew. I thought there was no point in telling them about my suspicions, since Stephanie's murder wasn't even in their jurisdiction.

After they left Jack said to me. "I hope you're not going to make a habit of people trying to kill you," as he attempted to look serious but couldn't help suppressing a smile.

"I'm glad my near-death experience is amusing to you. Just don't tell Susie or Alan. They'll want to put me in a straight jacket for the rest of my life."

He looked at me with his beautiful big brown eyes and held my hand. "I know you're going to continue looking for Stephanie's killer. There wasn't anything you could have done differently."

"Maybe if I was more aware, I would have spotted whoever it was long before they were on my ass."

"That's in the movies. Besides the fact you haven't been at this very long."

"So now what?"

"You keep doing what you're doing. Just have your antennas up. Are you sure you're all right?"

"Yeah, I'm more shook-up than anything else." Jack helped me out of my car and held me close. I was afraid to look at the damage. The back got the brunt of it. The lights were smashed and the rear was badly pushed in, but the good news, I could still drive it.

"Are you sure you're up to driving? We can get a tow truck and have it towed to my place."

"I'm okay now. I just needed some time to calm down." I didn't want to tell Jack that I was more frightened then I led him to believe.

Though I was very capable of getting ready for bed by myself,

Jack didn't seem to mind undressing me and getting me settled in. His body was nice and warm as he slid under the covers next to me. The last words I heard as I drifted off to sleep were "good night," as Jack pulled me close to him.

When I opened my eyes, Jack's side of the bed was empty and the sun was peeking into the room.

"Hey there sleepy head, how are you feeling?" he asked, holding two cups of coffee.

"Sorry I ruined whatever plans you might have had for us last night."

"You didn't," he said as he got into bed, placing the coffees down on the night table and kissing me gently on my lips. I softly moaned, his hands and mouth kissing me all over. I quickly forgot about any ruined plans.

"Well that was fun," I said playfully.

"I'm glad you thought so," cupping his hand on my chin and kissing me softly on my lips.

I started to get up. Jack said, "is the fun over?"

"Just until I take a quick shower." While I showered Jack made us breakfast and fresh coffee. We stayed in bed most of the day and took advantage of each other with great joy.

On Sunday afternoon we took a ride over to Goose Pond Reserve. In the summer you could rent paddle boats and fish. We walked for a few miles on the hiking trails and then went into town for dinner at the Morgan House, a very quaint Inn with a nice, cozy dining room with white tablecloths.

When we were seated, a young man who looked like a college student with curly black hair and wire-rimmed glasses came over. "How are you tonight?"

"Fine, thank you," Jack said. "Could I get a light beer on tap?"

"And I'll have a glass of Sauvignon Blanc."

"I'll be right back with your drink order."

"So how do you plan on tracking down someone from the group Stephanie was a part of in high school?"

"I'm waiting to hear from her daughter. She's checking with Stephanie's parents about the guest list from the funeral service."

Our waiter came back with our drinks. "Have you decided on

dinner?"

"Yes," I said. "I'll have the grilled salmon."

"And I'll have the same."

After he left, Jack said, "And what happens if there were no friends who attended from her high school days, what then?"

"I really don't know. Do you have any suggestions?"

"I'll put some thought into it. There has to be a way."

"I love your optimism. It's very comforting."

I left Jack's house late Monday morning with my damaged Beetle.

"Stay out of trouble. I'll see you on Thursday," Jack said to me as I drove away.

I made it home without incident. It was one o'clock when I opened the door to my apartment. When I checked my phone, I had missed a call from Christine. I quickly called her back.

"Christine, it's Tracey. Any luck with the guest list?"

"There were two people whose names we didn't recognize, a Greg Todd and a Linda Brent. I have no idea how they knew my mother."

"Did you speak to the police?"

"I did and they said they had nothing concrete to tell me. Apparently there were no fingerprints. Whoever it was must have worn gloves."

What a shocker, I thought to myself. "Friday night someone tried to run me off the road. Either they were trying to scare me or trying to kill me."

"Are you alright?" she said horrified.

"I'm fine. A little sore, but otherwise okay."

"I'm so sorry. What could my mother have possibly been mixed up in?"

"I don't know but I will do my best to find out. Thanks for the names."

After hanging up I took out Stephanie's high school yearbook. I found Greg Todd. He was a good looking kid with blond hair that looped around his ears. His blue eyes looked as though they could see right through me. Under his picture it was written, 'will charm his way to success.'

I searched for Linda Brent without success. There were several girls with the first name Linda. Brent was probably her married name. I wrote down the last name of the five Linda's in the book. Linda was certainly a popular name.

I then placed a few calls to auto body shops in the area and decided on one about two miles away. I told them I would bring in the car tomorrow. I then called my insurance company to report what happened and told them a police report was filed.

I scrounged around in my refrigerator for something to eat. The only thing I had was frozen macaroni and cheese. While I was heating it up, I began searching on my laptop for Greg Todd in the Westchester area, though he could be living anywhere. There were two Greg Todd's listed, but only one was the approximate age. There was an address in Connecticut but no telephone listing.

When I searched in my databases under his name and address it listed Greg as forty-eight and owned a house with a Julie Todd, most likely his wife. He lived in Ridgefield, Connecticut. There was a mobile phone number.

While eating my lunch I tried to locate Linda Brent. Christine had told me that there were no addresses listed in the guest book for either person. Linda was not as easy to find. There were several, though only three possible matches if she lived in the area.

Since I had her maiden name from the yearbook, I went through each Linda Brent. Finally, I got a hit. Linda Brent, also known as Linda Clark, residing in Eastchester, New York. It didn't appear she was married anymore but couldn't be certain. I decided I would contact Linda first.

I finished the last of my macaroni and cheese and was still hungry. I resorted to a half a pint of double chocolate ice cream I still had in my freezer. I took a spoon and sat on my couch indulging myself right out of the container. I really need to keep healthier food in my refrigerator. In my defense, I hadn't been home for a couple of days.

My phone buzzed, "Hey Susie." I knew she was going to ask

me about my weekend with Jack. "What's going on?"

"Not much. I'm trying to get my client a decent settlement. How's Jack?"

"Good. He's coming down Christmas morning and we'll go over to Alan and Patty's in the afternoon. I'm not sure we'll have a chance to stop by in the evening. If not, maybe we can all meet for breakfast Friday morning."

"We're having a Chanukah party on Friday. I thought you guys would like to come and take part in the festivities of Chanukah. I'm giving out chocolate dreidels."

"Well that cinches it for me."

"How was your weekend?"

I couldn't lie to Susie about nearly getting killed but I tried to downplay it. I held the phone away from my ear as Susie started yelling.

"This is serious. I hope you realize that."

"I know. I'll be more vigilant. By the way, I found out that two people on the guest list from the funeral service were not known to the family. They're next on my list to talk with."

"Have you thought about the fact that these people might have something to do with her death?"

"Why would they be at the funeral if that was the case?"

"Who knows, there could be any number of reasons."

"I promise I'll be careful."

I started to think about what Susie said. Could she be right?

CHAPTER 14

I was up Tuesday morning by six. I put on my running clothes and headed out. I ran on the streets instead of the park. It was cold and was glad I had on my knit cap to keep my head warm. When I got back I showered and added an extra layer of clothing since the weather was only going to be in the twenties. When I went to get my car I almost forgot what happened to my poor Beetle.

I stopped for my usual and headed up to Eastchester, about a mile south of Scarsdale. "Jack, hi," I said looking at the caller id.

"How are you feeling?"

"I'm fine. I'm bringing my car in later and then I'll stop at the rental place."

"Listen, I was thinking that you should start carrying your gun. I know you said you have a permit to carry."

"Between you and Susie you're scaring the crap out of me."

"I don't mean to. I just want you to be safe. Besides if anything happened to you I'd miss all those fabulous meals you slave over to feed me."

"If you hadn't scared the living shit out of me, I'd be rolling on the floor laughing at your attempt at a joke."

"See ya soon."

I found Linda's house with no problem. My database listed a Blue Honda Accord registered to her. The houses on the street were small ranch style homes. Her car was in the driveway. I sat across the street trying to figure out how to approach her. I waited until ten before ringing her doorbell.

"May I help you?"

"Are you Linda Brent?"

"Who's asking?"

"My name is Tracey Marks." I showed her my card. "I saw that you attended

Stephanie Harris' funeral and I was wondering if I could talk with you. Stephanie's daughter hired me to investigate her death."

"I'm very strapped for time," looking at her watch.

"Please, I promise I won't be long."

"There's a Dunkin Donuts down the road. I'll meet you there in five minutes."

I had no choice. I hoped she wasn't going to give me the brush off. But a few minutes after I arrived at Dunkin Donuts, Linda Brent showed up. Linda was probably a good four inches taller than me.

"So what's this about," Linda said as we sat down. She looked uneasy, brushing her wavy brown hair away from her face. Her black framed glasses sitting low on her nose.

"As you know Stephanie was murdered."

"Yes, but I thought it was a robbery," looking confused.

"The day Stephanie died she called me and was very upset. We were supposed to meet that day but she never showed, and she didn't call to cancel. I thought she might have changed her mind but then I found out she was killed. I think she was targeted."

"I can't believe it," she said shaking her head.

"How did you know Stephanie?"

"We were friends for a while in high school."

"Were you also friends with Maddie Jensen?"

"Why yes." She sounded surprised. "How did you know?"

"I wasn't sure but I spoke with Maddie's mother. Do you know anything about why Maddie committed suicide?"

"I'd really rather not talk about it."

"It could be important."

"I don't see how it has anything to do with Stephanie. None of us were in touch when Maddie committed suicide. She was in college when it happened."

"Maddie's mother said she began isolating herself in her senior year. Don't you think that's odd?" Linda was twirling her hair. I wasn't expecting the next thing she said.

"Maddie was raped," she whispered. "She never wanted to talk about it."

"Did she report it?"

"No. And I don't think she ever told her parents."

I was shocked. How could she never report it? "Did Stephanie know?"

"She did. Maddie begged us not to say anything."

"Did anyone else know? What about Greg?"

"I'm pretty sure he didn't. I still have nightmares about her suicide. I keep thinking if only I had told her parents she might still be alive. After she was raped our friendship couldn't take the strain. We had to keep a secret that was so horrendous. We all went our separate ways."

"Who else was in your group?"

"Joe and Donna." Linda told me that Joe and Donna were married and their last name was Connolly.

"I still don't understand how any of this is related to Stephanie's death."

"I don't know if it is," I said.

After leaving Linda, I called Susie. I filled her in on my conversation with Linda Brent.

"Wow, poor girl. One reason she might have been too scared to tell anyone except for her friends is because she may have been threatened. But I'm still not seeing the connection between Maddie's rape back then and Stephanie's death now."

"I still have no clue myself."

"I'm not saying there isn't a link, you just have to find it. Talk to the rest of the people in the group."

"Maddie's mother will never know why she committed suicide. How awful for her. I wonder if Maddie knew her rapist."

"You may never know but keep plugging along."

I didn't know what to think. Was there a connection or did I just want there to be one? I had no idea.

CHAPTER 15

On the way back to the office I dropped my car at the auto body shop and then took an Uber to the rental place. They gave me a black Honda Civic. I went back to the office and took my gun out of the safe. I cleaned it and headed to the Westside Rifle and Pistol Range on 20th Street. There was a different guy at the counter from the last time I was here, which was over a year ago. I took a quick look around but didn't see anyone suspicious. I knew I had to be more vigilant. When I took my last case it never occurred to me that I could be putting myself in danger. How naïve I was. I had no idea what I was getting myself in for working a missing person case.

I put on my goggles and earplugs and loaded my gun. At first the gun felt heavy as I extended my hand and pulled the trigger. But as I got used to it, I started to relax and it felt good as I tried to hit the bullseye. I never did, but it didn't stop me from trying.

As I was lying in bed, it occurred to me that Christmas was on Thursday. Jack and I never discussed gifts and I didn't know if he planned on getting me anything. What if I get him a gift and he doesn't have one for me? I called Susie and explained my dilemma.

"You have a real problem on your hands," she said sarcastically.

"Are you making fun of me?"

"Moi? I have no idea what you mean. Why don't you get tickets to a show and this way it will be for both of you?"

"Once again you come up with the right answer. Mark is a lucky guy."

"I'll put him on the phone so you can tell him."

Now all I had to do was think of what tickets to buy as I was trying to fall asleep.

In the morning I woke with a determination to be more in the holiday spirit. I also decided to take a break in the case until after the New Year. Maybe some time away from it would give me a new perspective and hopefully new insights on how to proceed.

I threw some clothes into my bag and headed to the gym. It felt good running on the treadmill. Thirty minutes later I was in the weight area working my chest and arms. I finished up with squats. I showered and stopped at a neighborhood coffee shop for breakfast. By the time I finished it was eleven a.m. It was time to do some Christmas Shopping.

I walked until I found a toy store. I had no idea what to buy a seven month old baby. The salesperson gave me several suggestions. After looking at baby toys for more time then I care to admit, I decided on a deluxe Busy Time Play Cube that looked like it could keep Michael amused for a while, though I might have trouble figuring it out. I wondered when baby toys got to be so expensive.

I had the day for myself so I walked over to the theatre district. I knew someone who had seen Tootsie and raved about it. Since I wasn't quite sure what Jack would be interested in seeing, I thought this might be neutral. On my way home I stopped at my local wine store and bought a bottle of French wine for Alan and Patty.

"Hi Wally."

"You look like you have your hands full. Can I help you?"

"Nah, I'm good." Wally held the door for me. "Oh before I forget," putting my packages down, "Merry Christmas Wally." I handed him a wrapped box with leather gloves inside.

"Thank you Miss Tracey; they fit perfectly. Is that handsome fella of yours coming for Christmas?"

"He is. Have a wonderful holiday with your family. I'll see you in the New Year." Wally always takes the week between Christmas and New Year's.

Jack arrived early on Christmas Day. I was totally surprised when he presented me with a pair of diamond-studded earrings. I was so relieved when he seemed genuinely happy after he opened up the tickets I gift wrapped. Though Jack never spent much time in New York before we met, he really enjoyed exploring the city with me. Even I ventured out with Jack to places I rarely went to.

My gift for Michael was a huge success for the ten minutes he played with it. Michael had more fun playing with the blocks Jack gave him.

"I'm pooped," I said later as Jack and I got into bed. Michael wore me out. How can one baby do that to you?"

"I take it you haven't spent a lot of time around kids."

"And you have?"

"Marty and Jen have two kids so I get to hang out with them when we're all together," Jack said as he pulled off his pants.

"How old are they?"

"I'm assuming you mean their kids," he said smiling.

I punched Jack lightly on the shoulder.

"Jennifer is five now and Bryan is six."

I was hesitant about asking my next question, but I forged ahead anyway. "How come you never had children?"

"Well for one I'm kind of old fashioned and I would like to be married if I did have children. But if I'm being honest with myself, I never felt a strong desire. I think if you're going to have a child it should be something you choose, not something that just happens. What about you?" he asked casually.

"I never had a strong maternal instinct. Sometimes I think there's something wrong with me. There are women who would do anything to have a baby." Jack pulled me closer to him.

"There are many women who choose not to have a baby. You just hear about the ones that do. There are women out there that have children that should never have been mothers."

"Yeah, you're right."

"On another subject, Patty is one heck of a cook."

"You certainly know how to kick a gal when she's down." He kissed me and thoughts of food went right out of my head.

The next day we went to Susie's Chanukah party. Mark made potato latkes, which Jack never had, but I noticed he went back for seconds and thirds. We brought in the New Year at Anton's with Susie and Mark and a few friends. Jack left late New Year's Day.

When I finally got into bed I was surprised that I missed him. I never spent a week with someone and I thought I would be happy when he left, a New Year's surprise. When I think about Jack and our relationship, it scares me. I don't like depending on anyone else because you never know when something suddenly could end it. What happened to my parents was never far from my thoughts.

Monday morning I was up by five-thirty. When I went outside it had the feel of snow in the air. I jogged my three miles and put on coffee as soon as I returned. The hot shower felt great. After I had my Cheerios and milk, I headed to the office. I stopped along the way at my favorite coffee place. Anna greeted me, "Happy New Year," as she handed me a cup of coffee and a banana nut muffin.

"Let's hope this is a great year for both of us," I said as I left.

As I sat glued to my office chair, I thought about what I knew for sure. I knew that Stephanie, Maddie, Linda Brent, Greg Todd, and Joe and Donna Connolly hung out together; Maddie was raped; she told Stephanie and Linda and swore them to secrecy; Stephanie and Maddie were no longer in the group after the rape occurred and withdrew from their friends; Maddie killed herself when she was in college.

So how come Linda Brent stayed friends with the others in the group? What does that mean, if anything? Did something happen to Stephanie also? Was she raped too? Always more questions than answers. I never asked Linda if either Maddie or Stephanie had a boyfriend in high school.

I picked up my cell phone and called Linda. She answered right away. "Linda, it's Tracey Marks. Would you happen to remember if either Maddie or Stephanie had a boyfriend in high school?"

"I vaguely remember Maddie had someone. I can't remember his name. I'm not sure about Stephanie."

"Do you have your yearbook?"

"I don't. Somehow it got lost in all the moves over the years."

"Do you think if you went through Stephanie's yearbook, you might be able to pick him out?"

"Possibly."

"I can stop by this evening if that works for you."

"I can't. I'm busy this evening. Can you come by tomorrow evening, say around six-thirty?"

"Okay, I'll see you then. Thanks Linda, I appreciate it." I wanted to insist on today but I thought better of it.

I arrived at Linda's house at six-thirty the next day. It took a minute or so before she answered the door. "Come in." She had on jeans and a ratty sweatshirt.

"I was just making coffee. Would you like a cup?"

"I would love one, black, no sugar."

"You're easy."

"Some people would beg to differ with you." We sat down in the kitchen. It was warm and inviting. There were pots and pans hanging from a black wrought iron structure attached to the ceiling.

"Where do you work?" I asked Linda.

"At Lawrence Hospital, I'm a lab technician. Are you married?" she asked me.

"No, never been, and you?"

"Once, and that was enough."

"Not a very glowing endorsement for marriage," I said.

"I guess not."

As Linda was pouring our coffee, I opened the yearbook. I handed it to her after she finished pouring.

"Wow, I haven't looked at this since I graduated. It brings back so many memories," she said as she turned the pages. "I can't believe our hairdos back then. So embarrassing."

"Did you date anyone from high school?" I asked.

"No one steady," she said, looking intently at the faces on the pages.

When she finished she looked up and said, "I don't recognize the guy Maddie was dating. I'm sorry. If he was older he wouldn't be in this book."

I was disappointed when I said goodbye. Was something going on with Stephanie that was connected to Maddie? And if it was, how did it connect to the present?

CHAPTER 16

Right now I had no answers. I needed to keep plugging along. Maybe the other people in the group would be able to fill me in on some of the questions I had.

When I got home I decided to wait until the morning to call Greg Todd. From the search I had previously done on Greg, it listed an address in Ridgefield, Connecticut.

I settled into bed and was watching a rerun of Law and Order with my pistachio ice cream when my phone buzzed. "Hey you," I said to Jack. "I was just about to dive into my ice cream."

"Well don't let the sound of my voice stop you. How's everything?"

"My usual frustration. I hope there's someone who could give me answers. I just find it weird that Maddie swore Stephanie and another friend to secrecy about the rape. I'm thinking she could have been threatened. Why else wouldn't you report it?"

"You watch enough TV shows to know that they might feel ashamed. Were they to blame? Did they do something to encourage the guy? Maybe you'll find out."

"It was so long ago. I wonder. By the way our show tickets are for next Saturday evening."

"I'm looking forward to the show and my date."

"I do declare; I am blushing all over."

"Enjoy your ice cream. Be safe."

The next morning I called Greg Todd. I was about to leave a message when he answered.

"Mr. Todd, my name is Tracey Marks and I'm looking into the death of Stephanie Harris. I was wondering if we can meet someplace at your convenience?"

"How did you get my name?"

"You signed the registry book at the funeral service."

"Right, but I thought it was a burglary."

"I was hired by her family since they aren't sure it was a burglary."

"That's interesting. But how can I help you? I haven't seen Stephanie since high school."

"Well you cared enough to come to her funeral service." I could hear him thinking.

"I have to be in White Plains later today. There's a place called City Limits Diner on Route 119. I could meet you there at one-thirty. I'll be the guy with blond hair and a brown leather jacket."

"I'll be there."

In the meantime I ran a check on Joe and Donna Connolly. All I knew about them was that they lived in Larchmont, New York. Nothing significant or alarming showed up.

As soon as I walked into the diner, I spotted Greg Todd in the waiting area. His blond hair was a lot shorter than in high school and he now wore tortoiseshell glasses. "Hi Greg, I'm Tracey." The hostess showed us to our booth and left menus. The diner was huge. It had two levels. It was kind of retro-looking.

"What can I get you?" the waitress asked.

"Just coffee for me. Oh, and I'll also have a corn muffin."

"I'll have coffee and a toasted bagel," Greg said.

"Thanks for meeting me Greg. I spoke with Linda Brent and she told me that back in high school you hung out with Stephanie and Maddie."

"That's right, but just for a few months."

"Did you know that Maddie was raped?" His eyebrows shot up.

"I had no idea. Who told you?"

"I can't tell you that. I just know that Maddie never reported it to the police. Did you know she killed herself?"

"I did."

"Do you know why?"

"No."

"Weren't you curious to find out?"

"When Maddie killed herself I hadn't seen or heard from her in two years."

"What do you remember about Maddie and Stephanie?"

"Before I tell you anything, why are you inquiring about Maddie when you're looking into Stephanie's death?"

"I believe somehow they're connected, though I'm not positive. I have no evidence that they are, just a gut feeling." Greg seemed to be mulling over what I said.

"We all hung out together. It was Linda, Stephanie, Maddie, Joe and Donna. I'm not quite sure how we all met."

"Did you guys do drugs back then?"

"We did some, nothing hardcore. But yeah we got high sometimes."

"Did you get into any trouble?"

"You would have to define trouble. Nothing that got us jammed up with the police. Maybe we were lucky."

"So what happened to the group?"

"Both Stephanie and Maddie stopped hanging out with us."

"Did you ask them why?"

"Linda did. They said they wanted to focus on their studies since they wanted to get into a good college. I thought it was a little strange but I didn't question it."

"They both said the same thing?"

"That was what Linda said. I had no reason not to believe her."

"Do you remember if either Stephanie or Maddie had a boyfriend?"

"I believe Maddie did. I think the guy was a year or two older than her. I don't remember his name. I'm not sure about Stephanie. I don't think she had a steady boyfriend."

"What about rumors of guys being aggressive with some of the girls?"

"Not that I'm aware of." He didn't sound very sure.

I couldn't think of any more questions to ask Greg.

The waitress came back with our check. "I got this," I said to Greg. "If you think of anything else please give me a call. Actually, are you still in contact with Joe and Donna?"

"I haven't spoken to anyone since high school except Linda Brent. And we speak rarely."

"Thanks. By the way, what do you do for a living?"

"I'm a therapist."

"Does therapy really help people?"

"It does if people are serious about wanting to be helped."

I didn't learn much more from Greg except that both Maddie and Stephanie left the group around the same time. Neither had a plausible answer why they didn't want to be in the group anymore. And it appears the guy that Maddie was dating was a little older than her.

I thought I would pay Joe and Donna Connolly an impromptu visit. Since it was almost three o'clock instead of heading back to the city, I went straight to Larchmont. I drove around for a while and wound up by the beach. Larchmont is a village off the Long Island sound. Though it was freezing out, I took a walk on the beach, something I rarely do. When I was young my parents, who were both teachers, rented a cottage on a lake in North Carolina during the summer months. I would spend every day down by the lake. That was where my father taught me how to fish. We'd take the rowboat out to the middle of the lake and he would show me how to bait the hook with worms. I was so happy to be out there, just the two of us. I loved wrestling with those squirmy worms trying to get them on the hook.

I headed back to my car and blasted the heat. As soon as I could feel my fingers and toes again, I drove into the village of Larchmont and parked my car. I walked around looking into the pretty shops. I found a Starbucks, sat inside and had a cappuccino. By the time I finished it was almost five-thirty. I put the Connolly's address in my phone and headed to their place. Their house was on a quiet street. It looked like the Connolly's had money. The house was a large center hall colonial. It was painted white with green shutters. I didn't see any cars in the driveway, so I waited.

At six-thirteen I saw a car pull into the driveway. On the driver's side a male got out and a female exited on the passenger side. I waited fifteen minutes before I rang the bell. I had to look up to see the face of the man who opened the door.

"Can I help you?"

"My name is Tracey Marks and I'm looking into the death of

Stephanie Harris." I gave him my card. "I'm sorry to disturb you. May I come in?"

"Okay," he said, looking as though he wasn't quite sure whether he wanted me to come in. "Let me get my wife." Joe led me into their living room. "Please sit."

"Thank you." Donna came into the room. She was maybe 5'3", slender with jet-black straight hair. Next to her husband she looked tiny. Besides being very tall, Joe was massively built. He could probably crush me with his bare hands.

"Did you hear about Stephanie Harris' death?"

"Yes, we read about it in the papers," Joe said.

"When was the last time either of you saw her?"

"If it was a burglary, why are you investigating her death?" Donna asked.

"It's possible it wasn't a burglary. It may be related to something else but it's too early to tell."

"We haven't seen Stephanie in years," Joe said. A weird look passed over Donna's face. I decided to leave it alone for now.

"I spoke with Greg Todd and Linda Brent. They were at the funeral. They told me that you had been friends in high school with Stephanie and also with Maddie Jensen."

"Poor girl," Donna said. "I had no idea she was suicidal. She seemed fine when we were friends."

"I was told that both Maddie and Stephanie had left the group kind of abruptly." I waited to hear their response.

Joe said, "I remember they stopped hanging around with us but I never knew the reason why."

"Did you know that Maddie was raped in high school?"

"Really, we had no idea. She never said anything," Joe said with very little emotion which I thought was weird.

Donna's face looked pale. It appeared Joe was talking for his wife also. I wondered why?

"Would you happen to know if either Maddie or Stephanie had a boyfriend in high school?"

"I can't recall," Joe said.

"Do you remember?" I said looking at Donna.

"I don't know. I'm sorry."

"Well I won't take up any more of your time." Joe got up and walked me to the door. I was hoping I could slip my card to Donna before I left, but Joe made sure I wasn't going to get the chance.

Joe was definitely lying, but about what? I needed to talk to Donna alone.

CHAPTER 17

It was after eight by the time I got home. I stripped down to my panties and put on a sleeveless tee shirt, my sleeping attire. I looked in the refrigerator. Nothing. I made myself a peanut butter sandwich and got into bed. I opened my laptop and tried to get a cell phone number for Donna Connolly. My database showed an AT&T mobile phone number. I didn't know if she would talk to me but I had to try.

The next morning I dropped off my rental car at nine and took an Uber over to the auto body shop. My Beetle looked as good as new. I was a happy puppy.

On my way in I picked up a salad at the deli near my office. Stephen, my regular mailman, popped in my office. "I hope you haven't brought me any bad news," I said to Stephen.

"Never for you," he said chuckling.

I called Donna's cell number praying she would answer. It went straight to voice mail. Maybe she was at work.

"Hey Susie, can we meet for dinner tonight? Talk soon."

As I was devouring my salad, my phone buzzed. "You sound disappointed. Were you expecting someone else?" Susie feigned being hurt.

"I was hoping it was someone calling that I needed to talk to about the case, but you'll do."

"Thanks. I feel so much better. I'll meet you at Anton's at seven."

By six o'clock, as I was giving up any hope that Donna would call, my phone buzzed. "Tracey Marks."

"Ms. Marks this is Donna Connolly."

"Thank you for getting back to me."

"I'm actually glad you got in touch with me. Can we meet somewhere tomorrow during the day?"

"Absolutely, whatever is convenient for you."

"I'm going to be in the city. Can I come by your office say around eleven a.m.?"

"Yes. That's perfect."

For a change I arrived at Anton's before Susie and went straight to the bar. "Hi John, can I have a glass of Merlot?" John was gorgeous and gay. By night he was a bartender and by day he was studying law.

"Here you go Tracey. How's everything?"

"Good. Are you taking the bar exam soon?"

"I am, in a few weeks."

"You never know when I might need a good lawyer."

"What's all the chatter about?" Susie said as she sat down. "John what do you suggest? I'm feeling adventurous."

John came back with a Margarita. "Looks delicious. Excellent choice," Susie said.

A few minutes later we were seated at a table. "I'm famished," I said.

"If you weren't I would think something was wrong. Did your call come in?"

"It did." I filled Susie in on the latest developments.

"Well now my curiosity is peaked."

"Mine too," I said just as our waiter came over.

"Are you new?" Susie asked the waiter.

"Yes, my name is Jason. I just started two days ago."

"Well we promise to be gentle," Susie said. "I'll have your house salad and a bowl of pasta with red sauce."

"And I'll have the linguini and clams and a house salad."

"Thanks ladies."

"He's really cute," Susie said. "He looks a little like Brad Pitt."

"Did you know John is taking the Bar exam soon?" I said.

"I did. I was here with Mark about a week ago and was giving John some pointers. I hope he passes on the first try, though if he does he may quit bartending and that would not be a good thing."

"Leave it to you to cover all the bases. Is Mark working tonight?"

"No, he's out with some of his friends. I think it's a birthday celebration."

"I'm kind of worried about the case. It's so different from the last one, and if it does have something to do with Stephanie's past, a lot more complicated."

"One step at a time, that's how you'll figure it out. Don't look too far ahead. It will just frustrate you. And this time you have Jack and me to use as sounding boards. By the way, how's the car?"

"All fixed. If I ever find out who ran me off the road, they'll be sorry."

"I'd like to be there when that happens," Susie laughed.

After inhaling my pasta, we both ordered Tiramisu for dessert. By the time we left it was almost ten.

It was drizzling when I woke up the next morning. By the time I walked out of my apartment building the rain had stopped and the skies were brightening up so I decided to walk to work.

I tried to keep myself busy, my mind wondering what Donna wanted to talk to me about.

At eleven-fifteen Donna came in. When I saw her yesterday she was dressed in a leather skirt and white turtleneck sweater. Today she was in jeans, a black pullover sweater and short black boots.

"Donna, please sit. Can I get you tea or coffee?"

"Tea, please, no milk or sugar."

"Do you work in the city?" I said trying to make small talk hoping it would make her feel more comfortable.

"I work for a small publishing house in White Plains three days a week."

While I was handing Donna a cup of tea she said, "I'm not sure if this was a mistake coming here. I really don't know anything that can help you."

Okay, now what. "Something prompted you to see me. I promise whatever you tell me will be held in the strictest confidence." I could tell she was nervous. I waited through the silence.

"When my husband told you we hadn't seen Stephanie in years, that wasn't exactly true. I saw her about two months ago when I bumped into her in Scarsdale. We went for coffee. While we were catching up, she seemed distracted. I asked her if something was wrong and that's when she just came out and said Maddie had been raped when we were in high school. I was flabbergasted. I had no idea."

"Did she tell you who raped Maddie?"

"Stephanie said she didn't know, but I didn't believe her."

"Why is that?"

"She seemed nervous, as if she was hiding something."

"Did you know who Maddie was dating back then?"

"I thought it might have been a teacher at the school, but that's just a guess. It was a feeling I had at the time, but I have nothing to back it up."

"Sometimes our first instincts can be right. What made you think it was a teacher?"

"I just thought it was odd that she wouldn't tell anyone who she was seeing. Whoever it was, she kept it a secret."

"Was there any particular teacher you thought it might be?"

"If it was a teacher it would be pure speculation and I wouldn't want to accuse anyone."

"I understand, but it's been more than twenty-five years."

"I'm sorry, but it wouldn't be right."

"Do you think Maddie might have told anyone?"

"If she did it would have probably been Stephanie since they were fairly close."

"Is there a reason you never told your husband you saw Stephanie?"

"It must have slipped my mind."

I didn't believe her for a second, but I knew I wasn't going to get anything more from Donna.

"Thank you for your honesty and if you think of anything else please give me a call."

Well that conversation was very illuminating. I wondered why after all these years Stephanie told Donna about the rape. Was Maddie seeing a teacher? That might be the reason Maddie was frightened to tell anyone about the rape, especially if he threatened her. But why would this teacher rape her if they were seeing each other? And why didn't Donna tell her husband about her conversation with Stephanie? Again more questions than answers.

CHAPTER 18

I took out Stephanie's high school yearbook. It had a list of all the teachers in her graduating class. Obviously I could eliminate all the women teachers. The good news is Hudson is a very small school and besides photos of the graduating class, they had photos of the teachers. I thought I would call Linda Brent and see if she knew anything about Maddie dating a teacher.

I put a call into Linda and left a voice message. Then I went to the deli three blocks away to get lunch. My phone buzzed as I was ordering a turkey sandwich. "Tracey Marks."

"Ms. Marks, its Linda."

"Thanks for calling me back. I have some information that Maddie may have been involved with a teacher at Hudson."

"I can't help you," she said.

"I don't understand. What does that mean?"

"I don't know what you want from me. I told you about the rape."

"Look, both Stephanie and Maddie are dead. Don't you want to find out why? These secrets you're trying to keep aren't helping anyone anymore. I really need your cooperation."

"Not over the phone. I have no idea if someone could be listening."

"I understand. I'll meet you." I thought she was being a bit paranoid but I had no choice.

"There's a parking lot opposite the movie theatre in Bronxville. I can meet you there at four."

"Okay, I'll be standing outside my car."

As I was eating my lunch, my mind was in overdrive. If Linda knew the name of the teacher it could be the break I was looking for. I tried not to get ahead of myself, one step at a time.

Since it was fairly mild out I walked back to my garage and picked up my car. The traffic was light and I made it up to Bronxville by three forty-five. Bronxville was an affluent community in Westchester County, a few miles from Scarsdale. I waited in my car until four and then stood outside. Linda spotted me and parked next to my car. She lowered her window and told me to get in.

"I'm sorry to make you come all the way up here but you hear all this stuff about cell phones. I just didn't want to chance it."

"It's no problem," and waited for her to continue.

"Maddie was seeing a teacher. She had no illusions that she was going off into the sunset with him. She knew she wanted a career, but she liked being with him. Both Stephanie and I thought he was taking advantage of her but Maddie didn't care. She made us promise we wouldn't tell anyone."

"Did she tell you his name?"

"She didn't, but she did say he wasn't married so I assumed he wasn't one of the older teachers."

"Well maybe he was older but divorced."

"I guess it's possible."

"Was Maddie seeing this teacher around the time she was raped?"

"I think so, but I never thought he raped her. Why would he rape her? They were probably having consensual sex."

"People don't always tell the truth, even to their best friends. Maybe she didn't want to see him anymore and he got angry. Maybe she lied and he was married."

"I didn't think of that."

I opened up the yearbook and showed Linda the photos of the teachers. She said she really didn't know which teacher it was and couldn't help me.

On the way back I called Susie. "Hey, this is the latest. Donna said she bumped into Stephanie and told Donna about the rape. She also thought Maddie was dating a teacher but it was just a hunch. Oh, and Donna never told her husband about the chance meeting."

"The plot thickens."

"I then met with Linda and she confirmed Maddie was dating a teacher but had no idea which one. She also thought he wasn't the one who raped her."

"This is getting good. If you need a sidekick, I'm available. I could always develop a case of the flu and call in sick."

"I'll definitely keep you in mind," I said smiling. "I guess now I'm going to have to check out possible teachers."

"Just be careful. Take your gun with you for precaution."

"Will do."

When I woke up the next day my window sills were covered with snow. Huge flakes were coming down. It was a good excuse to work from home, at least for part of the day. I took out Stephanie's yearbook and meticulously ran each name through my database. There were ten male teachers. Three I eliminated because they were in their sixties back then, and I just thought they were too old. As it turns out two were deceased and the other one was about ninety now.

The other seven were not as easy to eliminate. Four were around forty, thirty-two years ago which would make them in their seventies now. Two were in Florida, one lived in North Carolina and one lived locally. That left three teachers, Kevin O'Donnell, Larry McKinley and Jay Henderson. The only one in their twenties when Maddie was in high school was Jay Henderson; the other two were in their mid-thirties. All seven were possibilities though I thought I would start with the three youngest.

My database search listed Jay Henderson as fifty-two and employed at Hudson Prep. He owned his house in New Rochelle with a Rachael Henderson. I presume that Rachael was his wife. No criminal records listed.

I googled Jay Henderson. My, my, he is now the principal at the school. Well that's interesting.

Larry McKinley was now sixty-five and living in Scottsdale, Arizona. Hopefully he was not the one dating Maddie. Kevin O'Donnell was now sixty-seven and lived in Dobbs Ferry in Westchester County. His work employment is listed as Hudson Prep. He doesn't appear to be married, at least not currently. Two of the teachers back then are still at Hudson Prep. Maybe with a little luck it could be one of them.

I needed to tell Maddie's mother what happened to her. I had no idea where this investigation was leading but Mrs. Jensen had a right to know. I called her and she agreed to speak with me the next day.

I started to doubt whether I was doing the right thing by telling Mrs. Jensen what happened to her daughter. I can't imagine what a shock it was going to be. I was getting cold feet.

"Hey, I need your advice on something."

"Shoot," Susie responded.

"I want to tell Maddie's mother about the rape, but I don't know if it's the right thing to do. It seems at this point too many people know, and what happens if it comes out during my investigation?"

"I think you're doing the right thing. How do you think she'll feel if she finds out by accident?"

"I just feel awful telling her."

"She has a right to know. Maybe she won't have to wonder anymore why her daughter committed suicide."

When we hung up, I didn't feel much better.

On Saturday the sun was shining. I still wasn't looking forward to telling Mrs. Jensen that her daughter had been raped. It was enough that her daughter had been dead since she was a teenager and now to tell her this.

I found a parking spot in front of her building. Mrs. Jensen buzzed me in. Like last time Mrs. Jensen was waiting for me outside her apartment door. She took my coat and led me into a toasty warm kitchen. We sat down at a square antique wooden table.

My palms were sweating. I didn't know how to begin. "I've been speaking to members of the group Maddie was involved with trying to find out if there was any connection to Stephanie's death and what happened to Maddie. One of the girls in the group was a Linda Clark, her married name is Brent. Does her name sound familiar?"

"Yes, now that you mention it. Did she say anything about my Maddie?"

I was dreading the next words out of my mouth. "I'm sorry to have to tell you this but Maddie confided in Linda and Stephanie that she had been raped in high school, but swore them to secrecy." I waited. Mrs. Jensen started crying. It was heart wrenching.

Through her tears she said, "my poor Maddie."

"Can I get you a glass of water?" I asked.

"I don't understand why she wouldn't tell us," looking distraught.

"From what I understood she may have been threatened."

"But we could have helped her. The awful pain she must have been in," she said dabbing her eyes.

I didn't know what to say. I was at a loss for words. Mrs. Jensen was consumed with grief. I got up and brought back a glass of water and placed it in front of her. I doubt she knew anything about any teacher Maddie was seeing.

"Mrs. Jensen, I know it was so long ago but can you recall anyone Maddie was going out with in high school?"

"No, I can't," she said in a robotic voice. "When I moved from the house to the apartment I couldn't part with any of Maddie's things. I boxed them up and kept them in the closet in the spare room. Your welcome to look through her stuff if you think it might help. Just don't take anything."

"Thank you."

Mrs. Jensen showed me to the spare room where the boxes were and then left. The look on her face brought tears to my eyes. Wiping my face, it was time to get down to business. I took out the two boxes from the closet. There were a few trophies, books, photos, notebooks. I went through each thing. The notebooks didn't have anything personal in them. I turned each book upside down and shook them. A folded piece of paper came tumbling out of one of the books. It was a letter to someone that was never mailed. It was addressed to a Joe. It appeared she started the letter several different ways but never finished it. Basically, the letter said she couldn't see him anymore because she didn't want to hurt anyone. Since I didn't think Mrs. Jensen knew the letter even existed, I took it. I put the boxes back where they were and found Mrs. Jensen sitting in the living room looking lost.

"Mrs. Jensen," I said softly. Are you alright?" A stupid thing to probably say.

"If there is anything you can do to find this person who harmed my Maddie, I would be grateful."

"I'll do my best."

"Was there anything in the boxes you found that was helpful?"

"Not really. I will let you know if I find out anything."

"Thank you," she said as she walked me to the door. She looked smaller than when I first arrived.

CHAPTER 19

When I got back to my car I turned on my cell phone. There was a missed call from Jack. "Hey, I'm up in Scarsdale. I had an appointment with Maddie's mother."

"I miss you too."

"Sorry, I know I have a tendency to get excited and skip the normal rituals."

"That's okay. I'm just busting your chops. Your phone etiquette is very endearing."

"I'm glad. Can I continue now?"

"By all means."

"I decided to tell Mrs. Jensen about the rape. There were a few people in the group that knew and I didn't want her to find out from someone else. It was heartbreaking. It was like adding salt to a wound. Did I make the right choice?"

"I think you did. I know it was hard for you to watch her suffer, but this would probably come out at some point."

"I know, but the pain on her face." I filled Jack in on what I learned about Maddie possibly dating a teacher. Also I told him about the letter I found. "I wonder if it was the Joe in the group. Boy, this is getting to be a tangled web. I hope it's not too much for me to handle. And what if I'm completely off base and it has nothing to do with the past. I'm wasting a lot of time."

"It's your investigation. You have to go with what you believe. One step at a time. I would talk to this guy Joe first."

"What happens if he denies it even if it really is him?"

"The only reason he might deny it is if he was seeing his girlfriend at the same time. You are going to have to use your persuasiveness to get the truth. It works on me."

"Well you're easy."

"I beg your pardon. I will remember those words."

"I'm heading back to the city to the comfort of my warm apartment. What are you up to?"

"I have to do some additional follow-ups from my original interviews I conducted. Tomorrow is football."

"I didn't realize I was dating a football kind of guy. I might have to rethink this whole relationship," I said with a grin.

"Right back at you. Be safe."

"You too."

It was nice to get back to my apartment. I stopped at the supermarket and picked up fresh salmon and salad stuff for dinner. The rest of the day I binged watching Homeland and reading my John Grisham book.

Sunday flew by. Monday morning, after finding a cell phone number for Joe Connolly, I called him. He answered on the first ring.

"Mr. Connolly. I'm sorry to bother you again but something has come up and I really need your help. Would it be possible for us to meet?"

"Can't we do this over the phone? I'm very busy."

"That won't work. I can meet you wherever you are. It will only take a few minutes."

"I'm at a construction site in the Bronx." Joe gave me the address.

I quickly showered and scarfed down my Cheerios and milk. I was at the site by ten- thirty. I spotted Joe. He was in the middle of talking to some of the workmen. As soon as he saw me he stopped talking and quickly walked over to me.

"Why don't we go in here," leading me into a makeshift shed. "So what was so urgent you couldn't tell me over the phone?"

"I know you were dating Maddie." The look on his face gave him away. He tried to recover but it was too late. I didn't wait for a response. "I found a letter written by Maddie from high school. It was never mailed and it was addressed to you. Were you dating Donna also at that time?"

"What's the big deal? We were kids. What are you getting at?"

"Maddie broke up with you. Did it make you angry enough to rape her?"

"Are you out of your mind? Whatever we did was consensual."

"Did Donna find out?"

"Not that it's any of your business, but no. Maddie and I hooked up for just a short period."

"But you would have kept seeing her if she didn't break up with you?" He didn't answer me.

"If there's nothing else, I have to get back to work."

"Yes, one more thing. "Do you know why she didn't want to see you anymore?"

"I got the impression she started seeing someone else."

"Do you know who?"

"No, and I didn't ask."

I didn't believe Joe. He didn't strike me as someone who takes rejection in stride. But could he have raped Maddie? I certainly wouldn't rule him out. I wonder if Donna did know about his fling with Maddie. What would she have done about it if she had found out?

Finding a parking spot near the office was proving difficult. It took me fifteen minutes to find a spot five blocks away. On my way in, I stopped for a chicken salad sandwich at the deli.

Before going into my office I popped in next door to Cousin Alan. "Hey Margaret, how's everything?"

"Tracey, I hardly ever see you."

"I've been really busy. I'm working on a case that's taking a lot of my time. How are the kids and Mike?"

"Everyone's fine. No catastrophes at the moment. Alan is out with the flu. I think it hit him over the weekend."

"I'll give him a call. Take care."

I started the coffee machine and called Patty. "I heard Alan has the flu. How's he doing?"

"Terrible. He's a guy. You would think he was dying."

"How's Michael?"

"Fortunately we are both fine for the moment."

"Let me know if you need anything. I can stop by and throw whatever I get into the house."

"Well, let's hope I don't need eggs," she laughed.

"Tell the big baby I said hi."

I settled in, and while eating lunch I was debating what my next course of action was going to be. Did I really think any of the teachers were going to admit to having an affair with Maddie, let alone raping her, even with my gift of persuasiveness? What choice did I have? One step at a time.

I thought I would start with Larry McKinley since it was just a phone call to Arizona. So what would I say to him? 'Oh, I heard you were screwing Maddie Jensen, who by the way was a minor and she couldn't consent.' You think that conversation would go well?

I called. No answer. I left my name and number without leaving a message. It was twelve-thirty in Arizona. Maybe he was on the golf course. Why else would you move there?

I wrote up what I found out since my last report to Christine Harris and emailed it to her. I wish I had some positive news to give her.

My phone buzzed. "Tracey Marks."

"Ms. Marks, this is Larry McKinley returning your phone call."

"Thank you. I'm a private investigator in New York and I'm investigating the death of a Stephanie Harris. Her maiden name was Howell and she attended Hudson Prep back in 1987. Do you happen to remember her?"

"It was a long time ago. I can't really say for sure. I taught science and math. It's a small school so chances are she was in one of my classes. How did she die?"

"She was murdered. There may be a connection to something that happened back in high school. At this point I'm exploring all possibilities."

"I don't understand."

"Do you remember a girl by the name of Maddie Jensen? She was raped in high school but she never told anyone except two friends, Stephanie and Linda Clark. Maddie swore them to secrecy. I believe she may have been threatened."

"Poor girl. How is that connected to Stephanie Harris?"

"I'm not sure that it is. Stephanie may have known who raped Maddie."

"But even so, that was a long time ago. Why would someone kill her now?"

"That's what I'm trying to find out. Do you recall any rumors about Maddie Jensen seeing a teacher at the school?"

"No I don't. Even if that was the case, it wouldn't be something that a teacher would have broadcasted."

"There were ten male teachers that were at the school during that time period. Is there anyone you can think of that might have dated a student?"

"It sounds like you're accusing a teacher of raping Ms. Jensen. I'm sorry but I can't help you."

I heard a click. Well what did I expect? Without seeing his face it's hard to know if he was hiding anything.

My cell buzzed. It said unknown caller. I answered anyway. "Hello."

"Is this Tracey Marks?"

"Who's calling?"

"My name is Jeffrey Goldman. I knew Stephanie."

CHAPTER 20

I didn't recall that name coming up at all. "How did you get my number?"

"It will be easier to explain in person. I have a real estate firm in Manhattan. I could come by your office or you can meet me at mine."

Curiosity got the better of me.

"Why don't you come here? Do you know where my office is?"

"I do. I can come by tomorrow, say around noon?"

"I'll see you then."

When we hung up I was wondering if it was such a good idea to have him come to the office with no one here but me. For all I know he could have killed Stephanie. Then again, if he wanted to kill me, he could probably do it without announcing himself.

I called Susie as soon as I hung up. "Can you meet for a drink? I'm ready to pack it in."

"I'll meet you at the Vanguard Wine Bar in an hour."

The place was already hopping when I got there. I snatched a table and ordered a Malbec while I waited for Susie. Vanguard has great atmosphere. It's cozy inside with wooden tables, subway tiles on the walls and offers small plates with a flair for the French. I think I read that.

"Hi, I'm glad you were able to get a table. You started drinking without me?" Susie said.

"That's because I knew you would catch up to me in no time."

The waiter came over and we ordered a cheese platter and olives. Susie ordered a Cabernet Sauvignon.

"How's the trial going?" I asked Susie.

"I'm raking the bastard over the coals. He deserves to be destroyed."

"Do I sense a note of hostility in your voice?"

"Is that what you glean from what I said? What he has put his poor wife through, he deserves no mercy."

"I dare to ask."

"The guy, besides having an affair, was trying to drive her crazy and slowly turn their kids against her."

"Well it sounds like you're getting revenge."

While we were enjoying our cheese, olives and delicious crusty bread, I filled Susie in on everything that I had found out in the last couple of days.

"Hopefully this guy Goldman might be able to provide some helpful information."

"I'm keeping my fingers crossed," I said.

"I wouldn't expect too much from any of the teachers you talk with, though you might get a sense from their reaction to your questions. I wonder if someone else back then who worked at the school might know something."

"How would you propose I might find out?"

"How about going directly to the school? If you start inquiring, maybe something will shake out."

"Great idea. I know that two of the male teachers are still at the school. One is now the principal," I said.

"Also, this Joe Connolly, maybe he's the one that raped Maddie. He could have been jealous that she broke it off. If he was hot on her, maybe he didn't take it as well as he said he did."

"That's what I was thinking."

"How are you getting along without Carolyn?"

"As long as I have no pressing matters besides this case, I'm okay. Jack is coming down this Saturday. I thought you guys might want to come over on Sunday."

"Are you cooking?" Susie said with a straight face.

"If I was does that mean you're not coming?"

"Well it probably means Mark and I will eat first."

"Very funny. We'll order in. And there's always ice cream for dessert from the Corner Sweet Shoppe."

"Now that you should have led with."

On my way into the office the next day, I stopped for my usual. Anna seems to have a sixth sense, my muffin and coffee ready before she even sees me. "How are the kids?" I asked her.

"It would take up most of the day if I told you about all the trials and tribulations they put me through," laughing as she said it.

"Well it's good to see you still have a sense of humor," I said waving goodbye."

Sitting in my office, I bit into my muffin thinking about Jeffrey Goldman and what he might know.

I was just finishing up some paperwork when I heard the door open. I got up quickly to meet Mr. Goldman. He was a nice looking man, dressed in a business suit that fit snug against his six-foot frame. His eyes were a beautiful light green. We went back to my office.

"Can I get you anything to drink?"

"Coffee, only if you'll join me," he said taking off his coat.

"So what can I do for you?" I said trying to act all businesslike.

"There's something you need to know."

"Why don't you start with how you met Stephanie and go from there."

"Fair enough. Stephanie and I knew each other since high school. We never dated but we were friends."

"I'm sorry to interrupt but were you part of the group Stephanie was in during her junior year?"

"No. I met Stephanie in her senior year. When I met her she didn't seem to have any friends. I was kind of nerdy and shy. Maybe we were just two loners that found each other and felt safe sharing stuff. Anyway, throughout the years we stayed in touch, although our lives drifted in different directions. I guess our bond in some way stayed strong. We reached out to each other at different times in our lives."

"Did you both keep the relationship secret?"

"I know I did and I think she did also."

"Were you at the funeral?"

"I was."

"You didn't sign the book."

"No I didn't. I guess I still wanted to keep our secret."

"So what is it that you need to tell me?"

"About two months ago I got a call from Stephanie. She

seemed agitated. We arranged to meet. She told me to make sure I wasn't followed. I didn't know what to make of it. When we met up, Stephanie told me that she had been getting some threatening telephone calls recently. That's when she told me that Maddie Jensen was raped in high school."

"But why did she feel the need to confess now?"

"I don't know."

"Exactly what did she tell you about the rape?"

"She said she witnessed the rape but no one knew, not even Maddie."

I couldn't believe what I was hearing.

"Go on."

"Maddie was threatened and that's why she never reported it. She swore Stephanie and Linda to secrecy."

"Did she say who raped Maddie?"

"She told me that there were three boys. One was the ringleader who pushed Maddie down and raped her. It wasn't clear what the other two guys did."

"Did she tell you their names?"

"No. She clammed up and stopped talking."

"Where was Stephanie hiding when Maddie was raped?"

"I don't know. I didn't ask. I told her to go to the police but she said it was too dangerous. That's when she mentioned she was going to talk to a private investigator."

"So that's how you knew about me. Do you think she told anyone else what was going on?"

"I don't think so, though I can't be sure."

"Did she happen to mention what the threatening calls were about?"

"No. I think she was sorry she told me. She said it was probably nothing and to forget she said anything."

"Did she ever mention Maddie dating a teacher at the school?"

"No. Though it was a small school, I really didn't know Maddie very well. I wasn't part of the social scene back then. Maddie was very pretty and had a reputation of being a flirt. Even if I wanted to date her, she would never have had anything to do with me."

"When Stephanie was killed why didn't you go to the police with what she told you?"

"The papers said it was a robbery so I guess that's what I wanted to believe."

"So why come to me now?"

"I'm not really sure. I guess I'm not convinced it was a robbery and it felt safer coming to you than the police."

"Is there anything else you can think of that Stephanie said that might be important?"

"Not that I can recall. Do you think it was a robbery?"

"I don't believe in coincidences. She made an appointment to see me the very day she was killed."

"Do you think I should go to the police?"

"I can't answer that for you. I'm not sure if Stephanie's death was related to the rape but from what you've told me there's a good chance it may be. I'm definitely going to look into it."

"Thank you."

"If you think of anything else, please give me a call."

Wow, that was interesting. Stephanie was being threatened. It would appear to be someone who might feel threatened now but maybe not back then. But why would someone think Stephanie would talk after all these years? Did Stephanie think it was worth the risk to expose this person, and why now? Was Jeffrey Goldman telling the truth? Too many questions with no answers.

CHAPTER 21

Before I took everything Jeffrey Goldman told me as the gospel, I needed to check him out. For all I know he could just be fishing for information and he may be the killer. I think this job is playing with my imagination. I'm seeing a killer everywhere.

After searching all my databases, there weren't any flashing warning signals. He had no criminal records, his driver record was clean except for one speeding ticket and he did have a real estate broker's license. He lived in a condo in Hastings on the Hudson. I guess none of this means he's on the up and up. Let's just say for now he is telling the truth.

It was time to go back to where it all started, the school. Since it was after three I decided to go up first thing in the morning. So what was the plan? I thought I would wait before confronting Jay Henderson and Kevin O'Donnell. I wanted to gather as much information from people associated with the school back then. Maybe something would come to light.

I called Christine Harris to update her. "Ms. Harris, its Tracey. I had an interesting conversation with someone who knew your mother. Apparently they became friends in their senior year of high school. They confided in each other and throughout the years they remained in contact. I think Stephanie felt safe with this person." I filled Christine in on my conversation with Mr. Goldman.

"I don't know what to say. All these years and I never knew about him."

"I know it's hard to believe, but parents have secrets that they keep, especially from their children. The good news is that we may be on the right track. We just have to keep digging."

"Thank you," she said, though there was sadness in her voice.

On the way up to Hudson Prep the next day, I called Stephanie's business partner, Jennifer Daniels. It seemed odd that they worked so closely together and Stephanie didn't confide in her at all. "Jennifer, its Tracey Marks. Can you give me a call when you get a chance?"

I parked in the visiting area and found my way to the school entrance. It was weird being back at school, though mine was not private. I guess I looked lost since a woman came up to me and asked if she could help me.

"I'm looking for the office?"

"I'm going that way. Follow me. My name is Cynthia. Are you a parent to one of the students here?"

I was slightly insulted, but when I thought about it, I guess I could have a teenage kid.

"No."

"Well, here we are. Maybe I can help you. Would you like to sit?"

"Yes, thank you." Cynthia had taken me back to her office. On her desk the nameplate read, Cynthia Dunlop, Assistant Principal. She looked to be in her fifties, but nothing like the Assistant Principal when I was in high school, though all adults over thirty looked old when I was a teenager.

I took out my card and handed it to her. I noticed a tall guy with grayish hair walk by. I wondered if that was Jay Henderson. I turned my attention back to Ms. Dunlop. "I don't know if you've heard, one of your prior students, Stephanie Harris was killed. Her maiden name was Howell."

"Of course. What a tragedy. I felt so bad for her and her family when I read about it in the newspaper."

"I'm investigating her death. It appears she may have been targeted. I'm trying to find people who might have known her back in high school." I didn't want to mention Maddie.

"I have to ask, what does her murder have to do with Hudson Prep?"

"It may not, but I'm investigating several different possibilities." I was trying to be vague. If she knew it had to do with Stephanie's time here specifically, Cynthia might not be as cooperative as I need her to be.

"Well what is it you would like to know?"

"Were you here in 1987?"

"Yes, but barely. I started in 1986. There really isn't anything I could tell you about Stephanie."

"Maybe you remember any kids that were sort of trouble makers or that didn't fit in?"

"It was a long time ago, and as I said, I was relatively new and didn't know the kids all that well."

"Do you happen to remember anyone who might be able to help me?"

"There was a woman who worked in the office back then and recently retired. She's in her seventies now. Her name is Mary Stevens. I believe she lives in Ardsley."

"Was the principal here at that time?"

"He was, but he was a new teacher just like me." I left it alone.

"Thank you so much for your time Ms. Dunlop. I really appreciate it."

When I went back to my car I looked up an address for Mrs. Stevens. I thought as long as I was in the area I would drive over and see if she was home. Whitepages.com listed an address for a Mary Stevens, age seventy-seven, in Ardsley, New York. It seemed that all the towns in Westchester were relatively close to each other.

I pulled up to a small, but very pretty house. It was painted white with black shutters and had flower boxes outside on the upper and lower windows. I rang the bell. When she opened the door I was surprised to see a very pretty woman who could have passed for twenty years younger. She was tall and looked to be in great shape. Her hair was a silver gray, cut short which suited her face. She had on black slacks and a white pullover cashmere sweater. I could only hope to look as good as her when I'm her age. There was a screen door that separated us.

"Ms. Stevens, my name is Tracey Marks. Cynthia Dunlop at Hudson Prep gave me your name. I'm investigating the death of Stephanie Harris." She unlocked the screen door.

"Please come in. It's freezing out there."

"Thank you." We went into a kitchen that looked recently renovated with gray cabinets, stainless steel appliances and a light gray wood floor and white walls. We sat down at the kitchen table.

"I was just making myself a cup of tea. Can I offer you a cup?"

"Yes, thank you." The truth be known, I only drink tea when I'm sick but sometimes sacrifices have to be made.

"What a shame about Stephanie. The papers said it was a burglary."

"Yes, I know what the papers said, but I'm exploring the prospect it may have had something to do with when she was a teenager." Since Mary was no longer at the school I thought my best shot at getting any information was to be honest with her. "The day Stephanie was killed Ms. Harris was coming in to see me. When we spoke on the phone she seemed agitated. Unfortunately I never had the chance to find out why she wanted to see me. I've spoken to a few of her classmates. It turns out Stephanie and her friend Maddie were keeping a terrible secret. Maddie had been raped and I believe she was threatened to keep quiet. I also believe Stephanie witnessed the rape." Mrs. Stevens looked shocked.

"I had no idea."

"Why would you. Nobody knew. Not even Maddie's parents. I think that's the reason Maddie committed suicide."

"That poor girl, how can I help you," as she poured water into my cup, the teabag already settled inside.

"There were a few kids that Maddie and Stephanie hung around with before the incident, Joe Connolly and his girlfriend Donna, Greg Todd and Linda Brent. Can you tell me anything about them?" My phone was vibrating. I let it go to voice mail.

"Let me think. I remember Joe Connolly. He was a big guy if I recall correctly. I remember him because he was kind of a smart mouth. He was in the office more than once for mouthing off. He nearly got kicked out of school. Private schools don't tolerate insubordinate behavior."

"But he was never kicked out?"

"No. I think when he knew the school was serious, he changed his attitude. His parents were informed and maybe read him the riot act."

"Was he a bully?"

"I'm not quite sure you would call him a bully but because of his size he could be intimidating."

"What about Greg Todd. Do you remember any problems with him?"

"No, I don't."

"Can you recall anyone else that stands out?"

"Not really. Not that they were all saints but nothing that comes to mind. If I remember correctly Maddie Jensen was very pretty and definitely well developed, if you know what I mean. The boys liked her."

My segue into my next question. "There were rumors that Maddie was seeing a teacher at the school. Did you hear anything about that?" I took a sip of tea.

"I'm not saying yes and I'm not saying no, but I'm not naïve. I know it's a possibility."

"Please, if you know anything at all. Maddie has been dead for years. Nothing is going to happen to this person but I would like to question him. Maybe he knew who raped Maddie."

"I may have heard rumors but I have no idea who it could be even if it was true."

"Do you remember if there were any complaints filed by female students regarding rape allegations?"

"I don't, but if there were any complaints, those files would probably be long gone by now."

"Can you think of anyone who might have information that would be helpful to my investigation?"

"Leave me your card and if I think of anyone I'll contact you."

I've heard that before, most of the time it means I'll never hear from that person again. On the ride back I went over what Ms. Stevens told me. The one interesting thing I learned was that Joe Connolly was definitely not a saint. Though he told me he wasn't angry that Maddie broke it off, maybe Susie was right. Could he have raped Maddie because she didn't want to go out with him anymore? Maybe Joe didn't take no for an answer as well as he would have liked me to believe.

CHAPTER 22

On the ride back I thought about Maddie. How come Linda Brent never mentioned that Maddie was a flirt? Maybe Linda was jealous. Was Maddie raped because she got involved with the wrong guy, and was that guy Joe Connolly? Always more questions than answers.

I checked my phone. Jennifer Daniels had returned my call. "Ms. Daniels, it's Tracey Marks. Sorry to bother you but I was wondering if you thought of anything else that Stephanie might have told you, even if it didn't seem important at the time?"

"Like I mentioned to you, she seemed a little more anxious than usual but she never said anything to me."

"Okay, thank you." No point in beating a dead horse. It appears except for Jeffrey Goldman, Stephanie didn't confide in anyone else about her situation. I should speak to Linda Brent again. She is the only other person who knew about the rape at the time or at least that I know of.

I headed home instead of the office. It was after two o'clock and I hadn't exercised in a few days. When I got back I changed into my running clothes, grabbed a banana and ventured out into the cold. I didn't see Wally; maybe he was on a break.

One of the things I love about running is that I'm not thinking about anything. My mind is blank. Not today. All kinds of thoughts were running rampant. Gradually I was getting a clearer picture of Maddie but not fast enough for my liking. Could I be completely on the wrong track? Is it possible Stephanie's death had nothing to do with her past but something that occurred in the present? I think I'm driving myself crazy.

On the way back I stopped at a neighborhood Italian restaurant. It was mostly takeout, though there were a couple of tables if you wanted to stay. I ordered Eggplant Parmesan to go.

After showering I called Linda Brent and left a message in her voice mail.

While I was warming up my eggplant, I put together a salad. And who said I can't cook? I could hear my phone buzzing from across the room.

"Hello."

"Ms. Marks, its Linda Brent."

"Linda, since we last spoke I found out some additional information. Do you think we could meet at some point tomorrow?" There was a long pause before she answered.

"I don't think there's anything more I can tell you."

"I really need your help. It seems you're the only one besides Stephanie who knew about the rape." I decided not to mention Jeffrey Goldman now.

"Is this really necessary?"

"I wouldn't ask if it wasn't."

"I have an appointment tomorrow morning at ten-thirty. Can you be at my house by eight-thirty?"

"No problem."

I was up at the crack of dawn and was knocking on Linda's door on the dot of eight- thirty. She didn't look all that happy to see me. Who could blame her?

"Thank you for seeing me." We went into a small living room decorated with ultra modern furniture, lots of chrome and glass. I sat on a leather couch and Linda sat opposite me on a white leather chair with chrome legs.

"So what's going on?" Linda said crossing her legs several times.

"Since I last spoke with you I found out some things about Maddie. For one, she was fairly flirtatious which in itself is not a big deal, but it turns out she was involved for a while with one of the members of your group, Joe Connolly." I stopped talking, waiting to hear her response. There was none so I continued. "From what Joe said, it appears she broke it off and was seeing someone else."

"When we first spoke I didn't want to say anything negative about Maddie since she was dead. I guess I thought what would be the point."

"I can understand your dilemma but it's important that I know about Maddie."

"I still don't know why since you're investigating Stephanie's death."

I was trying to be patient. "As I may have mentioned to you, there may be a connection between Maddie's rape and Stephanie's murder. Right now I need to find out everything you know in case it is relevant to Stephanie's death. Were you aware that Maddie was having a relationship with Joe?"

"We all knew."

"You mean everyone in the group?"

"Yes."

"Does that include Donna?"

"Yes." Interesting I thought to myself.

"Was Donna upset that Joe was fooling around with Maddie?"

"There really wasn't much she could do about it. It's not like Donna and Joe were going steady or anything like that. We all knew Maddie and Joe would fizzle out and it did. Maddie broke it off and that was the end of it."

"Why did everyone think it would fizzle out?"

"Maddie never stayed with one guy too long."

"How did Joe take it? He doesn't strike me as the type that would take rejection well." I was just fishing.

"As far as I remember he was okay with it." Her face betrayed her but I didn't say anything.

"Did it cause a rift in the group?"

"Not really. Maddie moved on to someone else."

"Was that someone else a teacher?" Linda had a surprised look on her face.

"She never told us."

"But what did you think?"

"I had my suspicions."

"But you never tried to find out?"

"Not really." I didn't believe her. What teenager wouldn't be curious about something like that?

"I find it a little odd that Donna wouldn't harbor any bad feelings toward Maddie. I would think she would be furious at her. I know I would."

"Like I said there wasn't much she could do about it."

"Can you tell me a little bit about Joe?"

"What would you like to know?"

"I spoke to someone who worked in the office where you attended high school. She told me that Joe almost got kicked out." Linda didn't seem surprised.

"I knew Joe liked to stir up a little trouble but nothing serious."

"Do you think Joe is capable of raping Maddie because she rejected him?"

"No, of course not. I really have to get going now," she said abruptly. "I'll show you out."

Well that hit a nerve. I don't think she was telling me everything. At some point I'll have to speak to Donna again. This little group of theirs was not as harmonious as I thought. But was there something weird going on between them?

I found a parking spot two blocks from the office. Since I didn't have a chance to eat breakfast, I stopped to get an egg sandwich. The first thing I did when I got into the office, besides wolfing down my breakfast, was to take out my corkboard. It helps me organize my thoughts. I actually got the idea from the police show Law and Order, Special Victims Unit. If it's good enough for them, it's good enough for me. I have two, the other one I keep at home.

I took out my 5x7 index cards and wrote out the name of each person connected to the case so far. My phone buzzed. "Tracey Marks."

"Is this the infamous Tracey Marks, solver of all crimes?"

"The one and only," I laughed. "Are you in the need of the services of a private investigator?"

"It would depend on the services you offer."

"Well for guys with the first name of Jack, we throw in some extras."

"I'm very interested. How about we meet up this weekend?"

"Aren't you the eager beaver. I like the sound of your voice. I'm game."

"Now I'm not sure I can wait till Saturday."

"All good things are worth waiting for. At least that's what I hear."

"How's the case going?" Jack asked

"You don't want to know. I'll give you the complete low down when I see you."

I got back to the task at hand. I tacked each card up on the board with possible suspects connected to Maddie, on the assumption that whoever raped Maddie would connect to Stephanie.

Joe being my number one suspect for now, I speculated what would be his motive to kill Stephanie after all these years. I couldn't see one even if she had a change of heart and confronted him. It was too long ago and Maddie was dead. If it was a teacher what would be their rationale for killing Stephanie? I'm not sure. If Jay Henderson thought it would cost him his job, would that be a motive? It's possible, I guess.

Where do I go from here? I find it hard to believe after all these years Stephanie didn't tell one person. If she didn't trust the kids in her group maybe she confided in someone else besides Jeffrey Goldman. But why didn't she tell him who it was that raped Maddie?

CHAPTER 23

I still needed to talk to Jay Henderson and Kevin O'Donnell, if only to eliminate them. Maybe it's not anyone I know about, but I still think it's someone she knew, not a random stranger. A stranger would have no reason to threaten her. Maybe if I have a muffin I'll get hit with a bolt of genius and figure it out.

So how do I confront Henderson and O'Donnell? It would be better to do it away from the school, in a more relaxed environment. The only thing that would give them away would be their reaction to my questions because certainly they're not going to admit sleeping with a student. I thought I would wait and call them this evening when they're not at the school.

Wally was at the front door to greet me when I got home. "Hi Wally, missed you this morning."

"I came in late. I had a doctor's appointment."

"Is everything okay?"

"Oh yes, just a routine checkup. I'm afraid you're stuck with me for a while."

"You better not be going anywhere. I don't know what I'd do without you. Who else is going to make sure I stay warm and out of trouble?"

"What about that nice young man you're dating?"

"Well he's not around all the time so you're stuck with me."

"It is my pleasure."

My phone was buzzing just as I was unlocking my door. I fumbled around in my bag. "Tracey Marks," I said closing my apartment door behind me.

"Ms. Stevens I'm glad to hear from you." More like thrilled. "Has something come up?"

"After you left I remembered an incident with one of the students at that time. Originally she came forward and said she was raped but said she wasn't sure she wanted to bring it before the school board. She was in quite a state. The strange thing was a few days later she recanted and said she had been drinking and wasn't sure exactly what happened. She didn't want to get anyone in trouble."

"Do you remember her name?"

"Yes, it was Barbara Jorgensen. I don't know what happened to her."

"Okay, that's very helpful. By the way does Hudson have an alumni association? They might have updated information."

"They do. And I believe they also have a website."

"That's great. Thank you for letting me know." It sounds like someone might have changed Barbara Jorgensen's mind for her. This could be the lead I was hoping for.

After dinner I settled into bed with my laptop searching for Barbara Jorgensen. I tried Hudson's website. There didn't appear to be any information on her. I went into one of my investigative databases and put in her name, approximate age and limited the search to the New York area. If she was married, it might make my search more difficult. The good news is there were only three people with that name, two that fit the age criteria. I pulled up the first report. It appeared this person was a Jorgensen by marriage. Crap! I pulled up the next report. As I was looking through it I was getting excited. This person had at one time gone by the name of Barbara Grafton, but from what I could tell she was married to a Grafton and went back to her maiden name, Jorgensen. Old addresses had her living in the Westchester area. Parents listed were Thomas and Ethel Jorgensen. Both parents were deceased. A current address for Barbara was in Princeton, New Jersey. There was a mobile number listed. Do I call or just show up?

"Hey handsome." I explained my dilemma to Jack since he deals with these types of situations more than I do.

"In most cases it's always better to pay an unannounced visit. People's answers are more spontaneous and their reactions also reveal a lot."

"But it might turn her off if I just show up."

"That's a possibility, but the element of surprise is always better. You're going to have to think of a good opening line so she'll be amenable to seeing you. You might only get one bite of the apple."

"How prolific."

"I do have a way with words. Do you plan on going tomorrow?"

"I don't know. I might wait till Monday. I'll sleep on it."

I decided before I speak with Jay Henderson and Kevin O'Donnell I would talk with Barbara if she'll talk with me. I held off calling them.

As I was lying in bed I thought about my relationship with Jack. Neither of us had ever said the love word to each other. Do I love Jack? Love has never been a word in my vocabulary when it comes to men. Commitment is not my strong suit. Maybe I'm afraid to say it. Once I do I can't put it back in the bottle. Maybe I'm more afraid that he doesn't love me. Okay enough of this.

When I got up the next morning I made the decision to wait until Monday to see Barbara Jorgensen. It crossed my mind that I might have to be there all day if I didn't catch Barbara in the morning.

I spent part of Friday cleaning. I thought I would surprise Jack and make something for lunch instead of going out. That would require shopping. I headed over to the gym for a quick workout and then to the fruit and vegetable stand where I picked up some vegetables for an omelet. The rest of the day I spent reading and watching TV. I watched the last few episodes of Homeland and was disappointed when it was over. I would probably have to wait a year before the next season began again.

On Saturday Jack surprised me with flowers. "Is it a special occasion I don't know about and should have known about?" I asked as he followed me into the kitchen while I tried to find something to put them in.

"Yes. You don't remember the first time we had sex?"

"I do," I said not quite sure what Jack was up to since we met in early November if I recall correctly.

"You don't think that was something to remember?"

"I guess," still not sure what was going on. Then he gave me a big grin and I knew he was just playing with me.

"Well I think we should have a repeat performance," as he led me into the bedroom. A couple hours later we were both famished.

"I thought instead of going out for lunch, I would make us omelets."

"I'm game if you are."

The omelet was doing well until I tried to flip it over. A rookie mistake. Half of it wound up outside the pan, luckily not on the floor. Jack thought it was hysterical.

Tootsie was a big success. We both laughed a lot and loved the play. On the way home we stopped at a cafe for cappuccinos and dessert.

On Sunday we got up early and went to Balducci's to buy food for Sunday brunch with Susie and Mark. Jack's face couldn't disguise a look of uncertainty when I bought smoked trout. I told him not to worry.

Jack and I tried our hand at Bridge with Susie and Mark. It turns out Mark played Bridge in college and was quite good at it. Susie had been holding out on me, neglecting to tell me Mark has been teaching her the game. My head was spinning after two hours. Between learning how to count points in your hand, and what are trump and no trump and the bidding, I was exhausted. Jack was totally invested in it.

"I think we should learn how to play bridge," Jack said to me after Susie and Mark left.

"I can teach you a few things," I said. "And it won't require using your mind." That was the last I heard about Bridge for the rest of the night.

CHAPTER 24

Monday morning Jack and I left at the same time. I put Barbara's address into my GPS. On the way I stopped at Starbucks for coffee and a banana nut muffin. I really needed to clean the car. There were muffin crumbs everywhere. Traffic wasn't too bad and I made it to Princeton without any problems. I've never been to Princeton but I've heard what a great college town it is. I thought if I had the opportunity I would check it out.

Barbara's house was close to the town. It was a Tudor style home on a small plot of land. I rang the bell. Nobody answered. I rang it again. I could see a woman's face peeking out from behind a curtain. I knew she saw me. After a minute or so I heard a voice from behind the closed front door.

"What do you want?"

"Ms. Jorgensen I'm sorry to bother you. My name is Tracey Marks and I'm looking into the death of one of your former classmates from Hudson Prep, a Stephanie Howell. Her married name was Harris. Do you remember her?"

"Maybe," she said, though I could hear the hesitation in her voice

"She was killed recently and I've been talking to some of her classmates from Hudson Prep since I believe there is a connection to her time there. I wouldn't intrude if I didn't think it was important." No reaction, only silence. I tried again. "What you tell me will be held in the strictest of confidence. I need your help, please."

I was just about to give up when the door slowly opened. Mrs. Jorgensen looked older then her forty something years. Her light brown hair was streaked with gray and she was very overweight. I went inside. Though the sun was shining, there was very little light in the house. The place was a mess. We sat in the living room overrun with junky antique furniture and newspapers everywhere. I found a spot on a purple sofa that looked barely safe to sit on. I moved aside the pile of newspapers that took up most of the space. Barbara sat opposite me on a green upholstered chair that was so worn I wondered how it didn't break when Barbara sat on it. I noticed a vodka bottle on the table next to her. There was no glass. Clearly this woman was a mess.

"Recently Stephanie had received threatening phone calls. She contacted me, but before we had a chance to meet she was killed."

"What has this got to do with me?" she said as she reached for a pack of cigarettes on the table, her hand shaking.

"Did you know a girl by the name of Maddie Jensen?" Her eyes opened wide. I didn't wait for an answer. "I believe Stephanie's death is related to something that happened to Maddie."

"Maddie killed herself."

"Yes, but she was raped in high school and never told anyone except for Stephanie and another friend from high school, Linda Clark. Maddie was threatened and swore them to secrecy."

Barbara remained quiet.

"Did you know she was raped?"

"No," looking completely surprised.

"When I mentioned Maddie's name you seemed upset."

"I felt bad that she killed herself."

I didn't know if I believed her. Maybe she didn't know Maddie was raped but she was certainly hiding something.

"I was informed that you had told the school you were raped and then recanted. Can you tell me about that?" I said softly.

Barbara struck a match and lit a cigarette. I didn't see an ashtray nearby.

"There's nothing to tell. I was drunk and had sex. That's all there is to it," she said in a defensive tone.

"So why did you originally tell the school you were raped?"

"I don't know," she said looking down at the floor.

Watching Barbara I had the feeling her secret had been weighing on her for so long.

"I think Maddie killed herself because she couldn't cope with what happened to her. Were you threatened?" I said. Barbara looked like she was on the verge of breaking down. Tears were streaming down her face. I felt sorry for her.

"Is that true that Maddie was raped?" her face turning pale.

"Unfortunately it is true. If she wasn't so frightened she might have told her parents and gone to the police. Maybe she would still be alive today." I could see the wheels turning in her head. "I really need your help. Even if it is too late for Maddie, maybe Stephanie's killer won't go free." I waited.

"It happened so long ago I don't even know if it was real anymore."

"Sadly, that's your mind trying to cope. But you know the truth," her ashes from the cigarette falling onto her lap.

"I've held it in for so long. It's ruined my life. I was raped! I can't believe it. That's the first time I've ever said those words out loud in thirty years. I will never forget that day."

"Can you tell me what happened?"

"It was night time. I was walking home from the library. There's a park that I went through all the time, sort of a short cut," her hands shaking.

"Take your time," I said.

"He grabbed me and pulled me over behind a tree and pushed me down on the ground. He pulled my pants down and forced himself in me. I tried to scream but I don't know if any sound came out of my mouth. It happened so fast."

"Did you see his face?"

She nodded her head slowly up and down.

"Were you threatened?"

"Not then but a few days later. It wasn't the same person who raped me; it was someone else. He said if I tell anyone they would kill me and I believed him."

"Who raped you Barbara?" I could see the fear in her eyes. She didn't answer.

I tried a different approach. "Where do you work?"

"I work part time in the administrative office at Princeton University. I quit college and moved down here. My parents bought this house for me. How do I know I would be safe if I told you? If you confront this person they'll know it's me. If it's the same person that killed Stephanie I'd be in jeopardy also."

"I believe Stephanie confronted the person who raped Maddie and that put her life in danger. I'm just not sure why she would do it after all these years, though something prompted it."

"If my name is mentioned they might see me as a threat now."

"I don't see any reason why your name should come up. No one is going to hear it from me."

"I'd like to think about it."

I knew I would lose her if she didn't tell me now. "You're barely living your life. Isn't it time to take control? I can't imagine what you have gone through, living in fear all these years, but I know if it was me, I'd want to take the chance." I could see in her eyes she wanted to tell me. "Only you can decide what to do." There was complete silence. I could hear the humming of the refrigerator. Barbara was biting her lower lip.

"His name was Joe Connolly," she blurted out.

I needed to keep my emotions in check. I didn't want her to freak out. "Do you know who threatened you?" I asked.

"No, I don't."

"Would you recognize him, if you saw him again?"

"Maybe, it's been so long."

"Was Joe the only person who raped you? Was there anyone else there?"

"No."

"Would you happen to recall the names of any kids that Joe Connolly hung around with?"

"No."

"If I show you some high school photos, do you think you might remember?"

"Maybe, it's been so long ago."

I took out my cell phone and asked Barbara to look through the photos I had taken of classmates from the yearbook.

"I can't be sure but these two look familiar. I think they hung around with Joe Connolly. I think he's the one who threatened me," pointing to a kid named Ben Miller.

"Do you have someone you can call or you can be with if you're feeling anxious?"

"I have a sister in Philadelphia. Maybe I can call her."

"Would you like to go out and get something to eat? I thought I would go into Princeton. I've never been here before."

"I have to get ready for work."

"Are you sure?"

"Yes."

"I'm going to leave you my card. I will keep in touch to let you know what's going on. If you need me for any reason, don't hesitate to call me. Thank you for speaking with me. I know it was hard for you. Take care."

I had mixed emotions when I left. I now knew who raped Barbara but that doesn't mean Joe raped Maddie. If he did, and that's a big if, could these other two guys have been part of it?

CHAPTER 25

I drove into town and parked. I stopped at a coffee shop/diner on the main drag. Seeing college students walking about seemingly without a care in the world made me a little jealous. The diner was packed. I waited for a few minutes before I was shown to a booth.

"Hi," I said to my waiter. He looked like a college kid, maybe he was a student at Princeton earning some extra money. He put down a menu in front of me and filled my water glass. Before he had a chance to disappear I ordered pancakes, bacon crisp and coffee.

While I waited I took out my laptop and googled the names of the two boys Barbara pointed out. I first checked Ben Miller. Too many with that name came up. The second one was Randy Stewart. There were several in Westchester County. One Randy Stewart was interesting. He was running for Congress. That would be something if it turned out he went to Hudson Prep. I clicked on his name. It said that Randy lives in Bronxville and is running for Congress. He's forty-nine years old and his wife's name is Annie. He's been involved in local politics since graduating law school. I guess I better bone up on my Westchester County politics.

If it was the same Randy Stewart that was involved with Maddie's rape that might be a reason to feel threatened. He would definitely have a lot to lose. I was getting ahead of myself but the thought of this new prospect was getting my heart rate up.

My food came. I devoured it pretty quickly. Since it was still early, I walked around for a while and then thought it might be interesting to see the college before heading home. I asked a few students I saw on campus where I might inquire about taking a tour. Finally I got to the right place but there were no tours scheduled at the moment. I walked around the campus for a while before heading back home.

The ride back was going well until I hit the George Washington Bridge. I was stuck in traffic for about forty-five minutes. When I finally made it over the bridge it was almost five so I went straight home.

When I got settled in I took out my corkboard and added the names I just found out about. The possible suspects were mushrooming out of control. I still needed to find out more about Maddie. Was she a target because she was promiscuous? Does the reason really matter? I still needed to rule out the teachers, though it was looking less likely that one of them raped Maddie and killed Stephanie. It just didn't fit, but I knew I had to keep an open mind. Why didn't Stephanie confide in anyone about Maddie's rape? Why not tell Jeffrey Goldman, the one person she trusted according to him, who raped Maddie? Always more questions than answers.

I peeked in the refrigerator on the off chance there was something to eat. There was always tuna fish. I made a sandwich and brought it into bed with me along with my computer.

I called Susie. "What's up Sherlock?" she said.

"Cute. Do you want to hear the latest?"

"Always."

I updated Susie on everything I learned from Barbara and what I found out about Randy Stewart. "So what do you think?"

"First you have to find out if this Randy went to Hudson."

"I have an idea how I can find that out. There must be a photo of him somewhere on the internet, and then I can compare it to his high school photo."

"You're getting really good at this. Soon you'll have your own TV show solving crimes."

Ignoring her remark, I said, "if it's him, it's going to be a challenge interviewing him."

"Yes it will be, and I'm not sure you should go alone."

"I'll worry about that when the time comes. In the meantime I have other people to concentrate on. I need to confront Joe Connolly. We know he raped Barbara and he was a troublemaker in high school."

"Jack might know what the best course of action would be."
"Yeah, But I'd like to figure it out on my own."
"Okay, but be careful."

I slept fitfully, probably too many thoughts going through my brain. I woke up tired. After showering and a cup of java coursing through me, I felt at least half human. When I got into the office I sat in front of my laptop looking for a current photo of Randy Stewart. There was an article about Stewart with a black and white photo. I looked at the yearbook photo but it was hard to make a comparison against the grainy black and white on google. I continued searching since I needed to be absolutely sure I had the right guy. As luck would have it I came upon a photo that was taken a few years earlier but with a sharper image. In comparing the two I definitely had the right guy. The dead giveaway was the nose. It had a hook. Hook and all he was a nice looking guy. I was trying not to get too excited.

It appears Joe, Randy, and this guy Ben Miller were buddies. I wonder if they're still friends. I needed to tread carefully. I thought I would first tackle Jay Henderson and Kevin O'Donnell at Hudson Prep.

In the meantime I wanted to find out more about Joe Connolly and Randy Stewart.

I called someone I knew that could check statewide criminal records fairly quickly. I was curious if Joe got into trouble with the law. I knew Randy had no criminal record since he was a lawyer and would not have been able to maintain his law degree if he had a record. Until I can locate the Ben Miller who went to Hudson, I'll have to put him aside for now.

Before approaching Randy Stewart I wanted to gather as much information on him as possible. I started with my investigative databases. Looking through the report, it listed a divorce from an Emily Stewart over twenty years ago. That would explain the fact that he has two younger children from the article I read about him. If he had children with his first wife they would probably be young adults now. I wonder where his first wife is. Financially it looks like he is doing pretty well. He has a second house in the Hamptons, though it could be fully mortgaged.

My phone beeped. "Jack, I'm glad you called."

"What's going on?"

I explained everything to him.

"I'm very impressed. It sounds like you have your hands full."

"You think? I'm up to my eyeballs and don't know how to sort it out or what to do first."

"What about explaining to the Scarsdale Police what you found out?"

"What's your Plan B?"

"Be careful."

"A man of few words. Can you expand a little?"

"Tread lightly. No need to take a hard line on anyone right now."

"I get it but what about Joe Connolly? We know for sure that he raped Barbara Jorgensen."

"There are a few problems. One, it was over twenty-five years ago. She never came forward then. It would be his word against hers and there is no DNA from back then."

"So what you're saying is that Joe has nothing to worry about."

"That about sums it up. Right now you still have no idea who raped Maddie, and even if you did find out, it may not be the same person who killed Stephanie. Whatever you do be careful. If you need my help just ask."

"Thanks."

I needed fuel. I always think better on a full stomach. I bundled up and went to the deli near my office.

"Hey Mike," I said to the owner of the deli.

"What can I get you today Tracey?"

"I'll have a turkey sandwich with coleslaw and a pickle."

"For you I'll throw in an extra pickle."

"Thanks. Actually I'll take an order of very crispy French fries. A growing girl needs her energy." Mike smiled.

When I got back I made a pot of coffee and dug into my sandwich and fries. So what do I know for sure? Not much. Joe Connolly raped Barbara. Joe had two buddies, Ben Miller and Randy Stewart. Jeffrey Goldman, according to Stephanie, said that Maddie was raped by at least one person, though there were two other people there at the time. I don't know anything about Ben Miller except he threatened Barbara, according to her. Did he also threaten Maddie? It seems that Randy Stewart might have the most to lose running for Congress. I still don't have enough information to make any assumptions.

I called Jay Henderson later in the day. He answered right away. "Mr. Henderson my name is Tracey Marks. I'm investigating the death of Stephanie Harris, her maiden name was Howell and she attended Hudson around 1987."

"Yes, I read about it in the papers. I was sorry to hear about it. How can I help you?"

"I'm talking to former classmates, friends and staff at the school. I believe you were a new teacher at that time. Can we meet either later today or tomorrow?"

"What has this got to do with her time at Hudson?"

"It may not, but I'm exploring all avenues."

"I'm finished by six and then I can meet you for a few minutes. Why don't we meet at the Starbucks that's a few blocks from the school, say around six-fifteen."

I made a dash to pick up my car since it was almost five. Mr. Henderson had no idea that I wanted to talk to him about Maddie and that was how I wanted it.

When I walked into Starbucks, Jay Henderson was already there. The place was crowded. I walked over to where Mr. Henderson was seated and introduced myself. Mr. Henderson hadn't changed much in thirty years. He was tall and thin and still had a full head of dark hair with a little gray on the sides. He had a great smile.

"Can I get you a coffee," I asked him.

"I'm fine," he said.

I sat down trying to figure out how to bring up the subject of Maddie. At the moment I couldn't think of anything.

CHAPTER 26

"Do you remember Stephanie?"

"Not really. I don't think she was in any of my classes. She graduated not long after I began teaching at Hudson."

"Stephanie called me the day she died. We made arrangements to meet that day but she never made it. She was killed before she had a chance to see me. After talking to several people that Stephanie knew from high school, I'm pretty sure her death had something to do with an incident involving her friend Maddie Jensen." I paused. I noticed a slight twitch in his right eye. He didn't say anything so I continued. "Do you remember Maddie?"

"Vaguely, I don't think she was in any of my classes. I had just started teaching there."

"She was raped in her junior year of high school and committed suicide in college." His eye twitched again.

"She was raped? I can't believe it," sounding genuinely surprised.

"So you didn't know?"

"Absolutely not, why would I? This is the first time I'm hearing about it."

I needed to bluff and see his response. My hands were going a mile a minute under the table. "Mr. Henderson, one of Maddie's friends told me she was having an affair with you. I'm not trying to get you into trouble I just need to know what happened back then."

"Who told you that?" He said, sounding indignant.

"I can't divulge that information to you but it's from a reliable source." Was my nose growing? He shifted in his seat. I could see that he was agonizing over what to say. He could deny it and there was nothing I could do about it.

"Whoever told you was mistaken."

"I don't think they were. As I said before I'm not looking to jam you up or tell anyone. All I'm trying to do is find out who raped Maddie and how this involves Stephanie, if it does." I could see he was torn.

"I knew it was wrong but I was young and flattered that this beautiful girl wanted me. I don't have any excuse."

He couldn't look at me. I could see how Maddie would be attracted to this man. From what I have learned about her she probably didn't think about the consequences of her actions. She was bold enough to have a fling with Joe Connolly when Maddie knew Donna was seeing him.

"How long did it last?"

"It was a few months, maybe three. I wasn't married at the time. I know that's not an excuse but I wanted you to know."

"How did it end?"

"It was putting a strain on me, but to be honest she ended it."

"Do you know why?"

"I think it ran its course for Maddie and I was relieved. But I had no idea she was raped, and I swear I would never do anything to hurt her. I felt terrible when I found out she committed suicide. At the time I wondered why when she had her whole life ahead of her. Now it makes more sense. Did she ever tell anyone?"

"She told two friends but swore them to secrecy because she had been threatened."

"What does Stephanie's death have to do with Maddie?"

"I'm not quite sure but I believe it might be connected to the rape. I found out that Stephanie witnessed it but had kept quiet all these years. There were three boys involved. At this point I don't know who they were but I have my suspicions."

Mr. Henderson remained silent.

"Was Maddie the only girl you took advantage of?"

"I swear she was the only one."

"Would you happen to remember boys by the names of Joe Connolly, Randy Stewart and Ben Miller?"

"Why do you ask?"

"I was told they were buddies back in high school." I decided not to mention that Connolly raped Barbara. I only had her word for it even though I believed her.

"I really don't remember. Maybe some of the other students would. Why are you asking about them?"

"Just following up on some rumors."

"I do know that Randy Stewart is running for Congress. Do you suspect him of something?"

"No, I was just curious. What about Ben Miller. Do you know if he's still in the area?"

"I don't."

"Can you find out?"

"I'm sorry. It would be against school policy. Maybe you can check on the website if he's listed."

I left Mr. Henderson not knowing anymore then I knew before talking with him, except that he acknowledged his affair with Maddie. I was angry at him for taking advantage of her but I wasn't interested in getting him into trouble. Besides it would be his word against mine. I wanted to believe Maddie was the only one. I can only hope.

If Stephanie found out about Maddie's affair with Henderson and confronted him, would he feel threatened enough to kill her, and why after all these years? I wasn't convinced.

CHAPTER 27

By the time I got home I just wanted to flop into bed. I was even too tired to stop off and pick up something for dinner. I got into bed with my pistachio ice cream. The first summer I spent in North Carolina with my parents, they allowed me to walk into town all by myself. I was nine years old -- town being three blocks from our cottage. Every afternoon I would venture into town. My first stop was my favorite place in the world, Walter's Ice Cream Shop. Mr. Jones, the owner, would greet me with a big smile. I would marvel at all the different flavor ice creams he had. After a few days of sampling all of them, I fell in love with pistachio ice cream. Somehow the combination of the pistachios with the creamy vanilla ice cream made my mouth so happy. I would get a double scoop on a sugar cone and plant myself on the bench situated outside the shop and lick my ice cream slowly, wanting it to last forever while watching the tourists walking about. I was in heaven

The next day in the office I went on the school's website, but there was nothing on Ben Miller. As I was staring at my computer screen my phone rang. "Hello."

"Is this Tracey Marks?"

"Yes. Can I help you?"

"This is Barbara Jorgensen."

"Barbara, is everything alright?"

"Yes. There's something I want to tell you. I thought of it after you left."

The suspense was killing me. "What is it?"

"You mentioned Linda Clark. She was a bitch."

"Why do you say that?"

"Before I recanted, word had gotten around that I had accused Joe Connolly. Linda made a point of taunting me, calling me all sorts of names, telling me I was a crazy bitch and should stop spreading lies."

"I'm sorry you had to be subjected to that. Was there anyone else who was nasty to you?"

"There were people who snubbed me since they thought I had made up the whole story but Linda was especially cruel."

"Thank you for telling me. How are you doing?"

"Okay."

"Please call me if I can help in anyway. Take care of yourself."

I didn't know what to make of this new information. I'm wondering if Linda knew more then she had told me. And what about Donna, was she really okay with Joe fooling around with Maddie? Again questions with no answers.

An email came through that there were no criminal records on Joe Connolly. I didn't think there would be. I need to find this Ben Miller guy. Linda might know but would she tell me if she was somehow involved back then.

Maybe fresh air would make me think better. I put on my white parka jacket and locked up. There were snowflakes coming down as I stepped outside into the cold. I walked a few blocks heading absolutely nowhere. I picked up a hot chocolate at Starbucks and continued walking. I had the strange feeling that someone was following me but when I looked around, I didn't see anyone. It was probably my imagination. Ever since I was run off the road I've been a little paranoid. On my way back to the office I bought a salad with chicken for lunch. If I didn't get a green into me soon, my body was going to revolt.

When I got back I contemplated what to do next. If I confronted Linda about what Barbara told me, how would she react? There's only one way to find out, but this time I won't give her a heads up.

I left the office around four to pick up my car and head up to Eastchester. I called the hospital to make sure Linda was still working since I didn't want to make the trip for nothing. I rode passed her house and waited. At six-thirty she pulled into her driveway. I got out of my car catching up to her before she went inside.

"Linda."

"Oh, you scared me."

"I'm sorry. There's something I need to talk to you about."

"Did you ever think about picking up the phone and calling?" looking annoyed.

"We can talk out here, though it's freezing, or maybe we can go inside?"

She opened the door and we went inside. The hallway was as far as I got.

"What do you want," Linda said in an annoyed tone.

"Did you threaten a girl that was in your high school by the name of Barbara Jorgensen?"

"What are you talking about?" her demeanor becoming defensive.

"I have information that you were abusive to her when she came forward and said she was raped by Joe Connolly."

"If I was, and I'm not saying I was, it was because she was lying. She recanted right away."

"It strikes me as a very strong reaction, and why you? Wouldn't Donna be more upset since it was Donna that was seeing Joe?"

"You'd have to ask her. I have no idea."

"If my boyfriend was falsely accused of raping someone I'd be the one furious with her. You also told me that Donna didn't care whether Maddie and Joe were fooling around."

"I didn't say she didn't care; I said there wasn't anything she could do about it. Look I'm not sure what you're getting at but you'll have to ask Donna these questions."

"Did Joe threaten you? Did he tell you to scare Barbara Jorgensen?"

"Of course not, that's absurd," she said, her face turning red.

I wasn't so sure. What other reason would she have to frighten Barbara? It didn't make sense.

"Have you had any contact with Donna?"

"You asked me that already and I told you I hadn't. Now leave."

As she was opening the door I said, "by the way do you remember a boy named Ben Miller? I believe he was in your class or a grade ahead of you?" I noticed a flicker in her eyes.

"I'm sorry I can't recall the name."

Something didn't add up with Linda. I just didn't know what.

CHAPTER 28

On the way home I called Susie.

"Hi, you sound distracted," she said.

"No, just annoyed."

"What's going on?"

"I'm just not getting anywhere. People are lying and I feel discouraged."

"So what else is new? Is Jack coming this weekend?"

"I think so. I'll find out later."

"Talk to you tomorrow."

After I put my car in the garage, I walked four blocks to the Chinese takeout place. On the way back I had the feeling again that someone was following me. I turned back but didn't see anyone. There was one person about a half a block behind me. I quickly looked away. The person had a baseball cap on so I couldn't see their face though I was pretty sure it was a guy. My heart started racing. Calm down, he's half a block away and he's probably just some guy going wherever. But when I turned around again he was practically on top of me as I ran right into someone walking a dog.

"I'm sorry," I said to the guy I ran into. I was shaking. The person with the baseball cap was gone. I wondered where he went. I picked up the bag with my Chinese food that I dropped on the ground.

"Are you all right," the man asked.

"Yes, just a little paranoid. I thought someone was following me. I'm fine. Did you happen to see the guy who practically ran into me?"

"I'm sorry my back was facing the other way. Do you live nearby?"

"Just two blocks away."

"Do you mind if I walk with you?"

"But you're going in the wrong direction."

"My dog doesn't care what direction we're walking as long as he's outside doing his business."

"Thank you. So what's your dog's name?"

"It's Oscar named after Oscar Wilde. He's a miniature French Poodle. I'm John.

"Well Oscar's adorable. This is my building. Thank you so much. Bye Oscar. Thanks John."

When I got inside my apartment I pulled off my coat, went straight to the kitchen and poured myself a glass of wine. I drank it standing up over the kitchen counter. Halfway through my wine I sat down at the kitchen table and called Jack.

"I was just about to call you," Jack said. "What's going on?"

"I think someone was following me. I was walking back from the Chinese takeout place and I don't know if I was being paranoid, but I turned around and about a half a block away there was this guy wearing a baseball cap and when I turned around again he was practically on my heels. I ran right into this man walking his dog, practically knocking him over. I couldn't see where the guy in the baseball cap went. The thing is the other day I thought someone was following me. Am I losing it?"

"Between someone running you off the road, the weird phone conversation you had with the guy on the burner phone and now this, I know you're not going to like what I have to say next. I think it's time to quit the case. It's too dangerous."

"I can't believe you're saying this. If it was you, would you quit? No of course not. Of all people I would never have thought you were a sexist." I was livid.

"I'm sorry but that's how I feel. I don't want anything to happen to you."

"Well, why don't you just put me in a bubble, that way I'll be safe. I thought you knew me better than that." I was so angry I hung up. I finished my wine in one gulp, my hands shaking. I didn't know what to do with myself. My Chinese food was getting cold but I had no appetite. I needed to call Susie.

"What's the matter?"

I told her my conversation with Jack and what had transpired before that.

"Sweetie, he's just worried that something is going to happen to you."

"That doesn't give him the right to tell me what to do. You would never tell me to quit even if you wanted me to because you know me."

"Maybe I don't come out and say it because I do know you, but it doesn't mean I feel any different than Jack. Maybe he could have been a little more sensitive to your feelings."

"I was so sure he was different and understood me."

"He is different, but it's not as black and white as you want it to be. He has feelings too."

"I hung up on him."

"He doesn't strike me as the type that is thin-skinned. I don't think you bruised him too badly."

"I'll think about it."

"Good idea. I'll talk to you tomorrow."

I got into bed with my Chinese food and chopsticks. Was I kidding myself thinking I could be in a relationship for any length of time? I like my independence too much and compromise is not my strong suit. Yet, I was still hoping the phone would ring and it would be Jack. Maybe I deluded myself into thinking this could work. Susie did make a few good points, yet I felt suffocated when he told me I should quit. I would never tell him to quit. Does he even realize what he said?

I didn't sleep much and I felt like shit the next day. Jack was still on my mind. I had to concentrate on the case. I drank two cups of coffee before showering. I pushed myself to go to the gym since I knew it would help to relieve some of the stress. When I got into the office I called Donna.

"Hello."

"Donna, it's Tracey Marks. I need to talk with you. Can we meet somewhere?"

"I don't know. I'm really busy. Maybe some other time."

"It can't wait and it might help to find out who killed Stephanie." After what felt like an eternity Donna finally spoke.

"I'll meet you at your office around five p.m. today."

"I'll see you then."

I needed to be careful how I handled my conversation with Donna. I didn't want to turn her off. I could use Jack's expertise but I wasn't going to call him.

The day dragged. Between thinking about Jack and my interview with Donna, I was finding it hard to concentrate.

I heard the door open. I hadn't realized how attractive Donna was. Her beautiful dark straight hair complimented her olive complexion. I took her coat and we went into my office.

"Please sit. Can I get you anything to drink, coffee or tea?"

"No thanks."

"As you know I've been investigating the death of Stephanie Harris. Can you tell me what she was like when you knew her?" I hoped this would put her at ease to open up.

"Stephanie was fairly quiet, a little shy."

"How did she fit in with your group?"

"All our personalities were different. Greg was the most even tempered. Out of the four girls Linda was definitely the most vocal. Joe was probably the leader."

"And you?"

"I was more like Stephanie, more reserved. But we all got along."

"What about Maddie?" I noticed Donna stiffen up.

"She was a little wild and flirtatious."

"I heard she dated a lot of guys."

"I guess."

"When did you start to date Joe?"

"In high school."

"Was that after Maddie dated him?"

She looked up. Her face flushed. "It was after," she said turning her ahead away from me.

Her first lie. She was probably too ashamed to admit Maddie was screwing around with Joe while Donna was seeing him. I can't understand how she put up with it. Then again there are a lot of things I don't understand. I didn't see the point in bringing up the rape. It would just antagonize her.

"When did you find out that Maddie was dating Joe?"

"It wasn't a secret."

"I think it would bother me that someone who was part of our group was dating someone I was interested in."

"Well like I said Joe and I didn't start dating until they broke up."

I decided to leave it alone.

"Do you remember two guys by the names of Ben Miller and Randy Stewart?"

"Yes, they were friends with my husband."

"But they weren't in the group?"

"No. Joe was friends with them but they weren't part of our group."

"Do you know why that was?"

"I'm not sure. I think he knew them from football. The three of them played on the football team together."

"Do you know if they're still friends?"

"Why are you asking all these questions?"

"I'm trying to get a picture of who may have been in Stephanie's life back then."

"You certainly can't think that any of the people we hung around with had anything to do with Stephanie's death. That's crazy."

"In my line of work the more I know about someone, the better. Do you know if Ben Miller still lives in the area?" I asked casually.

"I think he lives in Armonk but I'm not sure."

Finally I have a lead where Ben Miller might live. "Oh by the way, you never answered my question. Is Joe still in touch with Randy Stewart or Ben Miller?"

"They may speak on the phone but we've never socialized with them."

"Well I appreciate you taking the time to come in and answer my questions. You've been very helpful."

When she left I wondered if she was going to tell her husband about our conversation. Could she be clueless about his behavior? If he raped Barbara Jorgensen, did he rape Maddie? Could there be others? It wouldn't surprise me if he's cheating on Donna. It may be worthwhile conducting surveillance on him. It could give me some leverage if I needed it.

CHAPTER 29

While I was still thinking about my conversation with Donna, my phone rang. "Hey."

"I thought you could probably use a drink," Susie said.

"I'm ready whenever you are."

"I'll meet you at the Dakota Bar in forty-five minutes."

I was sitting at a table with a glass of Sauvignon Blanc when Susie arrived. When the waitress came over Susie ordered the same, and we also decided on an order of fried calamari and chicken wings.

"So how are you doing?" Susie asked.

"I've been trying to keep busy so I don't have to think about Jack. I haven't heard from him and I don't plan on calling either."

"Why not?"

"I'm still angry, and if he really feels that way, what's the point?"

"It was one argument. If I walked out on Mark every time we had a fight, we'd be history."

"This was different than a fight. How would you feel if Mark said he wanted you to quit your job?"

"First of all my job is not dangerous so you can't compare."

"You know what I mean. I can't be with someone who is trying to run my life."

"I'm still not convinced that's what Jack was trying to do. At least talk to him. Tell him how you feel."

"Let's change the subject. In the meantime I just spoke with Donna, Joe's wife. She is definitely blind when it comes to her husband. Whether she knows what he's done, I can't say for sure. It wouldn't surprise me if he was abusing her. I was thinking it might pay to do some surveillance on him. See what he's up to. Would you like to come on a stakeout with me? It might be fun."

"When are you planning this fun outing for us?"

"How about one evening next week?"

"I'm in. Do I need to wear a disguise?"

"Yeah, how about what you wore last Halloween?"

"Ha ha."

The waitress came with our food and I reached for a chicken wing.

"Any plans for the wedding?"

"I think it's going to be sometime in April."

"That's pretty soon. January is practically over. You should start planning."

"Tracey, it's going to be very small, just close family and friends."

"Well you still need to find a place and get a dress. It would be fun to go dress hunting. We can make a day of it, first breakfast, then maybe Saks, then lunch, then Bloomingdale's."

"Are we eating or shopping?"

"We can do both," I said.

"If you need to talk over the weekend, we'll be around. You can always join us for dinner Saturday night."

"Thanks."

It was almost fifty degrees, very warm for a January evening. Instead of walking I decided to take an Uber just to be cautious.

As I was lying in bed, my mind was replaying my conversations with Jack and Susie. Was I overreacting? He didn't actually tell me to quit. Was I looking for a way out of the relationship? I'm thirty-eight and I've never lived with anyone. The thought of it terrified me. Cousin Patty said I would know when the right person came along. I actually thought it might be Jack. Now I was second guessing myself. How many times have I entertained the idea of seeing a shrink and then dismissed it. Maybe it was time.

When I got up Friday morning my first priority was to find out where Ben Miller lived. I had to put Jack out of my head for now. I put on the coffee maker and showered. While I was having cereal I opened up my laptop and began the hunt for Mr. Miller.

I found a Ben Miller in Armonk that fit the right age. One of my databases listed a Verizon mobile telephone number. I waited until nine to call him.

"Hello."

"Is this Ben Miller?"

"Yes," with reservation in his voice.

"My name is Tracey Marks, and I'm investigating the death of Stephanie Howell Harris. I believe you were both at Hudson Prep about the same time. Did you hear about her death?"

"Yes, I read about it in the newspaper. How can I help you? I'm just about to go into a meeting."

"I'm interviewing classmates and other students at the school. Would it be possible to meet?"

"I didn't know her so I have no information to offer you."

Think fast. I had to get this guy to agree to talk with me. "I understand but it would be helpful if I could speak with you anyway. As I said I'm talking to a lot of people at the school. I promise I'll only take up a few minutes of your time." I could hear the wheels churning.

"I work in Manhattan."

"That's perfect since my office is in the city. I could meet you for a few minutes either on your lunch hour or after work."

"There's a Le Pain directly across from my office. I'll meet you there at twelve-thirty."

After exchanging brief descriptions, we hung up. There was no point in beating around the bush. I had to confront him and see his response to threatening Barbara Jorgensen.

I took an Uber over to Le Pain and arrived just as I saw him walk in.

"Mr. Miller, Tracey Marks." We sat down after getting coffee. Ben Miller looked nothing like his high school photo, though in fairness it's been about thirty years. He had put on a few pounds and his hair was definitely receding. He wore black framed glasses. He couldn't be more than 5'8".

"I know you don't have much time so I'm not going to beat around the bush. It has come to my attention that you threatened a girl back in high school in order to get her to recant that she was raped."

"Is that what this is all about? Yes I did but only because she falsely accused my friend of something that didn't happen. Now if that's all I think we're done."

"How would you know if you weren't there?" He gave himself away when he shifted in his seat.

"Why wouldn't I believe my friend over some person who was an emotional wreck?"

"Why do you say that about her? Did you know her?"

"You just had to look at her, and I don't even think she had any friends. Now I have to go."

I didn't see any point in trying to stop him. I wasn't going to get him to admit anything to me. At least he confessed to threatening Barbara, but did he threaten Maddie? It felt like I was going nowhere fast. If either Joe Connolly or Randy Stewart killed Stephanie, how will I prove it? I should talk to Greg Todd again. He might be able to tell me more about Joe. Maybe Greg remembers Ben Miller and Randy Stewart. I should also question Stephanie's boyfriend again. For all I know he could have killed Stephanie. Maybe she was breaking it off with him and in a fit of rage he killed her.

CHAPTER 30

I called Greg Todd. "Mr. Todd, it's Tracey Marks. Do you think it's possible to meet sometime later this afternoon? I know it's kind of last minute."

"Has something come up?"

"Yes. I have some information I'd like to run by you."

"I finish up with my last patient at four. I can see you then."

Greg gave me his address in Ridgefield, Connecticut. Maybe I should pick his brain about my own problems while I'm there. I wonder if he has a couch you lie on and spill your guts out. That might be interesting.

I headed up to Ridgefield. It was probably a ninety minute drive to his office. When I arrived I walked into a waiting area. There was no receptionist. Dr. Greg came out a few minutes later.

"Come in Tracey. Sit."

"Thanks. I really appreciate making the time to see me." I noticed on his desk a photo of a boy about twelve in a baseball uniform.

"How can I help you?"

I wasn't sure how much I should tell him. Just because he's a therapist doesn't mean I can trust him. "When Maddie was raped she told Stephanie and Linda. It appears Maddie was threatened and swore them to secrecy. I subsequently found out that Stephanie witnessed the rape and that three people were involved." This is where it was going to get a little dicey. "It has come to my attention that Joe Connolly was accused of raping a female student but she recanted because she was threatened." I stopped talking waiting to hear his response.

"Joe and I were friends in our freshman and most of our junior year, but then he started hanging out with some other guys."

"By other guys, you mean Ben Miller and Randy Stewart?" His eyebrows shot up.

"Yes. How do you know about them?"

"That doesn't matter. Why didn't you want to hang around with them?"

"Let's just say our interests were different."

"Fair enough. Did you know that Joe was accused of raping a student?"

"I did but he swore to me it was a lie. And when she recanted I let him off the hook. I had no idea she was threatened."

"Did you hear about any other incidents with Joe and his friends?"

"Just rumors, nothing specific."

"Did it involve other girls?" I said.

"Again they were only rumors."

I decided not to pursue it for now. "What can you tell me about Maddie?"

"What would you like to know?"

"Now you sound like a therapist," I said. He smiled. "Whatever you can tell me. I heard that she was flirtatious, ran around with different guys."

"Well I never had the pleasure but you would be correct."

"I heard that Joe Connolly and Maddie were fooling around. How did Donna react to that?"

"If I remember correctly she was livid. Joe and Donna fought about it but he didn't seem to care what she thought."

"I find it hard to believe she married him."

"People do all sorts of things for different reasons. It's hard to get into someone's head."

'Ain't that the truth,' I said to myself. I switched gears. "I heard that Randy Stewart is running for Congress. Do you think if he was involved with raping Maddie, he could kill Stephanie if she confronted him?"

"You're asking me to speculate and without knowing him at all, I can't do that."

"One last question, how did you feel when Maddie took up with Joe? Did that make you angry?"

"I was angry at him for cheating on Donna."

"Did it make you mad that Maddie chose Joe and not you?"

"Maybe, but I wouldn't rape anyone because they didn't want to go to bed with me."

Now it was my turn to smile. I got up. "By the way is that your son in the photo?"

"Yes. He's on his junior high school baseball team. I'm one of the coaches for the team."

"Well again thank you for your time. If you think of anything else please contact me." We shook hands and I left.

I drove home thinking about what Greg told me. I learned a little more about Joe and Donna. What a pair. If Donna knew that Joe raped Maddie, would she be blind to it? She strikes me as the kind of person that no matter what Joe did she would stand by her man. Is that love or was she delusional? If Joe did rape Maddie could Donna have put him up to it? More questions than answers.

I wasn't hungry and it was past seven. I wonder if my lack of appetite had anything to do with Jack. I wasn't use to feeling this way over a break up. Jack was supposed to come down tomorrow but that wasn't happening. Snap out of it Tracey.

I brought home some wonton soup and spare ribs in case my appetite came back. I always have pistachio ice cream to comfort me.

"What's happening to me Susie?" I said when she answered. "I actually lost my appetite though I'm sure it will come back."

"I am so happy to hear that. It means you have feelings for Jack otherwise you wouldn't be so upset."

"You sound like the therapist I saw today."

"You saw a therapist?"

"Not the way you mean. It was someone who was friends with Stephanie back in high school."

"Oh, you scared me for a second. I think you should call Jack."

"I wish he would call me and apologize."

"You hung up on him. Remember."

"I'll think about it. How's Tuesday look for surveillance?"

"I have to check what's going on with work but so far Tuesday looks good. Call me if you're feeling blue."

I undressed, poured myself a glass of wine, heated up the

wonton soup and spare ribs and turned on the TV.

Just as I was about to bite into a spare rib, my phone beeped.

"Hey. How are you? Listen I wanted to give you some space before I called. I know you were pretty mad. I think the dead giveaway was when you hung up on me. You need to know that I would never tell you what to do."

"Well it sure sounded like that's what you were doing."

"I would say the same thing to a male colleague if I thought he was a novice handling these types of situations. It's just that I care about you and want you to be safe. You scared me and I overreacted. I really have no intention of trying to run your life. I just worry. What I love about you is your determination. I wouldn't want to change that. I need you to trust that you can tell me anything without thinking I'm judging you and vice versa."

"I'm glad you said that. Would you believe I almost lost my appetite because of you?"

"I wouldn't believe it, but I'm flattered you would say it."

"I was going to call you. I did need time. Thank you."

"Why don't I come down in the morning and we'll do a proper makeup."

"That sounds great. I'll see you soon."

I texted Susie that Jack was coming tomorrow.

Most of the weekend Jack and I spent having great makeup sex. We emerged Saturday night and met Susie and Mark for dinner at Anton's. When we told the guys about our surveillance outing they just looked at each other as if to say, 'there they go again.' On Sunday afternoon Jack and I took a walk through Central Park.

On Monday morning, after Jack left, I got a call from Christine Harris asking for an update. Unfortunately I had nothing concrete to tell her but she understood or at least she seemed to. I still didn't want to contact Randy Stewart yet. I wasn't exactly sure why. I thought I would try speaking again with Andrew Carter, Stephanie's boyfriend. He answered right away.

"Do you have any news about Stephanie?" without even saying hello.

"Nothing as yet Andrew. I know you told me that Stephanie was distracted. Can you think of anything else that she might have said or seemed odd at the time? It may be important."

"Did you check her computer?"

"I did. There wasn't anything on it that looked suspicious."

"Once I got up in the middle of the night and she wasn't in bed. When I went looking for her, I found her hunched over her computer. She must have heard me because she quickly shut it. I asked her what she was looking at, but she just said nothing important. She was definitely hiding something."

"Do you have any idea what she could have been looking at?"

"No. At first I thought she was emailing someone she was having an affair with or on a dating website. My imagination was getting the best of me. But nothing changed so I didn't bring it up again."

"I should probably take another look at her computer. Her daughter gave me the password to her email account but maybe she had another account. I'll check it out. How's the job hunt going?"

"Slow. I miss Stephanie."

"By the way, did Stephanie have a calendar where she wrote down her appointments?"

"Check her office desk. You should also ask her business partner, Jennifer Daniels."

Of course, I said to myself. "Thanks and good luck with the job search."

Could Andrew kill Stephanie thinking she was going to reject him? I didn't know what to believe anymore.

CHAPTER 31

I picked Susie up the next day at four at her place for our surveillance on Joe Connolly. I didn't want to miss him in case he left the construction site early. Besides I don't think construction guys work after dark. By five it would be quitting time.

"So how do I look?" Susie said to me all dressed in black, including a black baseball cap.

"I wouldn't recognize you at a distance."

"That's what I was going for. I brought snacks and water."

"Just don't drink too much water. If you have to pee you're out of luck."

"I didn't think of that."

When we arrived at the site I saw Joe's car. It looked like the crew had left already. At five forty-five Joe sprinted to his car. I was a little anxious since I didn't want to lose him and it was the height of rush hour. Joe drove to the Cross County Parkway and then onto the Bronx River Parkway where he got off at Paxton Avenue.

"Where the hell is he going?" I said.

"I think we're headed into Bronxville."

"How do you know?"

"Do you remember I once dated this guy Mike who lived up in this neck of the woods?"

"Oh yeah, that was so long ago."

"Look, he's parking."

We saw him walking into a place called Pete's Tavern. "Susie, he knows what I look like. You have to go in and pretend you're looking for someone. See who he's with. If you can't take a picture on your cell phone, get a good description of the person."

"Yes boss," saluting me as she got out of the car.

I was waiting for what seemed like an eternity wondering what the hell was going on. About five minutes later Susie came out with a big grin on her face.

"I am really good at this," she said getting into the car.

"Oh my God, this is Randy Stewart," I said looking at the photo. "He's the one running for Congress that may have been involved in Maddie's rape."

"Well I can tell you that they were in a pretty heated argument. The only thing I heard was this guy Randy saying something like you better not get me involved."

"Shit, Connolly must know I'm looking at him."

"Let's not get ahead of ourselves here. We don't know anything for sure. You may be right, but you have to take it slow."

"What I have to do is confront Randy Stewart. He might be the key."

"What you have to do is be careful. These guys may be dangerous. Did you forget what happened to Stephanie?"

"I just don't see how I can find out the truth without shaking things up a bit. Wait, they're leaving. Let's see where Connolly goes from here."

We followed Joe but he wound up going straight home.

"Nice house," Susie said.

"They all seem to live affluent life styles. Don't forget these kids went to private school. They grew up privileged and probably spoiled. It's still early. Why don't we go over to Stephanie's house and see if we can find out anything interesting. Two sets of eyes are better than one."

"I'm game. This is so much fun."

"I can always count on you to look on the bright side."

"Pardon me for being the optimist in this relationship."

"I'm getting hungry," I said. "What about you? Why don't we grab a slice of pizza before we search the house? I work better on a full stomach." Susie just looked at me as if to say, so what else is new?

We found a pizza place on our way to Scarsdale. We ate quickly and drove to Stephanie's house. Hopefully Christine had a cleaning crew come in by now, though I don't know if you can remove blood from a rug. Maybe she got rid of it.

I was glad to see the rug was gone and the place was tidied up.

"Let's start in her office. You can take the computer and I'll look through her desk."

"Sounds like a plan," Susie said.

"Is there any way we can see what sites she was on before she was killed?"

"I don't have a clue but I'll do my best. Did you check her emails?" Susie asked.

"I did, but it wouldn't hurt to give another stab at them. Maybe I overlooked something."

While I went through all the drawers, Susie searched the computer.

"I'm not sure what this means but it looks like one of the last google searches she conducted was on stalking," Susie said.

"That's very interesting. Can you print it out?"

The printer started humming. "Why would she be interested in researching information about stalkers? Maybe I'm looking at this all wrong and it has nothing to do with her past. Could that be?"

"Again one step at a time. Maybe the stalker is from her past and could be one of the guys you're looking at now. Let's keep all our options on the table. Anything in the drawers?"

"Nothing I found as yet. What about emails?" I said.

"Too many to go through. Why don't you call her daughter and find out if you can take the computer?" Susie said.

"Good idea." I called Christine and asked her to call me back ASAP.

Two minutes later my phone buzzed. "Christine. Hi, I'm at your mom's house. I found something interesting on her computer. It appears she was looking into information on stalkers. Did she say anything to you?"

"No," sounding upset. "Who the hell would be stalking her?"

"That's what we have to find out. I'd like to take your mom's computer back with me so I can look through it at my office. Would that be alright with you? I'll return it when I'm finished."

"Yes, that's fine."

"We're good to go," I said to Susie when I hung up.

"What about her text messages on her phone?"

"Any that may have come from her stalker were deleted or

were never there."

It was almost ten when I dropped Susie off. I was revved up and had trouble sleeping. The prospect of a stalker put a whole new spin on everything. But what was going on with Joe Connolly and Randy Stewart? It sounds like Stewart might be afraid Joe is going to be trouble for him.

The next morning I called Jennifer Daniels. "Ms. Daniels, I was wondering if Stephanie kept any personal papers in the office?"

"I don't think so but I'll check for you. Did you look in her home office?"

"Yes. By the way did Stephanie mention anything to you about someone who may have been stalking her?"

"No. Why do you ask?"

"Just curious." I didn't see any reason to explain what I found. "Thanks and please get back to me if you find anything."

Instead of going into the office first thing, I pulled up Stephanie's laptop and started going through her emails. It was slow and tedious. Most of the emails were from friends and clients. About an hour into it I saw an email from someone who was warning Stephanie to be careful. The email address seemed bogus.

I wrote back and waited. It was returned to me as undeliverable. Bummer. Who was trying to warn Stephanie and why? Was she coming to see me to find her stalker?

CHAPTER 32

After another hour or so I called it quits. My eyes were tired and I needed some caffeine and fresh air. While I was waiting on line in Starbucks I called Jeffrey Goldman. "Jeff, it's Tracey Marks. Did Stephanie happen to mention that she was being stalked?"

"She mentioned threatening phone calls."

"I know, but did she mention physically being stalked?"

"Now that you bring it up, she did tell me that she had a feeling she was being watched but she wasn't sure. Why do you ask?"

"Stephanie was looking at stuff on her computer about stalking. Can you think of anything she may have mentioned, maybe a name?"

"I think she said something about calling the high school."

"Did she say why?"

"No. I'm sorry I didn't ask."

Why would she be calling someone at the school unless she thought her stalker had some connection to Hudson or maybe it was something else altogether.

I waited until I got to the office before calling Linda. "I'm sorry to keep bothering you but would you happen to remember if there was anyone in your class that may have had a crush on Stephanie or was bothering her?"

"Not that I recall. Why are you asking?"

"Just wondering. If you happen to remember anyone please call me."

I needed to talk with Randy Stewart. I had a feeling Joe Connolly may have told him I was snooping around and mentioned my name, therefore, calling Randy wasn't an option. I would probably have to catch him at home, though I wanted to talk with him without his wife present. Since I didn't follow local politics, I had no idea whether it was too early for him to be out campaigning. Maybe waiting outside his building might be my best option.

My phone buzzed. "Jack. Hi. How's everything in your neck of the woods?"

"Good. How did the surveillance go?"

"Well I can report that Susie had a good time."

"As only she could. And you?"

"Probably not as good as Susie but it was kind of fun. I'm glad she was with me. I don't know how you do it all by yourself. Besides being boring most of the time, it's nerve racking following someone."

"If you do it enough it gets easier. The idea is not to get too stressed. If the first time it doesn't work out, the second might be the charm. So did you find out anything?"

"We actually did." I explained to Jack about the meeting between Connolly and Stewart and what we found on the computer.

"That's interesting, a lot of possibilities, which is good."

"It seems like there are too many possibilities. I would like there to be only one." Jack laughed.

"If only things were that simple," Jack said. "Unfortunately you are going to have to track down each lead. There are no shortcuts."

"You're no fun."

"Now you hurt my feelings."

"Poor baby, next time I see you I'll make it up to you."

I made a discreet phone call to the law firm Randy Stewart is a partner at and found out he was at work. Since I had no idea when he was planning on leaving for the day, I decided to be there no later than four-thirty. I was hoping I didn't have to wait out in the cold, but maybe I could hang out in the lobby. I think I would recognize him but I wasn't one hundred percent sure.

I took the train to his office on Lexington Avenue near 50th Street. I was happy to see that I could wait inside without looking too conspicuous. I went around the block to make sure there were no other exits Stewart could leave from.

Two hours later and still no Randy Stewart. There was no

place to sit and I was tired of standing. I had nothing to amuse myself except watching people going in and out of the building. I was beginning to think I either missed him or he left before I got here. Either way I was pissed. I walked over to the elevators to get a closer look as people were getting off when I spotted him walking out.

"Mr. Stewart," I called out as he walked passed me. He turned around but he kept walking. I rushed up to him. "My name is Tracey Marks and I'm investigating the death of Stephanie Harris."

"I'm sorry about her death but I don't know anything about it. I'm in a hurry."

Practically running to keep up with him, I said, "I'm not going away. If you don't speak to me here we can talk at your house." I don't know where I got the guts to say that to someone who's running for Congress.

"Are you threatening me?"

"No. But we need to talk."

He looked at me for a few seconds and said in a firm voice, "walk with me."

CHAPTER 33

We walked across the street to a coffee shop where the waitress seated us at a booth. We both ordered coffee.

"What is this about?" he said after the waitress left.

"I'm going to be completely honest with you. I believe Stephanie's death is connected to Maddie Jensen." His face gave nothing away. Though I had no idea if Stewart had anything to do with Maddie's rape, I had to try and get a reaction from him. "I know Joe Connolly raped Maddie and that you were there." It was a bluff.

"I have no idea what you're talking about."

"Yes you do. I have it from a reliable source you were there. This is just between you and me. I promise it doesn't go any further."

"I'm sorry I still don't know what you're talking about."

"I want this to stay between us but if you don't tell me the truth I can't make any promises." My right leg was shaking uncontrollably.

He remained quiet for what seemed like an eternity, and then he spoke.

"I have regretted that moment for my entire life. I wish I would have done things differently that night. I apologized to Maddie more times than I can tell you. When she committed suicide, I knew it probably had something to do with what happened to her in high school."

You mean the rape?" He flinched. "Who threatened her?"

"I didn't know she was threatened, I swear."

"Linda Brent, her friend at the time, said that Maddie told her and Stephanie that she was threatened not to tell anyone about the rape."

"Oh my God, I didn't know."

"What did Joe want when you met with him?" He looked up surprised.

"He told me you were snooping around and if you contacted me to keep quiet. I know nothing could make up for not coming forward and helping Maddie. I have been involved in women's issues for most of my adult life. That's one of the reasons I'm running for Congress."

Maybe he was remorseful, maybe it was an act, but he was also scared that I might say something and ruin his chances for Congress. I didn't plan on saying anything but I could use it for leverage.

"Tell me what happened that night?"

"Joe was angry at Maddie."

"Why was he angry?"

"Because she wouldn't sleep with him anymore. Joe was used to getting what he wanted."

"So then what?"

"He told us that he wanted to teach her a lesson, just scare her. I didn't know he was going to rape her. He asked Ben Miller to get Maddie to meet with him and take her into the park. When Joe and I showed up Maddie started freaking out. That was when Joe clamped his hand down over Maddie's mouth and shoved her on the ground."

"What did you and Ben do while this was happening?"

Sheepishly he said that they just watched. When Randy realized Joe was going to rape her he told Joe to stop but he wouldn't listen. Randy admitted he didn't try to push Joe off of her.

"Stephanie witnessed the rape. She saw the whole thing," I said. Randy put his hands over his face. "The only reason she never said anything was because Maddie was threatened. When she found out you were running for Congress did she tell you she was going to expose you and that's why you killed her?"

His eyes opened wide. "Are you crazy? I would never kill Stephanie and she never threatened me. I haven't seen or heard from Stephanie since high school."

I only had his word for that. "What about Ben Miller. Are you still friends?"

"We were for a while, but after high school we went our

separate ways. Every once in a while I hear from him. After that night I stopped hanging around with Joe."

"Did you know that Joe raped a girl by the name of Barbara Jorgensen and Ben Miller did his dirty work and threatened Ms. Jorgensen?"

"I didn't know any of this. I hadn't heard from Joe until the day he called to meet with me. He was worried and begged me to see him."

"Do you think Joe or Ben could have killed Stephanie?"

"When Joe and I met he was worried about me saying something to you about Maddie's rape. He didn't mention anything about Stephanie's murder."

"Did you hear from Ben Miller?"

"He did call to warn me that you might contact me. He probably spoke with Joe."

I sat there mulling over everything Randy Stewart told me. So if Stephanie didn't confront Randy as he said, then what does that mean?

"What are you going to do now?" Randy said to me looking nervous.

I took it to mean, 'are you going to tell anyone?'

"I told you it was between you and me." Just knowing I could cause him some trouble was enough for now.

"One last question, do you know if there was anyone that had a major crush on Stephanie back in high school?"

"I really didn't know Stephanie but you should probably ask Donna or Linda. Listen I want you to know if there's anything I can do to help you with your investigation, please don't hesitate to contact me. I have resources that might be beneficial to you. Please keep me posted."

I gave Randy my card as we were leaving. I didn't know if I believed Randy's story, but you never know, I may take him up on his offer.

I took the train back to my apartment building and picked up Thai food for dinner.

All the way home my mind was going through everything Randy Stewart told me. It appeared Joe Connolly was worried about what I knew. He ruined two lives that I knew of and there's nothing I can do about it. But what if he didn't stop raping women? What's that saying, 'a leopard doesn't change his spots.' And If Stephanie's death had nothing to do with Maddie's rape, I was back to square one with no possibilities.

CHAPTER 34

I wondered if Donna had any inkling of what Joe did. What would be the point in confronting her? Even if she believed me, what would I have to gain? I may never know if Joe raped anyone else since high school. My first priority is to find out who killed Stephanie. It might be worth a call to both Donna and Linda to find out if anyone back then had a thing for Stephanie.

Friday morning I went for a quick run. When I got back I called Donna and Linda and left voice messages. I also left a message for Greg Todd. If anyone knew someone was interested in Stephanie it would probably be one of her friends in the group.

My phone buzzed. "Hey are we still on for tomorrow," I said to Susie.

"Yes, I'll meet you for breakfast at the French Bistro at nine, and then we can go in search of a wedding dress."

"It should be fun."

"I never thought I would say this but for once you are more enthused than I am," Susie said.

"Bah humbug."

When I hung up I noticed a missed call from Linda Brent.

"Hi Linda, it's Tracey Marks. I was wondering if you remember anyone that may have been interested in Stephanie that she rejected or she might have mentioned was bothering her when you guys hung out together?"

"No one I can recall at the moment but I'll think about it and let you if someone comes to mind."

"Thanks."

As I was walking into my office my phone beeped. "Tracey Marks." The person hung up. It showed up as unknown caller. Was it someone who wanted to scare me or was it just a wrong number? This case was giving me the jitters.

I was just finishing up locating a deadbeat dad for one of my regular clients when Greg Todd called. "Mr. Todd, since we last spoke I came across something on Stephanie's computer. It's possible she was being stalked, though I have nothing concrete."

"What did you find?"

"She was looking through articles on the internet about stalking. The reason I called was to ask if you remember anyone back then that was paying particular attention to Stephanie?"

"I can't say as I do but I will think about it. I thought you said her murder was somehow connected to Maddie Jensen?"

"Yes, I did say that but I'm exploring all leads."

"Well that makes sense. Again I'll get back to you if anything comes to mind."

I placed a call to Cynthia Dunlop, the Assistant Principal. Maybe Stephanie called her.

"Ms. Dunlop, it's Tracey Marks. I was in your office regarding Stephanie Harris."

"Oh yes the private investigator. What can I do for you?"

"A friend of hers mentioned that Stephanie may have called someone in the school inquiring about a student. Do you know anything about that?"

"No but I would be glad to ask around if that would be helpful."

"Yes, that would be great. Thank you."

On the way home I stopped at the Corner Sweet Shoppe. While Mr. Hayes was waiting on a customer, I was salivating at the chocolates behind the case. My favorite was the dark chocolate covered marzipan. I decided to indulge myself and buy some marzipan and pistachio ice cream.

"Hi Tracey," Mr. Hayes said after finishing up with his customer.

"Hi Mr. Hayes. I noticed you added gelato ice cream."

"You have to try and satisfy all the customers or else they'll go somewhere else."

"Good move, but I'll have my usual, and could you also give me a few pieces of the dark chocolate covered marzipan."

"I hope that's not your dinner."

"Nah, I still have leftover Thai food."

At home I settled in and called Jack. "Nice to hear your voice," he said.

"Likewise, what's going on?"

"I'm up to my eyeballs in trying to find witnesses for a new case we just got in," Jack said.

I told Jack everything that was going on since we last spoke.

"What's your take?" he asked.

"I don't have a clue. It does seem like the original direction I was headed in is not panning out."

"That's not a negative. It just means a new direction has turned up."

"It's just the thought of this guy Connolly getting away with raping two people makes me sick."

"Is there anything tying him to Stephanie's murder?"

"Unless Stephanie somehow found out that he raped someone in the last few years, I don't see him as a suspect. But what if Stephanie threatened to tell Donna?" I said.

"Why now?"

"Maybe Stephanie felt guilty for not coming forward then. She must have felt horrible all these years, especially after Maddie killed herself."

"You can always come back to that. I would pursue the stalker possibility for now."

"I am but it's going so slow."

"I'm afraid that's investigative work, slow and steady."

"I've heard that before. On a different subject, Susie and I are spending the day tomorrow shopping for her wedding dress."

"You sound excited."

"That's what Susie said."

"You're just glad it's her and not you."

"Would you want it to be me?" I asked, not knowing if I wanted to hear the answer.

"That's a loaded question which I'm not sure I should answer. But I will. I'm not vehemently opposed to the idea."

"That's not exactly a ringing endorsement."

"Tell Susie I said hi."

"I will."

I would be lying if I didn't say I was surprised at Jack's answer. I never got the feeling he was interested in marriage. He left a slight opening, though I was scared to death.

CHAPTER 35

While having breakfast on Saturday with Susie I told her about my exchange with Jack.

"It sounds like he might be open to the idea of getting married or at least living together. The poor bastard must really like you."

"I beg your pardon."

"So how do you feel?" Susie asked.

"Like you felt when you first mentioned about moving in with Mark. Would I have to compromise? Would I lose my independence? Stuff like that."

My phone buzzed. "Mr. Todd, nice to hear from you, anything come to mind?"

"I believe so. I remember Stephanie complaining about this one kid. He had asked her out but she said no."

"Any reason she said no?"

"She just said he wasn't her type. The thing is she said that there were times when she would be someplace and he would show up, like it wasn't a coincidence."

"So what happened?"

"Eventually he must have gotten the hint since Stephanie never mentioned him again."

"How long did this go on for?"

"Not long, maybe a month, two at the most."

"Do you know his name?"

"It's Terry Brooks."

"How did you remember his name?"

"That's easy. We were in the same science class for two semesters."

"Do you know what happened to him?"

"I don't, I'm sorry."

"Thank you for calling," looking at Susie giving her the thumbs up.

Susie was halfway finished with her French toast and bacon

when I got off the phone.

"Well, good news?"

"Could be. That was one of the guys in the group Stephanie hung out with in high school. He's the one I told you is a therapist. He mentioned a boy that had followed Stephanie around. Now I just have to locate him. But getting back to why we are here."

"How can I try on dresses after I finished such a fattening breakfast? How about if we have a western theme at the wedding, jeans and cowboy boots? I'll wear a cowboy outfit."

"Sounds good to me. Now we just have to run it by Mark."

"Okay let's carry on. First stop Saks."

After an exhausting day which included shopping at Saks, Bloomingdales and a few small dress shops with lunch and drinks in between, we went back to Saks and bought the first dress Susie tried on there. It fit her beautifully and she looked gorgeous in it. It's not your typical wedding dress. It was a white silk A-line dress that tapered at the waist with a v-neck and gently fell right below her knees. Thank heavens she loved it and we could stop looking.

It was after seven by the time I walked into my apartment. While eating a bowl of Cheerios and milk in bed, I began to think about the direction of the case. I was so convinced that Maddie's rape had something to do with Stephanie's murder. How could I be so sure and maybe so wrong? I know I shouldn't rule it out. What if Ben Miller was lying to me? He did Joe's dirty work for him. But why kill Stephanie now unless there was something else going on that she found out about? Maybe Joe and Ben were in it together and needed to silence Stephanie.

The guy with the burner phone that I called from Stephanie's cell records denied that he knew her. I didn't believe him when he said it. Could he have killed her? Something about the call was bugging me but I didn't know what it was.

There was a loud knock at my door and it was getting louder. How could someone get passed the doorman? "Who is it?" I shouted running to the door.

"It's me."

"Susie?" I said opening the door. She was wearing pajamas under her heavy winter jacket. "What's the matter? Is it Mark?"

"No," tears streaming down her face. "It's Jack."

"What's happened to him?" I said frantically.

"You have to come with me. He's been in a terrible accident."

"Where is he?" pulling on my jeans and a sweatshirt.

"Hurry, he's in the hospital and they don't know if he's going to make it."

Susie was driving really fast. I had a million questions but I was too frightened to ask any of them. I was so scared thinking that Jack might die. We exited off the Taconic and out of nowhere there appeared a car behind us driving really fast heading right towards us. It was happening again. No, I have to get to Jack. The car smashed into us, Susie losing control. We were headed right into an oncoming car. I braced myself and reached out to Susie but she was no longer there. I opened my mouth to scream but nothing came out.

CHAPTER 36

My eyes shot open and for a second I didn't know where I was until I realized it was a dream, tears streaming down my face from relief. I was shaking. I got up and went to the bathroom and splashed cold water over my face. I sat down on the toilet seat trying to steady myself. The dream was so vivid I couldn't seem to shake it.

I didn't think I was going to get back to sleep, still disturbed by my dream. I went to the kitchen table and opened up Stephanie's yearbook looking for Terry Brooks. He was a pale looking kid with big black framed glasses way too big for his face. I can see why Stephanie didn't want to go out with him. Back then nerds never got the girl. He probably turned out to be a hunk and very successful.

Terry Brooks was a common name. How was I going to find him? First place to look was the Hudson Prep website. Searching through it I found a Terry Brooks that graduated in 1988. That seemed about right. It listed that he was a stockbroker at Morgan Stanley in Manhattan. Maybe he did become rich and successful.

First thing Monday morning I called Terry Brooks at Morgan Stanley.

"Hello, Mr. Brooks. My name is Tracey Marks and I'm investigating the death of Stephanie Howell Harris."

"Who?"

This guy is smooth. "Stephanie Howell Harris. You both went to Hudson Prep."

"Yes, Yes. Now I remember. She's dead?"

"Yes. She was killed a few weeks ago and I'm talking to other students from Hudson Prep. Would you be able to make time at some point later in the day to speak with me?"

"Yes definitely. I'm sorry, I just wasn't expecting this. Are you in the city?"

"Yes. I can meet you any time."

"Why don't we say at noon? We're located on Broadway between 47th and 48th Street."

"I'll be there. Thank you."

I have to say I was surprised at his reaction. Was he just a good actor or did he really have nothing to do with Stephanie's death. Hopefully I'll be able to figure it out after I speak with him.

When I arrived at Morgan Stanley the receptionist of course asked me to take a seat. I waited about five minutes when this tall, well-dressed man approached me.

"Tracey, I'm Terry."

Terry was nothing like his high school photo. His glasses were gone. He probably wore contacts. He seemed very comfortable in his own skin. Though he wasn't classically handsome, he certainly had sex appeal. I followed him to his office and he closed the door.

"Please sit. Can I get you coffee or water?"

"No thanks." I noticed a photo of a very nice looking woman on a credenza behind his desk. "Is that your wife? She's very pretty."

"Yes, thank you. Please tell me what happened."

Should I go through the whole story or give him a very short version why I'm here. I decided to go with the longer version and then hit him with what I was told about him. As I was talking he listened intently and seemed genuinely surprised at what I said. Nobody was that good an actor.

"When I was at Hudson I was a real book worm and didn't have many friends. I wasn't involved in sports or any after school activities except for the chess team. I was a shy kid."

"Well you seemed to have outgrown your shyness."

"That's true," he said smiling. "Things changed when I went to college. I was frustrated about my appearance so I went to the school gym and started working out. I began to gain confidence."

"In my interviews something came to light. It was mentioned that you had a crush on Stephanie." He looked surprised.

"I have to say I'm guilty as charged. I had forgotten all about that until you reminded me that Stephanie went to Hudson. I did kind of follow her around for a while, but then I realized how pathetic I was and stopped. She had no interest in me, and I couldn't blame her though I was disappointed that she was like most girls who wouldn't give somebody like me a second look."

"I found on her computer that she was looking at articles on stalking."

"Oh, now I see. You thought because I had a crush on her in high school I've never gotten over her and was stalking her now. You concluded I killed her. If it wasn't so ludicrous, I might be angry at you. I can assure you I am a happily married man and haven't thought of Stephanie since Hudson."

"I'm sorry if I have offended you but I had to ask the questions."

"I understand."

"Can you think of anyone at all that may have had a crush on Stephanie? Maybe somebody you noticed hanging around her."

"Most of the time I saw Stephanie with the kids in her group. I can't even tell you their names."

"Well if you think of something please call me," handing him my card.

I can't say I wasn't disappointed. I didn't know what to think anymore. After stopping for a salad I went into the office. My phone rang. "Hello," I said.

"Tracey, this is Cynthia Dunlop from Hudson Prep. I asked around whether Stephanie Harris spoke with anyone here. Apparently she asked to speak with the principal but before she was put through to him she changed her mind and hung up."

"Is the principal in?"

"He's away at a conference but I can have him call you when he gets back."

"Thanks."

I went next door to see Cousin Alan. "Hi Margaret, how's everything here?"

"Good, except the boss is in quite a mood."

"My dear cousin, couldn't be."

"Oh, it's not what you think. He's supposed to go to Chicago for an insurance conference next week which he really doesn't want to go to, besides the fact he hates flying."

"Poor guy, I'll see what I can do."

"Hi cousin, I heard I'm stepping in at my own risk. Anything I can do?"

"Yeah, you can take my place at the conference."

"Absolutely, but only if you find out who killed Stephanie."

"Having a hard time?"

"You can say. All roads seem to lead to dead ends. I'm just not sure that any of my suspects killed her. I keep rethinking everything. But I have a question. I have her computer and I need someone who is very savvy in getting information off of it. I just don't have the skills. Do you know anyone that could help me?"

"As it happens, I do. He's really good. A little expensive but maybe he would do me a favor and reduce his fee. We go back a long ways. I'll give you his number and you can call him directly. I'll give him a heads up."

"So what's the story with the conference?"

"I hate flying."

"Is Patty going with you?"

"It's just a two day thing and it's Chicago, not Paris."

"I guess you just have to suck it up. How's my main squeeze?"

"Life seems to be treating him well. No complaints as of yet. Though I'm sure they'll be plenty by the time he's talking."

"I'll call Patty and arrange a play date." Alan laughed as I left with Nick Jonas' card in my hand.

"Hello," I said answering my phone.

"Ms. Marks, it's Christine. I haven't been able to sleep. My mother's death has really upset me. The police are nowhere and I keeping envisioning how she died."

"Do you think you should talk to someone? It might help. Even when we find out who did this it won't change the fact that she was taken from you too soon."

"Are there any leads?"

"I can tell you that I am exploring every possible avenue and I won't quit. I'm having someone who specializes in computers see if there's anything on your mom's computer that might lead us in the right direction. I know it's hard to be patient, and I would feel the same way as you do, but I know something will break." If only I was as sure as I led Christine to believe.

When we hung up I hoped Christine would take my advice and see a therapist. I was also happy she didn't fire me.

Around four o'clock I called Nick Jonas.

"Jonas here."

"Mr. Jonas, my name is Tracey Marks. My cousin Alan said you're a whiz with computers and I could really use your help."

"No problem. Why don't I swing by your office and pick it up. It might take a few days before I have a chance to look at it. I've got some other clients ahead of you."

"That's fine. I appreciate it. When would you like to stop by?"

"I could be there in an hour if you can wait."

I gave Nick my address. I was hoping there was something on the computer that he could uncover. My thinking is that if Stephanie confronted someone and she was being threatened or stalked maybe it would show up on the computer.

CHAPTER 37

Nick was classically handsome. Perfect nose, beautiful blue eyes, and a dimple right in the middle of his chin. His smile showed off his straight, white teeth. His body was not bad either.

"Hi Nick, nice to meet you," shaking his hand.

"Likewise. Alan sings your praises. He's a great guy."

"I know. Well here's the computer."

"Is there anything specific you're looking for?"

"Anything she might have been looking into. The woman died and I'm trying to find out what got her killed. That's the best answer I can give you."

"Fair enough. Here's a receipt for the computer. Hopefully I can have some answers by the end of the week, Monday the latest."

"Thank you."

After he left I called Susie. "Alan recommended someone who is a computer specialist and hopefully will be able to discover what Stephanie was looking at before she died."

"That was a good idea."

"I spoke to someone that had a crush on Stephanie back in high school but I don't think he's our killer. I realized I was so fixated on trying to connect Maddie's death to Stephanie that I didn't leave room for the possibility that it might have nothing to do with Maddie."

"But that's where it originally led you. And you had to follow those leads. There's also the chance that someone you spoke to was lying. I wouldn't rule it out completely."

"Thanks. Did you show Mark the dress?"

"No, I don't want him to see it until the day of the wedding."

"I have to figure out what I'm going to wear. I'm not sure I have anything in the closet that's suitable for my best friend's wedding. I'm gonna take a look tonight."

"A simple black dress will do."

"I'll look like chop liver next to you."

"Well, it is my day."

"Good point."

On the way home I stopped off at one of these places that has prepared foods and bought half a roasted chicken. At the supermarket I stopped for salad stuff and a potato to bake.

While I was enjoying a glass of wine and catching up on the news, my phone buzzed. I was surprised to hear from Jay Henderson, the principal at Hudson Prep.

"Mr. Henderson, I thought you were away at a conference?"

"I am, but Mrs. Dunlop mentioned you called."

"Yes, she said that Stephanie Harris asked to speak with you and then hung up. Do you have any idea why she was calling you?"

"I don't. To tell you the truth I wondered if it had anything to do with what we discussed about my relationship with Maddie," he said.

"I actually don't think it did, but I have no idea what she may have wanted. Whatever it was, clearly she changed her mind. Maybe she was frightened of someone. Well thanks for calling."

I went back to my wine. My mind drifted to the various people I interviewed. I was still skeptical of the boyfriend. How do we really know Stephanie hadn't already dumped him? We have only his word on that. He may have been desperate, no job and now no girlfriend.

On the other hand, if Stephanie decided she could no longer live with the secret she could have confronted Joe. He had a strong motive to get rid of her even if he couldn't be prosecuted now. But if either of them did it, how do I prove it?

As far as Randy Stewart, even though he had the most to lose, I had mixed feelings about him. He seemed so sincere, but it could be an act. I just didn't know.

I had been wrestling with the idea of whether I should tell Joe's wife Donna what I knew. If he did kill Stephanie, confronting his wife might get a reaction from him since she would most likely tell her husband or would she?

My phone beeped. "How's my favorite PI?" Jack said.

"Contemplating my next move. I gave Stephanie's computer to an expert who will hopefully be able to trace Stephanie's movements on her computer."

"That was smart."

"Well I don't have many moves left. I was thinking about telling Joe's wife what he did but I'm not sure it's the right thing to do."

"If you're trying to get him riled up, you might get the same results threatening him instead of his wife."

"My objective is to find out if he killed Stephanie. If threatening him will do that then I'm game."

"Don't forget to make sure you take your gun wherever you go."

"I will. How was your weekend?"

"Worked most of it. Next time you come up we'll have to go cross country skiing."

"That sounds like fun, though I've never done it before."

"It's easy once you get the hang of it."

"Okay, I'm sold. Why don't I come up this weekend instead of you coming here?"

"Great idea, see ya soon."

Tuesday morning I went to the gym early and was in the office by eight-thirty. I put on coffee and contemplated how and where I was going to confront Joe.

For now I wanted to speak with Andrew Carter, Stephanie's boyfriend. I knew he lived in White Plains. Since he didn't work I thought I would try and catch him at home. I drove up to White Plains to an apartment building on Greenridge Avenue. The building didn't appear to have a doorman. There was a buzzer system in the lobby. I didn't want Andrew to know I was coming until I knocked on his door. There was an elderly man opening the front door so I held it for him hoping he wouldn't question whether I lived in the building.

I found Andrew Carter's apartment on the fourth floor. I rang the buzzer.

"Who is it?"

"Andrew, It Tracey Marks."

He opened the door. "What the hell are you doing here," looking more disheveled than the last time I saw him.

"Can I please come in so we don't have to talk in the hallway?"

"Why do we need to talk at all?"

"I'm trying to find out who killed Stephanie. That's why."

"As far as I know you have no leads."

"Can I please come in?" He stepped aside and I walked into a disaster. There were tons of books piled on the floor in the living room, along with newspapers that were probably going back several months if not longer. I wanted to say something but held my tongue.

"So what do you want?"

"Is there someplace we can sit?" He nodded towards the wicker chair in the living room. He sat opposite me on a beige couch that looked like he picked up at a garage sale.

"How's the job search going?"

"Did you come all this way to ask about my job opportunities? I think you could have picked up the phone for that."

"Not exactly, I was actually looking for your help." He seemed surprised. "I'm having a hard time making any headway. Maybe we can sort this out together. It appears Stephanie was holding on to a secret since high school. A friend of hers was raped and swore Stephanie to secrecy."

"How do you know all this?" he said, now fully engaged.

"From friends I interviewed and from people who worked at her high school. I think she confronted the person and that got her killed." I wanted Andrew to believe I was looking at someone else. "The thing is I have to prove it and that's a lot trickier. I think she would have been acting strange or scared in the weeks leading up to her death. I know you mentioned she was sometimes forgetful but can you recall anything else?" Andrew started to fidget.

"I didn't tell you this before because it didn't seem relevant at the time, but Stephanie and I stopped seeing each other a few weeks before she was killed."

"Why didn't you tell me?"

"I don't know. I just panicked."

I didn't say anything at first. Then I said, "did you break up with her?" though I was pretty sure I knew the answer.

"I was under a lot of stress trying to find a job, and it was putting a strain on our relationship. I guess it was mutual."

"Are you sure she didn't end it?"

"What's the difference who ended it? Why is that important?" he said raising his voice.

"I just need to know the truth. I've been in a few relationships and sometimes the guy broke up with me. It's nothing to be embarrassed about. Relationships are not easy. Take it from someone who's never been married."

"I wanted to give it a chance. I thought once I found a job the relationship would work itself out. Now it all makes sense. If Stephanie found herself under pressure because of whatever was going on in her life, I can see why the added pressure of my problems would be too much for her."

"So she broke up with you?"

"I guess."

That was as close to a yes as I was going to get from him. "Did you still have a key to her house?" From the expression on his face I think he realized where this was going.

"I would like you to leave now. I told you once and I'm going to say it only one more time. I loved her and I didn't have anything to do with her death. Now go."

I didn't see the point in pressuring him any further. I was curious whether the police had interviewed him but I could find that out from Christine. I left with my gut saying he didn't kill Stephanie but I've been wrong before.

CHAPTER 38

On the way back to the office I called Christine and asked her to check with the police whether they questioned Andrew. She said she would.

Where do I go from here? I'm thinking Joe Connolly might be my best hope. Maybe I should take Jack's advice and tell the police everything I know, but I wasn't ready to give up yet. I was determined that something would surface. I was hoping Stephanie's computer might reveal the answer.

I found a parking spot near the office pretty easily. That in itself was something to celebrate. I stopped and picked up a grilled cheese and tomato sandwich for lunch.

After spending some time handling administrative paperwork, I concentrated on how I was going to approach Joe Connolly and what I was going to say to him. I didn't think he would meet with me if I just asked him to. I didn't want to go to his house in case Donna was there, and I didn't want to meet him at the construction site after dark. So where does that leave me? Would he meet me if I told him I was going to the police with what I knew? I think he would. Maybe that was my only alternative.

I called Joe. I realized I was biting my lower lip. "Hello."

"Joe, it's Tracey Marks. I'd like to meet. You pick the time and place."

"Why the hell would I meet with you?"

"Why not, maybe we can help each other."

"I think I'll pass."

"Joe, I think it would be in your best interest to meet with me," holding my breath.

"You don't say. And if I don't?"

"I'll have no choice but to go to the police with what I found out."

"Is that a threat?"

"I guess it is," I said, my heart in my mouth. I can almost hear the wheels turning. He knew I had him.

"I'll meet you at Joe's Bar on Midland Avenue in Yonkers at six o'clock."

"I'll be there."

Now, how was I going to handle the situation? I didn't have many options. I had to lay out everything I knew. Why would he admit to killing Stephanie even if he did? Maybe there's a chance he might know something I wasn't aware of. Before I left I took my gun from the safe and slid it into my ankle holster.

A few minutes before six, I entered the bar. I didn't see Joe. I sat down at a corner table. The waitress came over and I ordered a glass of white wine. I saw Joe walk in and signaled him over. Joe ordered a light beer on tap.

"So what's on your mind," Joe asked in an apathetic tone.

"I'm going to lay everything out I know and see if you have any response."

When the waitress left after putting down our drinks, I continued. "I know you raped both Barbara Jorgensen and Maddie Jensen. I know there's nothing I can do about that unfortunately. You ruined two peoples' lives and you probably don't care. What you didn't know at the time is that Stephanie witnessed the rape of Maddie Jensen. You had Ben Miller threaten Maddie not to say anything. How did it feel as you pushed Maddie down on the ground and violated her? Did it make you feel like a real man?" His lips tightened. He didn't say anything so I continued. "It's now thirty years later and Stephanie can't live with the secret any longer. She confronted you and threatened to tell your wife but you couldn't have that so you killed her. It may have been an accident but that doesn't matter." I stopped talking.

"I hate to burst your bubble but Stephanie never confronted me. I haven't seen her since high school," he said trying to keep his cool.

"Well maybe your wife saw Stephanie and told Donna everything. How do you think your wife would react knowing she's sleeping with a rapist? Would that make you mad enough to kill Stephanie?" If looks could kill, I'd be dead.

"If Stephanie already told my wife what would be my reason to kill her?" he said, trying to regain his composure.

He did have a point, but I said, "logic doesn't always win out. You still could have been so angry at Stephanie you wanted her dead."

"Well since you have all this neatly worked out, why don't you go to the police? Why come to me?" he said with a smug look on his face.

I wanted to slap his face. Instead I said, "I wanted to give you an opportunity to explain yourself before I did." It was probably an idle threat. "I was willing to give you a chance that you might know something, information that would point me to someone else."

"Sorry, can't help you."

"Do you think your wife can?"

Before I had a chance to react, Joe reached across the table and grabbed my arm.

"If you dare tell my wife you'll regret it."

He stood up and walked out. Well that was fun. I sat there for a minute or so rattled. I asked for the check and left.

On the ride home I knew Joe had me over a barrel. I could go to the police but unless I had proof that he killed Stephanie what would be the point. Did I provoke Joe enough that he would try and come after me? Only if he did kill Stephanie, otherwise I was at another dead end.

The following day I woke up without any plan. I was struggling to start the day. I went through the motions of showering and eating breakfast. The walk to my office seemed longer than usual.

Sitting at my desk I was confronted with a horrible thought. What if nothing unusual showed up on Stephanie's computer? I quickly dismissed the thought out of my head. Now that I was aware that Andrew Carter hadn't seen Stephanie for weeks before she died, was it possible she could have confided in someone else? The only two people I could think of were her friend Mallory that she ran with in the mornings and Jeffrey Goldman. I would think she would confide in someone who was a constant in her life.

"Mallory, it's Tracey Marks. How are you?"

"I'm glad you called. I wanted to know what was happening with the investigation."

"Do you think we can meet? I'd like to talk with you."

"Can you meet me around lunchtime in Bronxville? There's a place in town called the Bronxville Diner.

"I'll find it."

Mallory and I arrived at the diner at the same exact time. We were seated at a booth right away. The diner looked like it was modeled from the fifties. Inside the walls were painted aqua and there was memorabilia from the fifties everywhere. There was a counter with stools with red vinyl cushions.

"Hi ladies, are you ready to order?"

I looked at Mallory and she nodded yes. "I'll have a hamburger and sweet potato fries." Mallory ordered a chef salad and we both ordered coffee.

"Tell me what's going on," Mallory said when the waitress left.

I explained as much as I could to her. I didn't go into too much detail.

"I had no idea what Stephanie went through. It must have been a burden for her to carry such a secret for all these years."

"Did you know that Andrew and Stephanie had broken up?"

"I knew there were problems. I had my suspicions but she never said anything to me."

I thought that was strange.

"Stephanie was a very private person. She wasn't the type to tell you everything that was going on in her life. Sharing wasn't her strong suit."

"You said you knew there were problems. Do you know what they were?"

"I think the biggest bone of contention was the fact that he didn't have a job. When she first met Andrew he had just quit teaching. That was alright with Stephanie at first, but after a year he still didn't have a job."

"Did you socialize with them?"

"My husband and I went out to dinner with them once.

Andrew can be charming. Maybe that's what drew Stephanie to him at first. But I guess charm can go just so far."

"Do you know if he was ever abusive towards her?"

"I don't think Stephanie would tolerate that kind of behavior."

"Why do you say that?"

"Once when we were running I mentioned that I had read in the paper about a woman who was raped. Her response completely took me by surprise. She said something like, 'if anyone even dared to put a hand on me, I'd kill them.' I had never heard Stephanie react that way."

"That's interesting. Can you think of anything that was different about Stephanie's behavior in the weeks before her death?"

"Besides the phone conversation I mentioned?"

"Yes. Looking back did she seem more edgy or distracted, like something was bothering her?"

"I'm not sure if this means anything, but she asked me if I had a security system in my house. I told her I did and gave her the name of the company I used."

"Do you know if she installed a system?"

"I believe she did."

Obviously Stephanie was afraid of someone, though I still didn't know if it was related to Maddie.

"Is there anything else you can think of?"

"I guess there's no point in hiding this anymore. She told me she started seeing a therapist."

"That's interesting. Did she tell you why?"

"She said she needed to work out some stuff but she didn't elaborate and I didn't ask."

I wondered if it was stuff from her past or something that occurred recently.

"She didn't by any chance mention the therapist's name?"

"No. I'm pretty sure I would remember if she did."

While Mallory was talking I got the impression she was holding something back.

"Are you sure she didn't tell you anything else?"

"Yes, I'm sure," she said avoiding my eyes.

CHAPTER 39

"Thanks Mallory. You've been a big help."

Mallory gave me the address of Strategic Security Systems located in White Plains. Since I was already in the area, I called hoping I could see the owner or someone in charge right away.

When I called I was told John Bento wasn't in the office and to leave a number. I figured I would stick around Bronxville hoping he would call me back soon.

I browsed in some of the clothing stores with fancy price tags. I wound up at Slave to the Grind, a place I knew from the last time I was here. They had several choices of different blends of coffee, plus an assortment of desserts. I sat at a table sipping a latte. I tried Strategic again. They wanted to know why I was calling but I only wanted to explain to Bento.

A few minutes later John Bento called. I explained who I was and told him I needed to talk to him in person.

"If you can wait till tomorrow morning I can take some time with you. Right now I'm too busy."

I agreed to meet with him at his office at nine-thirty the following morning. I was excited at the prospect of talking with him. I wondered if Stephanie had security cameras installed.

When I left Slave to the Grind, I drove to Stephanie's house but didn't see any cameras, in front or in the back of the house.

I called Susie on the way back. "How about a drink later?"

"Sure, I'll meet you at six at Jake's."

Jake's is a local bar situated between both of our offices. It's dark inside but has great fried Calamari.

I slid into one of the booths and I ordered a Malbec when the waitress came over. Susie walked in a few minutes later with a broad smile planted on her face.

"What's up?"

Susie sat down and signaled for the waitress. "I'll have whatever she's having."

"And we'll have an order of fried Calamari," I said.

"I got my client a great settlement. Her husband didn't think we would find out about all his other accounts but thanks to the guy you recommended, we found over $500,000 so tonight is on the firm."

"That's great. So listen to this. I was talking with Stephanie's friend Mallory. She's the one who ran with Stephanie in the mornings. She said that Stephanie put in a security system a few weeks before she died."

"Well, a lot that did for her. If she wasn't dead I'd tell her to ask for her money back."

"Very funny. I'm meeting the owner of the security place tomorrow morning. I went by her house but I didn't see any outside security cameras."

The waitress set down our drinks and a bowl of fried Calamari.

I plucked one with the tentacles out of the bowl and stuffed it into my mouth.

"That's too bad," Susie said.

"Any questions for him come to mind?"

"I'm not sure how much he's inclined to tell you. I wonder if Stephanie's daughter knew about the security system."

"I'm willing to bet she didn't know. I don't think Stephanie wanted to worry her."

"You may be right. Well if he's willing to help you out I'd want to know the exact date it was installed, but more importantly, did she say anything to the person who installed the system. Maybe she told him the reason."

"I actually don't know who it was. Bento might be a waste of time."

"Not really. You probably have to run it by him anyway."

"Mallory also mentioned Stephanie was seeing a therapist. Apparently she had issues she needed to work out."

"Interesting. I wonder what that was about."

"Maybe she was deciding to confront Joe Connolly after all these years and she wanted the therapist's opinion."

"I suppose," I said with no confidence. "I spoke with Joe Connolly, our neighborhood rapist."

"Oh yeah, what did he have to say?"

"Nothing good. He denied that Stephanie threatened him. He also didn't take the bait when I said I was going to the police with what I knew. But when I sort of threatened to tell his wife that's when he got upset. He didn't take kindly to that."

"Be careful. If he even thinks you might tell her he could cause trouble."

"I will. On a lighter note, I'm going up to Jack's this weekend. He's taking me cross country skiing."

"Well that should be a hoot. Make sure he takes pictures of you. I might frame them. By the way we finalized the wedding date. It's April 19th, a Sunday. We're going to have it at my parents' house. Both a rabbi and a minister will marry us. We'll set up a tent on the back lawn and hopefully the weather will cooperate since Mark and I both want to have it outside. I hope people don't mind traveling to Portsmouth, New Hampshire. There's a great hotel that everyone can stay at, though I'll have to book the rooms right away."

"I love it. I've never really explored the area. Since your parents moved there I was only at the house once when they threw you your thirtieth birthday party."

"Well, you and Jack will have to come a few days ahead and explore the area. It's very pretty and a lot to see."

"Aren't I supposed to choose my own escort?"

"It's my wedding," Susie said sticking her tongue out at me.

The following morning I met John Benito at his security business in White Plains. I sort of had a picture in my head of what he looked like, and when I met him I wasn't disappointed. He was on the tall side, solidly built with a peppered beard close to his face. He had beautiful green eyes.

"Mr. Bento nice to meet you," shaking his hand. Eyeing me up and down did not go unnoticed.

"So how can I help you?"

"Your company installed a security system in a house in Scarsdale for a Stephanie Harris maybe a few months ago. I'm not exactly sure of the date. She was murdered in her house about two months ago. You may have read about it in the papers. I was hired by her daughter to look into her death."

"I see, so you're wondering about the system we put in."

"I'm also curious about any conversations Ms. Harris had with the person who installed it."

"Well that would be me. Ms. Harris was concerned that she was being stalked. She didn't go into details."

"Did the police ask you any questions about the system?"

"Basically they wanted to know if there were any hidden cameras."

"I didn't see any."

"Because there aren't any. Most people think the security system is enough and don't install cameras."

"Are you sure she didn't say anything about the person who might be stalking her?"

"I'm positive," he said.

"So how would someone get in?"

"One obvious way is letting the person in not knowing that he/she is the killer."

"And if they had an idea who it was?"

"Sometimes people only set the alarm when they're not home to deter a robbery."

"Do you know if the police said a door was forced open?" I asked.

"You'd have to ask them."

"Well thank you for your time. If you happen to think of anything else please contact me. Oh, by the way, can you check when the system was installed?"

I thought since I was in the area I would take a run over to Stephanie's house again to see if there was any forced entry since I was in the dark about what the police knew. Also maybe knock on a few doors and see if anyone remembers a stranger hanging around her place.

I pulled my car in front of Stephanie's house. I noticed, Lottie, the neighbor I had interviewed, peeking out her window. I wonder if she did that the day Stephanie was killed. I waved.

I walked to the back of Stephanie's house and checked the

door that leads out to the patio. I opened it with the key I had and looked to see if it might have been tampered with. Unless it was fairly obvious I would have no clue if the door was jimmied.

Assuming the alarm system was on and she knew her killer, how did the person get in? What about through the garage? Besides the garage doors there was a side door that you can access to get into the garage and from there you could get into the house. I walked over to the side door and opened it with the key I had. I didn't know exactly what I was looking for. I pulled out my cell phone and called Jack.

CHAPTER 40

"Hey, got a question. I'm looking at a side door that goes into Stephanie's garage. How can you tell if it's been tampered with?"

"You probably can't, but it might be easy to get into. First go outside and close the door. Using a credit card, see if you can open it."

"Hold on; I need two hands."

I slid the card up and down. At first the bolt wouldn't move. I kept trying and then it gave way. "I'm in. I can't believe it."

"Now go over to the door that leads into the house and see if it's locked."

"Wow, I can walk right in. You mean she paid all that money for a security system and it was that easy to get in? Why wouldn't she have a better lock on the side door to the garage?"

"Who knows?"

"I'm going to knock on a few doors while I'm here to see if a neighbor saw anybody lurking around Stephanie's place."

"Can you come up tomorrow?"

"Yeah, I should be able to leave here no later than three o'clock since I'd like to get to you before dark. I don't want a repeat performance of last time."

"I agree. See ya soon."

I went across the street to Lottie's house. She opened the door before I had a chance to knock.

"Come in, it's freezing out."

I smelled freshly baked bread. My mouth was salivating.

"I just made some homemade banana bread. Would you like a piece?"

"I would love a piece." I followed Lottie into the kitchen where coffee was brewing. I wondered if she knew I was going to stop by.

"How is the investigation going my dear?" she asked while we were seated and I was biting into a piece of her banana bread.

"I think I'm finally making some headway. Lottie, did you know that Stephanie put in a security system?"

"I did. A lot of good it did her. Paying all that money and someone just walks in and kills her."

"Do you remember seeing any strangers mulling about Stephanie's place?"

"Well there was one guy but when I asked him what he was doing he told me that he was installing a security system. Of course I checked with Stephanie and she told me not to worry."

"What about a couple of weeks before that. Did you notice someone checking out the house?"

"Well let me see. Actually, there was a car that was sitting outside Stephanie's house. I remember it because the car sat there for a while."

"Did you happen to see who was in the car?"

"I could only tell you it was a man but I couldn't tell you what he looked like."

"Do you remember anything about the car?"

"Well I have no idea about cars. But I do remember the color. It was blue."

"Are you sure it was blue and not black?"

"Very sure. I remember thinking it was a very bright blue. You wouldn't forget it."

"Would you happen to remember if the car was fairly new?"

"If I had to guess I would say pretty new. I think there was some sort of sticker on the back bumper but I couldn't tell you what it said."

"Did you ever see the car before or since?"

"Now that you mention it, I haven't. Oh my, do you think he might have been the killer?"

"No way to know right now. Are there any other neighbors home during the day?"

"Everyone pretty much works except for the woman three houses on Stephanie's left. She has a young daughter, but I doubt if she would be of any help. I believe she has a drinking problem."

"Well I think I've taken up too much of your time. You've been a big help and thank you for the delicious bread."

"If I see that man again, I'll be sure to call you. You take care of yourself and I hope you find the person who killed Stephanie."

I didn't have the heart to tell her if he was the killer she wouldn't be seeing him again.

I knocked on the door where Lottie mentioned the woman with the child. There was no answer. I left my card in the door.

Instead of going into the office I went straight home except for a detour to pick up some wine to take to Jack's, and dinner for tonight, Roast Pork Lo Mein and an egg roll. I couldn't recall Joe Connolly's car. I've only seen him with the pick-up truck. I wondered what his wife drives.

While I was contemplating what to wear for cross country skiing, my phone buzzed.

"Nick, I wasn't expecting to hear from you so soon."

"I just quickly glanced at Ms. Harris' computer and probably won't have the search completed until next week sometime, but I thought I would tell you what I found so far in case it might be of some help."

"Shoot," trying to keep low expectations.

"She was looking at the statute of limitations regarding rape."

"That's interesting. Thanks for letting me know."

While finishing up the last of my Lo Mein noodles, I was mulling over why Stephanie would be searching that particular statute. I guess that would make sense if she wanted to come forward with what she knew. I opened up my computer and looked up the law. It appears it was only five years back though in certain cases it can be up to twenty years. But since the rape occurred in high school she was out of luck. Now I am really curious what else she was searching?

I arrived at Jack's before dark. Jack has a small but really nice house. Some of the inside walls are brick which gives the place a cozy look. The first floor is completely open with steps leading up to a fairly large bedroom and a smaller room that Jack turned into an office. His furniture was mostly modern, with a few antiques scattered around. On the patio he had a barbecue which he used all year round. We usually grill which I love since there is no place for me to grill at home.

This time it was Jack's turn to greet me with only a towel wrapped around his waist. Just looking at him made me horny. We rectified the situation pretty quickly.

"So what's for dinner?" I asked.

"Sure, now that you're satisfied the only thing on your mind is food."

"Yes, that's true. But isn't food one of the essentials of life, second only to shelter?"

"Well I have to give it to you, you do know your rules of survival."

"Yes and I make sure I follow them."

Jack grilled salmon steaks. I did help make the salad. We sat down with our wine glasses filled with the Cabernet I brought.

"I heard from the computer expert. He only had a chance to briefly look at Stephanie's computer." I told Jack what he found.

"You're right, it would make sense. Something recently prompted her to look into the statute."

"We just don't know yet. I think the key to it is on the computer. Or I'm hoping. I wish there was some way Joe Connolly could be punished for what he's done. It doesn't seem fair that he's gotten away with two rapes that we know of and ruined two lives. I never even got the feeling from talking to him that he was the least bit remorseful. His only concern was that I would tell his wife. I'd love to ruin him, make him pay for what he's done."

"For now I'd concentrate on finding out what happened to Stephanie. You can always revisit Connolly at another time. Just be careful he doesn't try anything since your last encounter with him did not end well."

"I spoke with Stephanie's friend Mallory and she told me that Stephanie was seeing a therapist."

"She probably needed someone to help sort out her feelings."

"You are so insightful," I said giving him a squeeze on his leg. "So here's the latest on Susie's wedding. They're having it in Portsmouth, New Hampshire at her parents' house. Have you ever been to Portsmouth? It's really a very pretty place."

"I have and it is, though I haven't spent a lot of time there. When is it?"

"It's April 19th, a Sunday. I didn't even have a say in whom I'm bringing. She designated you as my escort."

"Well Susie is a very wise woman," Jack said.

"I'm sure you think so. Since it is her wedding I'll default to her."

"And you're very wise also."

With that Jack hauled me over his shoulder and carried me up the stairs and into the bedroom.

CHAPTER 41

The next morning after breakfast we went to the ski shop in town and rented cross country skis for me. Jack had his own.

We drove over to Monument Mountain Reservation in Great Barrington. Along with gloves, a knit cap and a ski jacket, I had long johns underneath my pants. If nothing else I was prepared. Jack gave me a quick lesson on going downhill and stopping. I followed him and thankfully he didn't take me down any steep trails. I was getting the hang of it and enjoying being outdoors when I landed right on my butt. Jack thought it was hilarious. He held out his hand while I attempted to get up with my feet attached to the long skis. I have to say even I thought it was hilarious.

After a few hours we called it quits. When we got to the car I said to Jack, "isn't it time for hot cocoa?"

"Why am I not surprised. But since you were a real trooper, I'm going to take you to a place that makes the best hot cocoa in the county."

We went to the Chocolate Springs Café in Lenox. It was a really cute place with a few wooden tables. I got a hot chocolate and a cappuccino mousse cake. Jack got a cappuccino and attempted to take a forkful of my cake.

"You're lucky I love you," I said letting him steal a little piece of my cake. I realized what I said as soon as it came out of my mouth. I was hoping Jack didn't catch it. Did I mean it or was it just a playful remark that people say?

When we got back to the house we showered, and Jack and I sat in front of the fireplace both wearing our sweats while enjoying a glass of wine. I was completely relaxed, something that doesn't often happen to me. Jack pulled me close to him and kissed me, a deep, hard kiss and I was putty. He drew away and said to me, "I love you."

I was taken aback. I wasn't expecting it. But I responded with a deep, hard kiss back. And then the words came out, "I love you. I can't believe I just said that."

"Are you taking it back already?" he said with a half-smile.

"No, of course not, except you're the first man I've ever said that to except for my father. It scares me Jack."

"Why does it scare you?"

"I guess because I've relied on myself for so long. You can't be disappointed if you're not involved with someone. You can't get hurt."

"That's true but there is no real joy in it either."

"Have you ever been in love before?" I asked, not sure I was ready to hear his answer.

"Once, a long time ago."

"What happened?"

"A long story short, when it came down to it I wasn't ready to marry her or anyone. I was only twenty-five and I knew it wasn't fair to her."

"Very wise, so what now?"

"Now we enjoy the rest of our wine."

On Sunday Jack and I spent a leisurely day inside, enjoying the comfort of his bed. At some point we both showered and went into town for dinner.

Monday I left Jack's place at the crack of dawn. I was hoping Nick Jonas would have some news soon. I went straight to the office, stopping first to pick up a muffin and coffee. My phone rang as I was opening my computer.

"Is this Tracey Marks?"

"It is."

"My name is Sandra Peters. You left your card a few days ago."

"Oh yes. Thank you for getting back to me. I'm investigating the death of a neighbor of yours, Stephanie Harris."

"Oh. That was just terrible. I really didn't know her. Just to say hello. She was always friendly and made a special point to talk to my daughter. Some people don't bother talking to children; they just ignore them. How can I help you?"

"I'm asking neighbors if there was anyone suspicious hanging around Stephanie's house before she died."

"Let me think. It was a while ago."

"Yes. It was before Christmas."

"Well, I was coming out of the house with Jaime, my four year old daughter and my little poodle, Jasper. I noticed this car pull up in front of Stephanie's house. We were taking the dog for a walk. At first I didn't think much of it but it was still there when we got back. I started walking toward the car, more out of curiosity, but he drove away before I had a chance to approach him."

"Can you tell me about the car, the color, anything?"

"It was definitely blue. I'd say probably maybe a year or two old. I think it was a BMW but I'm not positive."

"You didn't by any chance get the license plate number?"

"I didn't."

Too bad, I said to myself.

"Can you tell me what he looked like?"

"I really didn't get a good look at him. I think he was wearing a baseball cap or some sort of cap. Other than that, I can't tell you anything about him."

"Thanks. If you remember any more details please give me a call."

I dialed Susie. "Can you meet for lunch?"

"Oh boy must be something important. I can meet you at one o'clock at Gino's."

After hanging up I went back over my conversation with Sandra Peters. Could this guy be the killer? I wondered if he was in the area twice to check out the house or did both Lottie and Sandra Peters see him on the same day.

While waiting for Susie the hostess seated me. I was looking at the menu when Susie sat down.

"This must be really good or really bad to meet during work hours. Not that seeing you anytime isn't one of the great joys of my life."

"Yeah, blah, blah, blah. Let's order first."

"Are you ready to order?" the waitress asked.

We both nodded in the affirmative.

"I'll have a veal parmigiana sandwich and the house salad," I said.

"That sounds good. I'll have the same. So what gives?"

"First, I heard briefly from the computer guy. He only had a chance to take a quick glance but it looks like Stephanie was researching the statute of limitations on rape."

"If she wanted to blow the whistle on Joe that doesn't seem odd."

"You're right, but it appears that if it was about Maddie she would have confronted Joe a long time ago."

"I'm not sure I'm following your logic," Susie said.

"I'm not sure myself. I keep thinking what if it's not about Maddie but something that happened to Stephanie. I know it may be far reaching. Her friend Mallory told me that Stephanie was seeing a therapist, something about unresolved issues."

"She may have had a guilty conscience because she witnessed the rape and never told anyone."

"I guess. Maybe I'm overthinking it. Hopefully this guy will be able to uncover more information that might give me another lead."

"Here you go," the waitress said putting down our food.

When she left, I blurted out, "Jack told me he loved me."

"Wow. Tell me everything. Don't leave out a single detail."

I told Susie everything starting from when I let slip out about sharing my dessert.

"Before you get ahead of yourself, it doesn't mean Jack and I plan on living together. We both like it exactly the way it is."

"How did you feel when he said it?"

"Actually my first response was surprise, but the bigger surprise is when I said it back. I wondered afterward if I said it just because I thought that's what he wanted to hear or if I really meant it."

"You really do know how to overthink something. Knowing you, I don't believe you would have said it to Jack so his feelings wouldn't be hurt. You're not that nice."

"Thanks."

"I love Jack. He's a great guy. I wonder how he puts up with you," Susie said smiling.

"I must have some endearing qualities. You put up with me."

"You got me there."

My cell phone rang as I was heading back to the office. "Hello."

"Ms. Marks. This is Greg Todd. I was calling to find out if you had gotten in touch with Terry Brooks, the guy I mentioned who liked Stephanie."

"I did but my instincts tell me he didn't have anything to do with her murder. I'm glad you called though. I'd like to ask your professional opinion on something."

"Shoot."

"Why do you think someone would be looking up the statute of limitations on rape now if the rape occurred over thirty years ago?"

"I guess I would need more information to give any type of credible answer."

"I was thinking, if Maddie's rape occurred over thirty years ago why wait all this time to look into it."

"Well one explanation would be that guilt finally got to her. You said she witnessed the rape and never said anything because Maddie was threatened."

"Yes, but why wait all these years. Maddie died two years after the rape. Why not then?"

"You have to remember Stephanie was around nineteen when Maddie died, and maybe she thought she would be in trouble for waiting to report it."

"That makes sense. I never thought of that."

"If I can be of any further assistance let me know."

"Thanks doc."

I was running out of ideas. The one thing that kept coming back to me was my gut feeling that this was about Stephanie and not Maddie. It's not usually wise for an investigator to go with instinct as opposed to facts but I was at an impasse.

I called Linda hoping she'd pick up since the last time we

spoke I got the feeling she never wanted to see or hear from me again.

"Hi Linda, it's Tracey Marks, quick question. Do you know if Joe Connolly has been in contact with Stephanie in recent years?"

"No. I would have no idea. Why do you ask?"

"I'm reserving judgment. He did rape two people in high school. Is it possible he hurt Stephanie? Did you have any problems with Joe?"

"Joe was a loud mouth and a lot of other things but I can't recall anytime he tried anything with Stephanie or me."

"Okay, just checking."

"One other thing, someone told me that Stephanie had witnessed the rape. Do you know anything about that?"

"No. This is the first I'm hearing of it. I can't believe Stephanie never told me. I'm flabbergasted."

"Thanks Linda."

I guess Stephanie had her own secrets. What else was she hiding?

When I got back to the office I charted everything I learned recently. It looks like somebody was definitely targeting Stephanie. Was it the guy sitting in front of her house with the blue car? If someone was targeting her now how would it be related to her past? What was her motivation for seeing a therapist? So many secrets Stephanie kept.

CHAPTER 42

Thursday afternoon I got a call from Nick Jonas.

"Mr. Jonas. You have news?"

"I do. I'll stop by at four-thirty to return the computer."

"I'll be here."

It was three o'clock and I was on pins and needles. My mind was engaging in all kinds of theories on what was on the computer, none that made any sense. I was clueless. I was also getting antsy. I needed a distraction. I grabbed my coat and walked over to the coffee house near my office and bought a blueberry muffin and a cappuccino. One day I'm going to suffer from all the junk I eat, but hopefully not today.

I sat down at a small round table and became a voyeur for the next forty-five minutes. It was mindless, but it calmed me. If people could see themselves with all their mannerisms and gestures, they might be horrified. I was amused.

I got back a few minutes before Nick walked in. We sat down in my office.

"I wrote down everything I found out. If you have any questions you can call me," as he handed me his report.

"Can you give me a general sense or a basic overview of what was on there?"

"A lot of the searches were centered on a therapist by the name of Greg Todd. Where he lives, whatever she could find out on google. Stephanie was also checking court records on this guy. Does any of this make sense to you?"

"I'm not sure," my foot jackhammering as Nick was talking.

"Well, like I said it's all there in my report."

I stood up. "Thanks Nick, this is great. I'll pay your invoice as soon as I get it."

"This is on me. Alan has helped me out of jams more times than I can count."

"Thank you."

When he left, I sat rooted in my chair. I was trying to absorb what I just learned. I read the report twice. I wondered if Stephanie was checking on Greg because she was thinking of seeing him as a therapist. But would you go to a therapist you once knew in high school? I was having trouble sorting this out. I should probably check with Mallory and see if Greg's name ever came up.

I called Stephanie's daughter.

"Christine, how are you doing?"

"It's hard. My dad has been very supportive but I still can't believe it."

"Have you heard from the police?"

"Not really. They're not telling me anything."

No surprise there.

"Did you know your mother was seeing a therapist?"

"No. I had no idea," sounding bewildered. "I feel like the last few months my mother had all these secrets. Do you know the therapist's name?"

"I don't, but I do have some leads now that we know more about what your mother was searching for on her computer. As soon as I have a solid lead I'll contact you."

My next call was to Susie.

"I'm just leaving the office," Susie said. "What's going on?"

"I got the report back from the computer guy."

"And?"

"She was searching information about Greg Todd who Stephanie went to high school with. He's a therapist."

"That might make sense if she was checking him out before she went to see him."

"But why would she go to someone she knew and why didn't he tell me?"

"It is confidential. That doesn't surprise me."

"Maybe, I'm just not as convinced as you are."

"Well this is where your sleuthing abilities come in."

"It will be interesting to see where this Todd guy leads to," I said.

Before I left the office I called Mallory. I left a voice mail message asking her to call me back as soon as she receives my message.

I went straight home and changed into my running clothes. I needed to work off the anxiety that I was feeling. I couldn't shake off the dreadful feeling that something was rotten in Denmark.

When I got back I showered and put on my sweats. I scrambled up some eggs and toast, at least it was whole wheat, and ate in bed while watching the news. Why do I torture myself listening to all the bad stuff going on in the world? My phone rang as I was taking a bite of my toast.

"Ms. Marks, it's Mallory. Your message sounded urgent."

"I need to talk with you in person, something has come up. Can we meet at some point tomorrow?"

"Can we meet early, before work?"

"Absolutely, just tell me where and when."

"How about Slave to the Grind at eight a.m.?"

"I'll be there." That place was becoming way too familiar, though the coffee was really good. Before going to sleep I set my alarm for six.

I was pushing down on the stainless steel coffee holder that contained hazelnut coffee when Mallory walked in. After she filled her cup we both sat down.

"I had a computer expert look through Stephanie's computer and the name of someone she had gone to high school with came up. Did she ever mention a guy by the name of Greg Todd?"

Mallory's face turned ashen, coffee spilling from her cup.

"What's the matter Mallory?" looking at her shocked face.

"I'm sorry you just caught me off guard."

"Well obviously something is the matter. What is it?"

"It's like I said, you caught me off guard."

"Why would Greg Todd's name upset you?"

"Because she had talked about the kids she hung around with in high school and I was surprised that she was looking into him. That's all," not sounding very convincing.

Her explanation did not seem plausible to me. I didn't think she was telling me the truth. But what would be her reason for lying?

"Well, you told me she was seeing a therapist. Is it possible she was checking him out?"

"She never told me who she was seeing."

"Mallory, if you know why Stephanie might have been looking into this guy Todd I need to know. It's possible he might be the one who killed her."

"I'm sorry I can't help you," as she quickly got up, practically knocking over her chair.

CHAPTER 43

On the way back I called Jack and told him what transpired with Nick Jonas and Mallory. "Are you still there Jack?'

"I'm processing the information. You have to take things slowly. Figure out what you need to do next."

"Okay. I can do that. What's your take on the situation?"

"I don't know. Find out why Stephanie was looking into Todd. There has to be a reason. Also, it does seem as though Mallory's reaction to Greg Todd's name doesn't add up. She's hiding something. What about Connolly. Is he still a possibility?"

"I guess I still can't rule him out, but Greg Todd just became my main focus."

"Okay, just don't confront him. Find out whatever you can on him first."

"I agree. I thought I would check with the Connecticut State Licensing Board."

"Not sure how cooperative they'll be, but it's a start."

I was pretty hyped up after talking to Jack. When I got back to the office I popped in next door to Cousin Alan. "Hi Margaret, did the big baby make it back from his conference?"

"Oh yeah, if you don't count the fifty times he called me. Go ahead in."

"I see you made it back in one piece. How did everything go?"

"These conferences are more for socializing than anything else. I'm glad it's over."

"How's my favorite guy?"

"He was asking about you. He wanted to know when you two were going to have play date," Alan said smiling.

"I've been so busy lately, but I'll call Patty to see when Michael is available. By the way Nick came through big and he didn't charge me, said he owed you."

"He may be exaggerating. We go way back, a story for another time."

"I can't wait to hear it."

"So you're making progress on the case?"

"I am now. I just have to prove who I think it is."

"Ah, the hard part."

"See ya."

I was glad it was Friday. The weekend would give me time to recharge and time to assess my next move.

I picked up the phone and called Patty.

"Hi Tracey, I'm glad you called. How are you?"

"Good. I wanted to know if you and Michael might be interested in lunch tomorrow and a stroll in Central Park, or is it too cold for him to be outside."

"I speak for Michael also when I say we're in. And I have to give you a crash course on little people."

"You pick the restaurant and the time," I said.

"Okay, I'll text you."

Before leaving the office I did a quick check on Joe and Donna Connolly's cars. Besides the pick-up truck the only other car registered to them was a Gray Toyota Camry. Too bad, I was hoping it was a blue BMW.

Saturday I met Patty and Michael at Sarabeth's on Amsterdam Avenue on the Upper West Side. The weather was beautiful for the third week of February. It was in the fifties and the sun was shining.

"You have gotten so big. I hardly recognize you," I said to Michael as I poked him in his belly. That got a smile out of him.

The hostess showed us to a corner table and the waitress brought over a booster seat for Michael.

"He took his first steps last week. Of course it was so exciting as only a parent would think."

"Well I'm proud of you Michael. So what looks good on the menu?" I said asking him in a serious tone.

"If he answers you I will eat my napkin," Patty said.

When the waitress came over Patty ordered Mac and Cheese for Michael. I ordered a crab cake and a salad and Patty ordered the same. We both ordered a glass of Sauvignon Blanc.

"So tell me everything that's going on?" Patty said. "Thank heavens I work part-time otherwise my day would be all about my intellectual conversations with Michael, though he is a captive audience. We haven't started playdates yet."

I filled Patty in on the case. "Any thoughts?"

"First I'd love to see this guy Joe crucified. Do you think his wife has any inkling of what he's done?"

"I do. I just think she has a blind spot when it comes to her husband, otherwise how could she have married him?"

"She must have zero self-esteem to be with someone like him. I wouldn't put it passed him if he was cheating on her," Patty said.

"If you could have seen his reaction at the prospect of me telling his wife, he did not handle it very well."

"He has a lot to lose."

"It wouldn't surprise me if she didn't divorce him even if she knew."

At that moment the waitress came over with our food. Michael squealed with delight.

"Maybe he takes after me," I said. "Mac and Cheese would make me squeal."

"Well, hopefully you don't eat with your hands also."

As we were talking Patty was feeding Michael and herself. Quite an art.

"If we were home I'd let him use his fingers but he might make too much of a mess here.

To get back to the case, do you have any idea where you're going with this guy Todd?"

"Legwork. No getting around it. Jack wants to make sure I find out everything I can on him."

"Whatever you do, just be very careful."

"Who's going to teach Michael how to drive his parents crazy if I'm not around? Isn't that right my little man?"

"How's Jack?"

"He's fine. He took me cross country skiing last weekend. I have to say it was a lot of fun. And I know you'll be happy to hear that Jack told me he loved me."

"I'm ecstatic. What did you say?"

"I told him the same."

"You don't seem that happy about it."

"I am, but I'm also afraid. Remember when I told you I didn't know if I could be in a relationship for the long haul. Well, I'm still not sure."

"You don't have to worry about that now. As long as he knows how you feel it will be fine."

"He definitely knows I'm scared."

"Well I'm happy and apparently Michael's happy." Michael was putting his little hands together and giggling.

After we left the restaurant we took a walk over to the Central Park zoo. I thought Michael would get a kick out of seeing the animals. After about forty-five minutes Michael conked out and Patty and I strolled through the park for a while until it started to get chilly. Patty took a cab home and I walked home.

I had no plans for the rest of the weekend which I was thrilled about. I spent part of Sunday cleaning. I finished a mystery book I was reading and then flipped on Netflix. There were new episodes of Frankie and Grace, a comedy series with Lily Tomlin and Jane Fonda about two women who forge a friendship after their husbands dumped them. It turns out the husbands were in love with each other. Mindless TV.

In the evening I took out my computer and looked up the telephone number for the State Licensing Board in Connecticut and the address for the County Clerk's Office in Ridgefield, Connecticut. I wanted to check the court records in person since not all records are listed on my databases.

First thing Monday morning after showering, I called the State Licensing Board. They provided me with an email address for the Investigative Unit. After some back and forth I was told to submit a request in writing under the Freedom of Information Act to the Department of Public Health. I was informed it might take from one to six weeks for a response.

I dressed quickly, had my cereal and headed to the County Clerk's office in Ridgefield, Connecticut. The Clerk's office was on Main Street. From interstate 684, I took Exit 6 to Route 35, a one lane road in each direction. It had the feel of a country road with antique stores, a small grocery market and cute little houses miles apart. I reminded myself to stop on my way back at the market I passed.

I found the County Clerk's Office without any trouble and parked in their lot. When I located the right department, I went straight to the young man behind the counter and asked for his assistance. I am never beyond asking for help. It saves me a lot of time having to figure out things on my own.

"Hi there," I said. "I was wondering if you could help me?"

"I'll try." He looked about twelve with deep set brown eyes and a big crop of black hair. He was skinny and hopefully was due for a growth spurt.

"Can you please show me how to look up records on an individual?"

"What kind of records?"

"Anything you have."

He led me over to one of the computers and gave me a crash course on how to use it. As he walked back to his post I searched the name Greg Todd. I found one divorce record on file. It looked like Joan Todd filed for divorce in 2007. Good to know. There was nothing else I could find on him.

When I got back to the car, I reached for my computer that I left on the floor behind the driver's seat. I looked up Joan Todd who was now Joan McGraw. She lived about five miles out of town. I thought I would see if she was at home.

On the way to her house I passed through the Town of Ridgefield. It was one long street with shops on both sides. Joan's house was a small, two story yellow house with black shutters on a narrow street. There was a green sedan parked in her driveway.

So what is my opening line when she answers the door? The problem was I didn't know if the divorce was amicable or not. Would she let him know I was asking about him? I guess I would eventually find out.

I rang the doorbell. A very attractive woman, probably in her mid-forties with very curly brown shoulder length hair wearing tight jeans and a blue sweater answered the door.

"Hi, my name is Tracey Marks. I'm a private investigator." I'm looking into the death of a woman named Stephanie Harris. I believe your ex-husband Greg was a friend of hers at Hudson Prep High School."

"Why are you inquiring about Greg?"

Good question. "I was wondering if you knew anything about Ms. Harris' relationship with Dr. Todd?" I was floundering. It didn't look like she was going to take the bait or let me in.

"And you thought since I was the ex I would be a likely candidate to talk."

"You got me there," I said trying to suppress a smile.

"Since you're being honest I can tell you Greg and I have not talked since the divorce. Maybe that says something."

"Can you at least tell me why you divorced him?"

"That's personal."

"In case you change your mind, here's my card. Thank you for your time."

I walked back to my car. It was a long shot, but I was still disappointed. My phone rang. "Hi Susie. I think I screwed up my one chance to talk with Todd's ex. I'm not sure what I should've said."

"Start from the beginning."

CHAPTER 44

I explained what I found out at the Clerk's Office and my conversation with Joan McGraw.

"Don't be so hard on yourself. I would have reacted the same way she did. Unless she hated the guy she's not going to talk to a perfect stranger about him."

"Oh, by the way, I spoke with Mallory, Stephanie's friend from college. Her reaction was very weird when I mentioned Stephanie was looking into Greg Todd. I think she's hiding something."

"That may very well be. You might have to press her on it again. How's dinner tomorrow?" Susie said.

"Good. See you then."

I had all intentions of heading right back but changed my mind. I thought I would drive pass Greg's house and check it out. Greg lived not too far from the town. It was a very upscale neighborhood with large center hall colonial style homes. His house was on at least a half-acre. I guess being a therapist pays very well. There was a gigantic weeping willow tree on his front lawn. Next to the house was a two car garage with a basketball hoop attached.

I parked down the block and ran a search on Greg while sitting in my car. It listed that he owned the house with Carrie Todd, age 42. Well at least he didn't marry someone half his age. There were two cars registered in his name. One was a leased 2017 Blue BMW, and a 2018 Green Dodge. I wonder if his Blue BMW was the same one Lottie and Sandra Peters saw.

I drove slowly passed his house, my stomach growling. I was looking for any signs of the BMW so I could take a few photos. I wasn't sure if anyone was home since the garage doors were shut. I didn't want to circle too many times around the street and have someone report a suspicious car in the area. Unfortunately it's harder to do surveillance in a richer neighborhood. My car is a sitting duck. As I was making my last go around I saw a car pull into the driveway. Not the BMW. From the car to the front door of the house I couldn't get a good look at the woman's face. From behind she was tall, with dark brown straight hair that was up in a ponytail. Her long black parka was covering most of her. As she was opening the door I heard a dog barking. The door shut. I'm thinking I would have to come back another time, maybe early in the morning, see if I could catch a glimpse of his car.

On my way back I stopped at the country market I had passed on the way to Ridgefield. I was starved. It had everything from candies in glass jars, maple syrup to kitchen towels. It even had a case with deli meats, tuna fish and egg salad.

"Well hello there," the gentleman said. "Can I help you with anything?"

He was probably in his sixties, almost bald, on the heavy side, with a friendly smile.

"I'm just browsing. Has the store been here long?" I asked.

"It's been here for thirty years. The missus is usually at the store with me but she's home babysitting a sick granddaughter. My name's Frank."

"Frank, I'm Tracey. Can I get a tuna fish sandwich on that crusty multigrain bread you have. And I'm dying for a cup of coffee."

"I just made a fresh pot. There's a small table where you can sit and eat."

"Thanks." I called Jeffrey Goldman while I was waiting and left a message. Maybe Stephanie confided in him about Greg. If Mallory was hiding something there had to be a way to find out what she knew. I also put a call into Stephanie's business partner to see if Greg Todd's name came up in their conversations.

"Here you go Tracey," putting down my sandwich and coffee.

"Thanks for bringing it over. It looks yummy."

"And if you're still hungry, my wife makes a mean Apple Pie."

"No need to ask me twice." My phone rang.

"Mr. Goldman thanks for getting back to me so soon. I was wondering if Stephanie mentioned someone by the name of Greg Todd to you?"

"No. The name doesn't sound familiar. Why?"

No harm in telling him. "It appears she was searching his name on her computer. He's a therapist in Ridgefield."

"Was she seeing him?" he asked.

"I don't know. Are you sure she never mentioned him?"

"Positive."

"Okay, Thanks."

"How's your sandwich?" Frank said.

"Best tuna ever. I wish I lived closer."

"I didn't mean to overhear your conversation but you mentioned the name Greg Todd. Is he the therapist in Ridgefield?"

"Yes," I said caught off guard. "Do you know him?"

"Not me personally but I have a friend who went to see him for a while. Small world."

"I know you can't give me their name but I thought if you could pass on my information," handing him my card, "maybe you can ask your friend to call me."

"Is Greg Todd in any sort of trouble?" he said studying my business card.

"Not that I'm aware of. Just involves a case I'm working on."

"Private Investigator, well I'll be darned. I never met a female private investigator. I bet you have plenty of stories to tell."

"Not as many as you think. Most of the work is pretty mundane."

"I'll pass your information on. Now are you ready for that apple pie?"

Before leaving I bought some maple syrup and some miniature size tootsie rolls for the ride home. Maybe it was fate that I walked into that store.

CHAPTER 45

The following day I was up by five-thirty and went for a run. It was still dark out and the air was biting. No one was out on the streets. My body was prepared with a knit cap and wool gloves but my mind was going to a dark place. It's been more than two months since I started the case and all my leads have turned into dead ends. If this possible lead with Greg Todd doesn't pan out, I was ready to throw in the towel. I needed to stay positive.

As I was heading back the streets were no longer empty. The city was waking up. I saw a few people walking their dogs and the neighborhood deli was open, ready for their regular customers wanting their morning coffee fix.

Just before leaving for the office my phone rang. I didn't recognize the number.

"Hello."

"Is this Tracey Marks?" a female voice asked.

"Yes."

"My name is Nancy Jamison. Your name was given to me by Frank Santulli."

It took me a moment to realize it was Frank from the country store. "Oh yes. Thank you for calling. I'm not sure what he told you but I'd like to talk with you about Dr. Todd."

"I'd rather do it in person."

"I understand. Let me know when and where you want to meet."

"I'm coming into the city today. We can meet at your office. I'm having lunch with a friend at Fiorello's at noon. I could be at your office say around three."

"That's perfect. See you then."

Ms. Jamison arrived on the dot of three.

"Please take off your coat and have a seat. Can I get you coffee or tea?"

"No. I probably had too much caffeine already," Ms. Jamison said avoiding my eyes.

Nancy was very attractive. Her straight black hair came just above her shoulders. Her olive complexion complemented her dark chocolate eyes. She was about 5'6" tall and looked as though she was in great shape. I didn't know how she was able to sit in her tight leather pants.

"So tell me why you're asking about Dr. Todd?" Nancy said.

"I can just tell you he's a person of interest regarding a case I'm working on. I'm sorry I can't be more specific."

I could see by the look in her eyes that she was contemplating what to say or how much to tell me.

"I went to see Dr. Todd about a year ago. I was having marital problems and was afraid to make any rash decisions."

I didn't want to interrupt with any questions so I let her continue.

"At that point I was seeing Dr. Todd for about three months. In one of the sessions I started crying."

Ms. Jamison became very quiet, tears slowly running down her cheeks.

"Dr. Todd came over and sat on the couch next to me." She paused. "He put his hand gently around my shoulder and pulled me close to him. He told me my husband didn't deserve me. At that point I thought he was trying to comfort me so I didn't pull away, his fingers softly caressing my hair. I could smell the spicy aroma of his cologne. Maybe I was being naïve but in that moment I didn't think he was doing anything inappropriate. It wasn't until he tried to kiss me that I began to realize this was not normal behavior for a therapist. I pulled away from him. He stood up abruptly and told me he thought that's what I wanted. I didn't know what to say or do. At the time I thought maybe he was right. I was confused."

"Where was his assistant?"

"I believe I had the last appointment of the day. His assistant had already left."

"Did you report him?"

Looking ashamed, she said she didn't.

"How come?"

"I never told my husband I was seeing a therapist. I wanted to forget the whole incident. I was just relieved he didn't try to go any further. If I reported it, my husband would have found out that I was thinking of leaving him."

Being a woman I know I shouldn't judge other women so harshly but I was angry at her. Who knows how many other female patients he tried to take advantage of. I kept calm since I didn't want my anger to show.

"I know I should have reported him. I was being selfish, just thinking of myself."

I ignored her comment. "Are you still married?"

"I am but I don't know for how much longer."

"Did you continue being his patient?"

"No, of course not."

Thank heavens.

"Did you tell anyone what happened?"

"My best friend, but I knew she would keep my secret."

CHAPTER 46

I was meeting Susie at six-thirty at Marcello's. They make a stuffed artichoke to die for. I was a little early and sat at the bar sipping a glass of Chianti.

"Hi there," Susie said. "I'll have whatever she's having," signaling to the bartender.

"Shall we get a table before the rush?" It was a small place, but very lively, always packed.

The hostess seated us right away.

"So how are you two love birds doing?" Susie said.

"Are you going to ask me that question every time I see you?"

"Just until it gets old which I gather from your response it already is."

"Talking about love birds, any more news on the wedding plans?"

"All the invitations are in the mail. It could be in your mailbox at this very moment."

"Just don't aim the wedding bouquet in my direction because I won't catch it."

"Party pooper."

"Hello ladies, would you like to hear the specials?"

In unison we both said no.

"I'll have the stuffed artichoke, and for my main dish I'll have a bowl of linguini and clams," I said.

"And I'll have the house salad and the eggplant parmigiana."

"By the way, what's the wedding menu?" I said when the waitress left.

"So if you don't like it you won't be coming?"

"Well normally that would be a deal breaker, but for you guys I'll make an exception."

"On behalf of Mark and me, we are both honored. What's happening with the case?"

"Some progress, I think. On my way back from Ridgefield I

stopped at a country store. While I was having lunch there I was talking on the phone to a friend of Stephanie's and I mentioned the name Greg Todd in my conversation. When I hung up the storeowner, Frank, a very nice man, asked if that was the same Greg Todd who was a therapist in Ridgefield."

"That's interesting."

"Well it gets more interesting. He said he knows someone who went to see Dr. Todd for a while. I gave him my card and Frank said he would pass on my information. This morning I got a call from the woman and she came into the office earlier." I told Susie what transpired between her and Todd.

"That's quite a story. It doesn't surprise me she didn't report him, but it certainly puts a definite light on Dr. Todd, the scumbag. I wonder how many other women he's tried this with."

"Here you go ladies," the waitress said as she put down our food."

"Thank you. It looks scrumptious," Susie said.

"I'm waiting to hear from the State Licensing Board to find out if there are any complaints filed against him. After speaking to someone in their Investigation Unit I was told to put in a Freedom of Information request. It could take from one to six weeks to hear back. In the meantime I was thinking of doing some surveillance on his house and office. Maybe I can recruit Jack to go along since he's coming down this weekend."

"Wouldn't it be cool if you and Jack started your own private investigation firm?"

"I don't see that happening, not if our relationship has any chance of surviving."

"You are very bossy," Susie said grinning at me. "Talking about being bossy, I'm trying to convince Mark to move."

"Isn't his place big enough?"

"It is, but it's his place. I thought we would both sell our apartments and buy a two bedroom. This way it would be ours and I can decorate it. Now I'm living in a man cave."

"It makes sense. So what does Mark have to say?"

"I think he's leaning my way, but we'll wait until after the wedding. Spring is a good time to go apartment hunting."

On our way out my phone rang. "Hello."

"Ms. Marks this is Jennifer Daniels returning you call."

I signaled to Susie that I had to take it and waved goodbye.

"Ms. Daniels, I had Stephanie's computer checked out. It seems she was looking into an old high school friend of hers, Greg Todd. He's a therapist in Ridgefield, Connecticut. Did she happen to mention his name to you?"

"I don't think she did, but now that you bring it up I remember one afternoon she came in looking upset. She said something about her friend Mallory and some therapist Mallory was going to. She was very vague and then dropped it."

"It may be important. Do you remember anything else Stephanie said at the time?"

"I'm sorry, that's all she told me."

"Okay. But if you remember anything please call me."

"Can you tell me what's going on?"

"I can't right now, but I'll be in touch."

It started drizzling as I was walking to my apartment. All I could think about was Mallory, was she a patient of Todd's? And if she was, did something happen between them? Was that why Mallory was so upset when I mentioned Greg's name? All these questions and right now I had no answers. I had to find out what happened.

I had trouble sleeping. I couldn't turn off the noise in my head. The clock said four-thirty. Since all I was doing was tossing from one side to the other I got out of bed. I put on the coffee maker and waited until it was finished dripping and poured myself a cup. I took it back to bed with me and turned on the TV. I happened upon an old Law and Order show with Chris Noth (Mr. Big from Sex and the City) and Jerry Orbach. At some point I must have dozed since the next time I looked at the clock it was six-fifteen. I turned off the TV and went into the kitchen and made a fresh pot of coffee. While I was having my Cheerios I contemplated what to do next.

"Hey, I didn't wake you?"

"Nah. I was just sitting down to eat breakfast," Jack said.

"And what does a big, strong boy like you have for breakfast?"

"Well aren't we playful so early in the morning."

"That's what happens when you're sleep deprived." I explained to Jack what Jennifer Daniels told me.

"Do you think Mallory might talk to you knowing what Daniels told you?"

"I could try. But I wouldn't count on it. Are you game for a little adventure tomorrow?"

"My idea and your idea of adventure might be very different," Jack said. "Mine involves basically one room."

"Well, if you do what I want on Saturday, we can come to a mutually satisfying agreement for Sunday. Are you in?"

"I'm definitely in. I'll see you bright and early tomorrow."

By the time I got into gear it was almost eight-thirty. I put on my running clothes and jogged over to the park. Nannies with baby strollers were taking advantage of the mild February temperatures. I on the other hand was thinking about Greg Todd as I was on my second loop around. My plan was to take Jack with me to stake out Todd's house. Not too thrilling, but a start. If I could get a photo of the car I could show it to the neighbors.

"Hi Wally," I waived as I approached my building. "How are you?"

"I'm doing just fine Ms. Tracey. What a beautiful morning."

"It is. Did I tell you that Susie is getting married? And don't give me that when are you getting married look." I could see on Wally's face that he was trying very hard to suppress a grin.

"I like the way things are just fine," I said heading to the elevator.

I decided to spend the day working from home. I had a case that came in that needed my immediate attention. The attorney asked me to locate a witness for a trial that was starting in a few days. Since I had nothing planned until my surveillance tomorrow, this was the perfect opportunity to try and find this guy.

As I was finishing up my phone rang. "Christine, I'm glad you called. I might have a possible lead on someone, but until it pans out I would rather keep the details to myself for now. By the way,

I got your additional retainer yesterday. Thank you."

"Is there anything you can tell me? I've spoken to Detective James who's handling my mother's case. When I ask him anything he just says he's pursuing leads."

"I promise when I have something I'll let you know."

If this Detective James looked into Stephanie's computer and found out Stephanie was searching Greg Todd he might question him, but would he have any reason to suspect him?

CHAPTER 47

"You're dressed," Jack said as I opened the door.

"That's usually how people answer the door."

"May I come in? Can this be a subtle hint that we're not staying for a while?" he said following me into the kitchen.

"You catch on really quick. I'm quite impressed. Yes, you're right, we have to get going. No time for..." as he leaned in and gave me a wonderfully, delicious kiss.

"That," I said.

"Okay I know when to quit."

"I've packed some snacks. I thought we'd pick up coffee before we leave."

"I'm just going to take a quick bathroom stop, if that's allowed," Jack said grinning.

We took Jack's car since my Beetle was probably too conspicuous. Jack has a dark colored car with tinted windows. We stopped at Starbucks for coffee and two blueberry muffins.

"I hope I don't pick up your muffin habit," Jack said as I gave him directions to Greg Todd's house.

"There are worse habits you can acquire."

We arrived at Greg's house by ten o'clock. One of the cars was in the driveway. We had to be careful since we didn't want any cops knocking on the window. Every ten minutes we circled around and changed where we sat.

"This isn't the easiest place for surveillance," Jack said.

"I know. Let's hope something happens quickly." As soon as the words came out of my mouth, the front door opened. It was a teenage boy, maybe around thirteen or fourteen walking a little brown and white dog. This must be the boy who plays baseball that I saw a picture of in Todd's office.

"There's only one way out to the main road," Jack said. "I think there's a place to sit where we can see Todd if he comes out where no one's going to bother us."

"Good idea. I have the license plate numbers for both cars."

We moved Jack's car and waited. Unfortunately surveillance is tedious. We needed to make sure we weren't distracted so we wouldn't miss him when he came out.

While we were waiting, I said to Jack, "so did you date a lot in college?"

"Now that you have me cornered the inquisition begins," he said playfully.

"You can ask me anything you want. I have no problem. There's his car," I said practically jumping out of my seat. "It looks like he's alone and he's driving the Blue BMW."

Twenty minutes later I was wondering where the hell he was going.

"It looks like he's driving into Norwalk, Connecticut. I heard they have great seafood restaurants."

Jack just gave me his look that said, only you can think of food no matter what was happening. Jack told me if we were in a life and death situation I would be telling him what I want for my last meal. He could be right.

"Look, he's pulling into an Econo Lodge," I said all excited. He went into the office and when he came out he parked his car in front of Room 16.

"What a creep. Do you think there's a woman already in the room?"

"I would think not, unless that person's car is parked somewhere else," Jack said.

"Why the hell would he take someone to this cheesy motel?"

"Because it's out of the way, more private than a fancy hotel."

"Only a guy would think of that," punching him lightly on the arm. While we were waiting I took photos of the car.

Fifteen minutes later a car pulled up next to Greg's.

"Holy shit," I said. "It's Mallory, Stephanie's friend. No wonder she was shocked when I had mentioned his name. What the hell do you think is going on?"

"Not sure. We know Stephanie was looking into this guy on her computer. We don't know why as yet. She was also checking out the State Licensing Board. There could be two explanations for that. One, she was looking into it for herself. Maybe she wanted to see him as a patient, but I highly doubt it. Two, she found out something that he might have been involved in, possibly with a patient, and she was checking to see if there were any complaints against him."

"So let's go with the second one. If she found out somehow that Mallory was having an affair with him why would it upset Stephanie?" I said.

"Let's say Mallory was a patient of his. It can't be ethical having an affair with your patient."

"What about the fact that he's preying on vulnerable women."

"It's a big leap to murder. You need to gather more information," Jack said.

"I'm still waiting to hear back from the State Licensing Board."

"I wonder if his assistant might know something. I'm sure she hears a lot," Jack said.

"Maybe I can figure out a ruse that she'll fall for."

"I'm sure you could," Jack said smiling.

"Would you like a banana or one of my health bars?" I asked Jack.

"I'll take the banana."

"Wise choice. The health bar tastes like sawdust," as I bit down and then took a big gulp of water.

"How long would you like to stay?" Jack asked.

"I'm not sure. This is not my area of expertise. What's your opinion?"

"We can wait a while. Maybe we'll catch them kissing when they leave."

"So you never answered my question I asked you before we were rudely interrupted."

"The truth is I didn't date much in college. I spent most of my time studying. Don't get me wrong, it wasn't as if I was a monk but it wasn't a priority for me. I did most of my dating post college. What about you or did you save yourself for me?" pulling me close to him.

"None of that, we're on the client's dime and if you continue I might jump you right here. But to answer your question, I was fairly shy. After college I dated, but I was never in a long term relationship. Especially after my mother died, I didn't want to get close to anyone. I would be a great study for a shrink. It's too bad Todd knows what I look like. I could let him analyze me."

"I'm sure you would be a great study."

Two hours later Mallory and Greg emerged from their room. I got some good pictures as they embraced and said goodbye, each going their separate ways.

"Well this was quite an afternoon. Mallory looked like she was head over hills in love with this guy. I wonder what stories he's feeding her," I said.

"He could be giving her the line that he's going to leave his wife and she's buying into it. That would be my guess."

"Do you think I should tell her what we found out?"

"I wouldn't. If she's crazy about him she's not going to believe anything you say. Just gather the information. At this point you don't need to inject Mallory into it."

"How about going for a late lunch at a seafood restaurant in Norwalk? There's probably a place right by the water."

"I like it."

"Thanks for helping me out. And I did promise to make it up to you."

"You did indeed. I look forward to it."

"I'm sure you do."

We found a restaurant with a view of the water. The Restaurant at Rowayton was very pretty inside. It was simple with wood tables and chairs and cloth napkins. We sat by a window table where we could look out on the water.

"Can I get you something to drink?" the waiter asked us.

"I'll have a glass of Sauvignon Blanc."

"And I'll have whatever light beer you have on tap, thank you," Jack said.

The waiter left leaving menus.

"Wow everything looks great. Would you like to share the lobster spring roll?"

"Happy to."

The cute waiter came back with our drinks. "Are you ready to order?" he asked.

"I think we are," I said. "We're going to share the lobster spring roll. I'm going to have a cup of your New England clam chowder and the Grilled Swordfish."

"I'll have the Sesame Crusted Yellowfin Tuna and your house salad, thank you."

When he left I said, "I'm hoping to hear from the Licensing Board sooner rather than later. It should be very interesting to see what they have on him, if anything."

"It's never a good idea to set your hopes too high though it's nice to see you're so optimistic."

"I saw they had Maine Steamers on the menu. Whenever I see Steamers on a menu it always brings back memories of my parents and me at the summer cottage we rented each year. My father used to take me digging for clams. He told me if I step on one it would piss on me. I thought that was so funny, having a clam pee on you. It turns out it's not really pee, it's sea water that squirts out."

"It must have been hard on you when he died."

"I was lucky to have such a great father." A few months ago Jack had told me his father left when Jack was young and his mother raised him. He's never had contact with his father. His mother passed away a few years ago.

"Here's your lobster spring roll. I also brought your salad and clam chowder."

"Thank you," Jack said.

"Oh my God, so delicious," I said biting into the spring roll.

When the waiter came back with our main dishes, I ordered another glass of wine and Jack had another beer.

"I noticed there was an Obama sticker on Todd's car. The neighbor said there was a sticker on the blue car. If it is his car, what was he doing there?"

"Any number of possibilities, but if he was there to stake out her house he wasn't trying to hide it, which doesn't make any sense. Not to switch topics but I think we should get some coffee before driving home," Jack said.

"Good idea and we can save dessert for later," I said in my

most seductive voice.

CHAPTER 48

On Sunday morning I left it up to Jack what he wanted to do and he had no problem coming up with something. We spent most of the day having a great time in bed. We stopped only for bathroom breaks and fortification. At some point we showered. By nine o'clock we turned on the TV and watched an old Law and Order episode.

Monday morning Jack and I parted on the street, but not before we held each other tightly. On the way up to Scarsdale, I called Lottie, Stephanie's neighbor, to tell her I was coming to show her some photos.

"Hi Lottie, how are you," I said as she opened up the door and led me into her kitchen.

"I made coffee when you called. I also baked date-nut bread yesterday. Would you like a piece?"

"You're going to spoil me," I said as we sat down at the kitchen table. Lottie gave me a big slice of the date nut bread and a cup of coffee.

"How is the case coming?"

"Unfortunately, I can't tell you very much but there are some leads I'm working on."

"Does it have anything to do with the man in the car?"

"It may, but it's still too early to tell. By the way have the police been back to question you?"

"No, and I'm glad. The detective who came by to question me was not very nice."

I laid the photos of the car on the table.

"It was a few months ago but it looks like the same one. The color's the same, I think, but I can't be one hundred percent sure. I'm sorry I'm not being more helpful."

"You're doing great. How about this man, does he look familiar?" I showed her a few photos of Greg.

"Wait. Let me get my glasses."

I was anxious and was playing with the crumbs on my plate.

"Okay, that's better. Again I only saw him from across the street and he was sitting in the car. As I said, I didn't see his face. I can't be sure it's the same person."

"You've been a big help Lottie. Is there anything else you remember?"

"If I do I will be sure to call you."

I then went across the street and rang Sandra Peters' bell to show her the photos. No answer. There was no point in sticking around.

I found a parking spot three blocks from the office. On my way in I picked up a turkey sandwich for lunch. I got settled in and turned on the coffee maker. The phone rang. "I was just about to call you," I said to Susie.

"How did the surveillance go?"

"You are not going to guess who Greg Todd is having an affair with."

"Okay, I give."

"Stephanie's friend Mallory. They were going at it hot and heavy at a motel, or I assumed they were. They were in the room for over two hours and when they came out they were all over each other."

"Holy crap. I wonder how long it's been going on. I guess it's possible Mallory confided in Stephanie and she freaked when she heard who Mallory was having the affair with."

"Maybe that's why Stephanie was looking into this guy. I'm still waiting to hear if there are any complaints on file for him," I said.

"What about his secretary. Who knows more about what's going on in an office than the secretary," Susie said.

"Already thought about it, now I just have to come up with a strategy."

"Just be careful. Not to change the subject but the wedding is about seven weeks away and I need to go up to New Hampshire and get things ready. I have to order the flowers and meet with the caterer. I'd rather take care of it myself though I know my mother would be glad to do it. If you're free this weekend would you come up with me? Mark needs to finish this deal he's working on though I guess ordering flowers and meeting with the caterer is not something Mark would relish to do."

"Sure, it will be fun, I think."

"Great. Could we leave maybe late Friday afternoon? I made an appointment to meet the caterer at twelve on Saturday and we still have to pick out the flowers. I also want to go over to the place I'm renting the tent and the table and chairs from to see what they look like."

"Just let me know what time and I'll be ready."

I needed to speed up the investigation on Greg Todd. I knew it was a possibility that I was completely wrong about him. Though he may prey on the vulnerable and cheat on his wife, does that mean he murdered Stephanie? Not necessarily. If he didn't, I'm out of suspects and out of luck.

CHAPTER 49

Talking to Greg Todd's receptionist was my next step. To do that, I have to stake out his office, waiting to see if Greg leaves at some point during the day. With a believable story, maybe I can get some information from his receptionist.

I was anxious to find out if there were any complaints against Todd. It was only a little more than a week since I submitted my request and I was keeping my fingers crossed that it wouldn't be much longer. I was informed that the name of the complainant is redacted from the complaint as I was pretty sure it would be, but it didn't stop me from being bummed out.

Munching on my sandwich, I googled Greg Todd. I wanted to see exactly what other information was out there besides what Nick Jonas reported. There was info on the schools he attended, his age, the location of his office, etc. This looks very interesting. He is on the Board of Selectmen for Fairfield County. It lists him as a part time Selectmen. What the heck is that? I googled Board of Selectmen. It is an elected position. The Board gives recommendations for projects, goals and issues affecting Fairfield County. It looks like the first Selectmen is a full time position and the rest are part time and receive a stipend. I don't think the Board would take too kindly if they knew Greg was seducing his patients and having an affair. Did Stephanie threaten to expose him?

From my conversations with Greg, it's hard to believe the stuff I've uncovered about him. He seemed so mild mannered, trusting, just what I would envision a therapist to be like. Maybe I'm still naïve. What's that saying, 'people see what they want to see.'

Next I went to his website which was pretty low key. There was a photo of him and under that he listed his credentials. His areas of specialty in his practice included relationship issues, anxiety, depression, loss. He takes all forms of insurance. Good to know.

While I was checking out a few other things on the good doctor, my phone rang. "Tracey Marks."

"Ms. Marks this is Donna Connolly. I was wondering if you had some time to see me. I'm in the city and I could be at your office by three-thirty."

"Sure. I'll see you then."

What was that all about? My curiosity was definitely piqued. I was anxious to hear what she had to say.

At three thirty-five Donna came in. I could tell by the way her eyes were darting all around she was nervous.

"Come into my office. Can I get you a cup of coffee or tea?"

"Nothing for me, thank you," she said sitting down.

I sat down and waited for her to speak. She kept crossing and uncrossing her legs.

"Actually, can I have some water?" her voice croaking.

After handing her a glass of water, I sat down. Donna took a sip.

"Ever since you told us that Stephanie died Joe has been on edge," Donna said.

"When you say on edge what do you mean?"

"I'm not exactly sure how to put it into words. Joe can sometimes have a temper especially when he's under stress. And it seems like ever since you've been investigating Stephanie's death he's not quite himself."

"When you say he has a temper, does he hit you?"

"No, no, nothing like that," Donna said not looking directly at me.

I wasn't sure if I believed her. "Like what then?"

"I came here to find out if you had any conversations with Joe that might have upset him."

"Any conversations I had with him are confidential. You would have to ask him. Is there something you're worried about?"

"When Joe was younger he was kind of wild and…"

"You were wondering if something happened back then that had to do with Stephanie and Joe."

Donna slowly nodded without looking up at me. Finally, we got to the real reason Donna was here.

"Did the police question your husband?"

Donna picked her head up looking alarmed.

"No. If the police questioned Joe he would have told me. I think I would know that."

I would beg to differ with her, but the police probably had no reason to even know about Joe or anything that went on during high school.

"Again, anything Joe and I spoke about is in confidence. You would have to ask him."

Donna's shoulders slumped. I was biting my tongue. I wanted to tell her everything that I knew about her rat bastard husband but ethically I couldn't.

"Are you still investigating Stephanie's death?" Donna asked.

"I am." I didn't want to mention Greg's name to her since she knew him from high school. "Donna, do you know anything that could assist in my investigation?"

"I don't. I swear."

"Okay. If you think of anything, please contact me."

I walked Donna out. I knew what Joe was concerned about. Even if he couldn't be charged with the rapes, I could still cause him trouble. He's probably worried about who I would tell. I wanted him to suffer but chances are that wasn't going to happen.

CHAPTER 50

The following day I got up early and went to the gym. I ran on the treadmill for twenty minutes and then went to the weight area where I worked on my biceps and triceps. I finished with sit-ups and push-ups.

I came home, showered, had a quick cup of coffee and filled my backpack with water, almonds and a banana for my stakeout at Greg Todd's office.

I was at Greg's office by eleven o'clock. I found a spot to sit where no one would bother me and where Greg couldn't see me when he left.

Since I wasn't going to tail Greg, I didn't need to be as vigilant as I would normally have to be. Surveillance could be so boring, that's why I never liked doing it besides the fact I was probably terrible at it.

By three I was having my doubts whether he was going to leave. If he brought his lunch, I'd be screwed. I was running out of mindless games to keep me occupied. And I was dying to go to the bathroom. After a while all the songs on the radio sounded alike.

"Hey Jack, I'm at Greg Todd's office, well not in his office. I'm bored out of my skull. Call me back if you can."

Five minutes later the phone buzzed. It was Jack. Hallelujah. "Hey Jack. I'm so happy to hear your voice."

"I think at this point you'd be happy to hear Jack the Ripper's voice."

"That is true, and it would probably make for very interesting conversation."

"Nice to know."

"But just to make it clear, I love hearing your voice."

"I do declare. I'm flattered."

"Is that your attempt at a southern dialect?" I said.

"I try. So what's going on there?"

"Well, I've been here since eleven and no sign of him leaving. I hope I don't have to do this again tomorrow."

"Practice makes perfect."

"Wiseass. By the way guess who came to my office yesterday?"

"Sidney Poitier."

"No, though I did see an old movie of his and he was quite sexy in his younger days. Listen he just came out. I'll call you tonight," I said in a hurry.

"Good luck."

I didn't know how much time I had. I knew he had fairly late hours today so at some point he would be back. Maybe he was on a rendezvous with Mallory.

As I opened the door, I said to myself, 'try not to screw up the conversation.' The receptionist was sitting at her desk eating what I presumed was a very late lunch. She got up as soon as she saw me.

"Hi," I said. "I'm sorry if I'm interrupting you." The nameplate on her desk said Lucy Cramer. She was probably around my age, not as tall, but slender with light brown curly short hair.

"Can I help you?"

"I hope so. My name is Sally Watkins. I saw the sign outside. I'm sorry, I'm a little nervous."

"Take your time."

"I've been thinking for a while I should talk to someone about my husband. It was just an impulse to come in. Maybe this isn't such a good idea," trying my best to seem genuinely conflicted.

Lucy bit down on her lower lip looking as if she wasn't sure what to say to me.

"Were you considering coming in with your husband or did you want to see Dr. Todd by yourself?"

"I think I would rather see him by myself since I wasn't planning on telling him," I said sheepishly for effect.

"I'm sorry but the doctor specializes in couples therapy," playing with a pencil she picked up from her desk.

"Oh, I didn't know." I was stunned by what she said since I knew she was lying, but why? "Well, thank you for your time."

"You're welcome."

I walked slowly back to my car. I was baffled. Did Lucy know what was going on behind closed doors? I only knew of the one patient he tried kissing. Were there more? I wish I had the damn information back from the State Licensing Board. Was Lucy looking out for me or did she see right through me?

CHAPTER 51

I went straight home and left my car in my garage spot. I walked over to the fruit and vegetable stand three blocks from my apartment building and bought some fresh asparagus and sweet potatoes. Next stop was the fish market where I purchased a piece of organic Salmon. I was determined to have one meal that wasn't from a Chinese or Thai takeout place. Of course there was no way I was going to preclude the Corner Sweet Shoppe.

"Tracey, so nice to see you."

"Hi Mr. Hayes, how's everything?"

"Everything is wonderful. My son, Jonathan got a scholarship to Northwestern."

"That's terrific. You must be so proud."

"His mother and I are both excited for him."

"So I guess that means he won't be joining his dad in the family business," I said with a smile.

"Thank Heavens, no. It's hard enough cleaning the ice cream off of my aprons," he said laughing.

"So what scrumptious flavor did you concoct today?"

"It's called coconut surprise."

"What's the surprise?"

"Well it wouldn't be a surprise if I told you. Now would it?" he said with a twinkle in his eye.

"I guess not. Well in honor of Jonathan, I'll try it."

"Good. Let me know what you think?" handing me a spoonful.

"Yum," as I licked the ice cream off the plastic spoon. "I think there's a hint of amaretto. Is that right?"

"You are correct. Now what can I get you?"

"I'll have half pistachio and half deep dark chocolate."

"I'm not sure why I bother to ask," suppressing a smile as he dug his ice cream scooper into the pistachio ice cream.

Walking back home a thought occurred to me. Why would Greg Todd's receptionist continue to work for him if she knew what was going on? Always questions with no answers.

As I was preparing dinner I called Jack. "Are you home?" I asked when he answered.

"I just got in. How'd it go?"

"Definitely not as I expected. After I gave Lucy, Greg's receptionist, a star studded performance, she told me he basically only does couples therapy, which we know is not true. Why do you think she said that?"

"I'm not sure. It certainly is highly unusual."

"Exactly what I thought, unless if she believed, me she didn't want me as his patient. So if that's the case she has to know what he's been up to. But why would she still work for him?"

"Let's back up. She actually told you he only does couples therapy?"

"Yes."

"Let's just say she does have some idea what he's up to. We don't know the extent to what that is. Maybe she's not sure what actually is going on. If she somehow identified with you she may have thought she was doing you a favor. I'm sure they rarely get walk-ins. It was an opportunity for her to steer someone away from him."

"I guess that's a possibility."

"You don't know her situation," Jack said. 'She could be a single mother and needs the money. There may be all sorts of reasons that she still works for him."

"I wish I would hear from the damn Board already. What's going on there?"

"A new case came in. It's a he said/she said. We're representing the husband. The wife claims her husband has been physically abusing her. I hate these types of cases."

"Does she have proof?"

"That's what I have to find out."

"Let's say she does have proof. How could your boss defend him?" I said raising my voice.

"Unfortunately, everyone under the law is entitled to a defense. I don't always like the cases that come in, but I don't get to pick and choose."

"But your boss can."

"May I remind you everyone is presumed innocent unless proven otherwise."

"That's bullshit and you know it."

"Tracey, it's not that I don't feel the same way as you do. The thing is he may be telling the truth. There may be a reason she's making it up. It would be up to us to uncover that reason. Not everything is black and white."

"We'll continue this conversation another time."

"I look forward to it."

I could vision the smile forming on Jack's face.

"On another subject, Susie and I are going up to Portsmouth, New Hampshire on Friday. She asked me to help her with some of the arrangements for the wedding. Can you believe it, it's only about seven weeks away."

"I thought her mother was going to take care of everything."

"Susie wants to do it herself. It is her wedding."

"I get it."

"Jack, suppose that there were some minor complaints, nothing that he would lose his license over. Would he have reason to kill Stephanie?"

"Let's look at this first from Stephanie's perspective. She uncovers the affair with Mallory. She finds out there are some complaints against him, though they may be minor and hard for the Licensing Board to act on. Stephanie puts together a pattern. She goes to Greg and threatens to expose him to his wife, Mallory and the Selectmen Board. From his perspective he has everything to lose."

"I see your point. I just thought of something unsettling. Mallory would probably mention to Greg my conversation with her, and though he isn't aware that I found out about his affair with Mallory, he might surmise it."

"That makes sense."

"Do you think he would come after me?"

"If he felt trapped, maybe," Jack said in a concerned voice.

"That's comforting to know."

"Until we figure out what to do, you should stay with me."

"Jack, I can't live like that. Every time I'm in a dangerous situation I won't hide."

"You're not hiding; you're being cautious."

"Still."

"Well what do you plan on doing?"

"At some point I'll have to confront him. Don't worry I'll do it some place where there's people around."

"That's not what I'm worried about. It's after you confront him. I think you need to go to the police with what you have and let them take it from there."

"I don't know if I can do that."

"You are one hell of a stubborn person. Do you know that?"

"That's one of my endearing qualities."

"This time your humor isn't going to charm me."

"Let me think about it. In the meantime I'll be in Portsmouth for a few days."

"I want you to promise me while you're in New York you'll have your gun on you at all times."

"I promise."

"How come I don't feel comforted now," Jack said.

CHAPTER 52

On Friday Susie picked me up at four o'clock.

"Buckle up. I can't have anything happen to my maid of honor," Susie said.

"With you driving, I should've worn full on protective gear."

"Very funny. I want you to know I have never been in a single accident."

"That's true. You just go through red lights, go down the wrong way on one way streets, and drive sixty miles an hour on a forty mile road. Should I go on?"

"Don't you think you're exaggerating a little bit?"

"Maybe just a tad."

"I promise to drive safely. Besides I have a stake in staying alive. I would like to wear my wedding dress on my wedding day."

"It is a beautiful dress."

"It is, so nothing to worry about."

"Jack's concerned the good doctor might be coming after me. He wants me to stay at his place."

"Let me guess. You told him no way."

"I did. What kind of investigator would I be if every time I was threatened or might be in danger, I ran away?"

"Are you planning on confronting the doctor?"

"I am. If Stephanie threatened him, it would definitely give him motive to kill her. He has a lot to lose."

"Well, let's put the case aside for now and enjoy ourselves for the rest of the weekend," Susie said.

"Is Mark getting any pre-marriage jitters?"

"Not that I can tell. But thanks for planting that lovely thought in my head."

"You're welcome."

"I made a reservation at a small hotel in Portsmouth."

"Won't your parents feel bad we're not staying with them?"

"I think my mother was relieved. They have so much going on

all the time with their busy social functions. I told them we would have breakfast with them tomorrow. They're looking forward to seeing you."

"The last time I saw your parents was about four years ago. It was when they still had their apartment in the city before moving to Portsmouth full time."

"Now they have so much going on they barely fit me in."

"They do have quite the social life."

"I told my mother she can only invite her very dearest friends to the wedding since Mark and I only want close friends and relatives attending.

The ride to Portsmouth is almost a four and a half hour drive. We stopped around seven at a place called the Crab Shack for dinner. We arrived at the Hotel Portsmouth around nine-thirty.

"Wow, the outside of the hotel is very interesting," I said.

"It's set in an 1881 Queen Anne Mansion."

When we walked in there was beautiful wood paneling that went halfway up the walls. The upper half was painted a light gray. The thick carpet was a design in gray and white. Our room was very sparse. The theme was gray and white. There was a sofa opposite the two beds and the bathroom had a clawfoot bathtub.

"I don't think I've ever taken a bath in a clawfoot tub," I said.

"There's a shower if you would rather not take a bath."

"No, I think this will be cool." I filled the bathtub up and added soap bubbles. After undressing, I lowered myself into the tub. Wow, this is so relaxing. All I need is some wine and I might never leave. "Hey Susie, I think I can get used to this."

"Well, try not to."

I stayed in the tub until my fingers and toes looked like prunes. I put on one of the plush bathrobes the hotel supplies and plopped down on the bed. By eleven we were both fast asleep.

In the morning Susie and I drove over to her parents' house. To say the house was beautiful is an understatement. It's a huge farmhouse with a wraparound porch. It must be over hundred years old. There are about twenty rooms inside. The whole house was completely updated including state of the art appliances and a fireplace in the kitchen, living room and master bedroom, and that's just the rooms I knew about.

"Tracey, my dear, I'm so glad to see you. Come sit down. I want to hear everything that's going on in your life," Mrs. Jacobs said kissing Susie and then giving me a hug.

Mrs. Jacobs and Susie could almost pass for sisters. Her hair was red like Susie's though I'm sure it was not her natural red. She's a little taller than Susie, slender, with porcelain skin. She had Susie's bubbly personality. On the other hand Mr. Jacobs was tall, stout, on the quiet side and smoked cigars. I liked him the moment I met him more than twenty years ago. He made me feel right at home. If you look at the Jacobs you would say they were a mismatch, but they seemed very devoted to each other. I guess like Susie and me.

We all sat down at a long wooden antique kitchen table that was covered with every breakfast food you could imagine.

"This looks delicious," I said as Mr. Jacobs passed me the pancakes.

"So how are you?" Mrs. Jacobs asked me.

I gave her a compact update of my life. She did not disappoint me when she asked about my love life.

"I've been seeing Jack for about a year. You'll meet him at the wedding." Shifting the conversation, I said, "so you must be excited about Susie's wedding."

"We both love Mark," Mr. Jacobs said. "I'm very happy the wedding is going to be right in our own backyard," looking lovingly at Susie.

I was trying very hard to hold back the tears. The thought of my parents never walking me down the aisle if I married was unbearable. Eloping might be a better choice.

When I composed myself, I said, "it's a lovely place for a wedding." Their back lawn overlooked the Piscataqua River.

When we got into the car, Susie said, "if I turn into my mother just shoot me. Hey, I'm sorry I didn't mean…"

"It's all right," I said squeezing Susie's hand. "Your mother is pretty overbearing."

"Okay then, off to the caterer."

"Maybe I shouldn't have stuffed myself at breakfast. I

completely forgot we'll be sampling food for the wedding," I said yawning.

"I can't make up my mind whether I want the wedding to be elegant or more on the homey side."

"I say somewhere between the two. Just have the wedding reflect who you and Mark are."

"It's hamburgers and hot dogs for everyone."

"I think your mother would disown you, maybe something in between hamburgers and hot dogs."

"I guess that rules out corn dogs."

The woman who greeted us at the catering place looked like she came straight out of a business magazine. She was tall, elegant, well dressed in a red suit, her skirt coming down right below her knees. Her blond hair was pulled back in a bun. Susie and I looked at each other as Ms. Prim and Proper escorted us into the main room. If Susie wasn't Mrs. Jacobs' daughter we wouldn't have made it past the front door. Wearing jeans didn't help.

"It's Susie, isn't it," said Ms. Ryan.

"Yes and this is my friend Tracey."

"Your mother is so excited about the wedding. She said you can choose whatever you like. Here are the menu selections. You can sample anything on the menu. I'll leave you two to look everything over and I'll be back in a few minutes."

"Now you know why I didn't want to leave it up to my mother. If I did, we would all be having pheasant under glass."

"That wouldn't be so bad. I've never had pheasant; maybe we should try it just for the hell of it."

"Good idea."

After sampling about half the menu, Susie decided on a combination of dishes for the hors d'oeuvres, including, sliders, shrimp cocktail, sushi rolls, and little baby lamb chops. For the main menu, mixed greens, and a choice of scallops or rack of lamb.

Next stop was the flower shop. After looking at every flower in the shop, Susie decided on simple white roses.

We just made it to the rental place before closing.

"Sorry we're late. This won't take long," Susie said.

The guy looked like he was ready to leave. Susie quickly picked out the chairs. The tent looked strong enough to withstand rain but probably not much more than that.

"My mother will call you with the number of chairs and tables we'll need. Do you also supply the table cloths, napkins and silverware?"

"Yes, we'll take care of everything."

"Okay, I'll let my mother know she has to give you a headcount. Thanks for waiting."

"Time for our own party," Susie said. I know this restaurant two blocks from Market Place called Jumpin' Jay's Fish Café. Great food and they make a mean Margarita."

The Café was tastefully done. There was wainscoting half way up the walls painted red and the top half was painted white. The chairs were black and the tables were a marbled white.

"Why don't we sit at the bar for a while," Susie said.

We snuggled up to the bar and ordered Margaritas.

"I'm glad that ordeal is over," Susie said.

"Well if I ever get married I'm eloping."

"You can't. I have to be there."

"Well, you can be at the court house with me while I'm taking my vows."

Our drinks came. "To a fabulous wedding," I said as we clicked our glasses.

CHAPTER 53

After finishing two Margaritas each, Susie and I were starved. The hostess seated us and left menus.

"I think I'm a little high," I said. "Those Margaritas were really strong."

A few minutes later the waiter came over. He was maybe twenty with a ponytail. All the waiters were dressed the same, dark trousers, white shirt and a red tie decorated with little fishes.

"Would you ladies like to hear our specials?" he said trying to be enthusiastic.

"Don't you ever get tired of repeating the specials to the customers?" Susie asked.

"Don't mind my friend I think she's a little high from your fabulous drinks."

He chuckled. "To tell you the truth I do. Most of the time people order from the menu. Half the time they're not even listening to me."

"Well, I'm listening very carefully," I said.

After reciting the list of specials which I was attentively listening to, Susie and I both ordered from the menu.

"I'll have the house salad and the grilled Swordfish, though the specials sounded great," I said, feeling a little guilty.

"And I'll have the house salad and the Yellow Fin Tuna. Oh, and we're going to share an order of the crispy Calamari as our appetizer."

"And we'll have two more of your fabulous Margaritas," I said as the waiter was walking away. "What the heck. We're not driving back to New York tonight. Maybe I'll even take another bath in my new favorite tub."

I could tell Susie had something on her mind. I was praying it wasn't second thoughts about the marriage.

"What gives?" I asked Susie.

"I told you that Mark and I had several discussions whether

we wanted to have children, and we both had decided we didn't want to at this point in our lives. Well I'm not quite sure anymore."

"You're entitled to change your mind."

"Not if that's what we agreed upon. And besides I'm not sure if I do want children."

"I think you need to talk to Mark about it. He might have doubts also."

"I'm afraid if he absolutely doesn't want children he'll change his mind about the wedding."

"Don't you think you should find out now no matter what the outcome? If you marry him and decide you want children and he doesn't, you'll regret it."

"I know you're right."

"So you're going to talk to him?"

"I will," Susie said as she bit her lower lip. A sign of anxiety for Susie.

The waiter brought over our margaritas and our order of crispy Calamari.

"Delicious," I said as I squeezed some lemon on the Calamari.

While I was eating my flan that I ordered for dessert, I said to Susie, "something has been nagging at me about the case but I can't seem to figure it out."

"It will come to you."

"I hope."

On Sunday we stopped at Susie's parents for a little while before heading back. Susie told them about the wedding menu. I thought I saw her mother cringe slightly. By twelve o'clock we were on the road back. We stopped at a diner around two for lunch and we were in front of my building by six. As I opened the car door I reminded Susie to talk to Mark.

On Monday morning I was raring to go. The walk to my office was invigorating. It was the first week of March and the morning sun was bright. The days were getting slightly longer but my patience was getting shorter. The case was driving me into an early grave. Something needs to happen and soon.

As I was waiting for the coffee to finish dripping, I rummaged through my emails. I heard a ping and saw it was an email from the Connecticut Department of Public Health. My finger was shaking as I pressed on the mouse to open up the email. I saw two separate attachments. I printed them both out.

I poured myself a cup of coffee and started reading the first complaint. The incident took place about two years ago. A woman claimed Todd came on to her. He alleged she became infatuated with him and was the aggressor, and filed the complaint because she was angry at him for rejecting her.

The second complaint took place about a year ago. It was basically the same story that Nancy Jamison told me. He touched her inappropriately, but he claimed he was trying to comfort her when she began crying in the session.

What a dirt bag. I wasn't sure to the extent the Board looks into these cases, if at all, but he deserves to lose his license. I wanted to tell Mallory but would she believe me? I wasn't sure. I know Jack said that he didn't think there was any point in speaking to her since chances are she wouldn't be cooperative, but I wanted to take a shot at it. Now that I had more incriminating information on him, she might be willing to talk. Maybe it was my ego or maybe I was just angry at both Greg and Mallory.

I picked up the phone and punched in Mallory's number. It went straight to voice mail. "Mallory, it's Tracey Marks. Some new information has come to my attention. Please call me back. It's important." Hopefully the urgency of my message will do it.

I thought about the complaints. Because the two complaints were a year apart he may have been careful, that or no other women wanted to file a complaint, Nancy Jamison being a prime example.

I heard my phone ringing. "Tracey Marks."

"Ms. Marks, it's Mallory. What's going on?"

"I would rather not talk about it over the phone. Are you working today?"

"Yes, but I'm free after four."

"Would it be too much of an inconvenience if you come to my

office?" I thought it would be better if our conversation was not in public.

"What is it? You're scaring me."

"I didn't mean to. I just meant it's easier to talk without people in earshot of our conversation," hoping this would calm her.

"I could be there between four-thirty and five."

"Great. Thanks. See you then."

What if I was all wrong about this? What if I don't convince Mallory what a sleaze ball Todd is? What if she runs to him with everything I've told her? I have to take the chance.

CHAPTER 54

"Mallory, thanks for coming in. Please have a seat."

"Do you know who killed Stephanie? Is that why I'm here?" trying to contain her excitement.

"Unfortunately, not yet." I needed to tread carefully. "Do you remember me telling you that Stephanie was looking into a guy named Greg Todd?" I paused. Mallory was shifting uncomfortably. "It turns out she found some disturbing information about him." I paused again. Mallory was no longer looking at me. "He had two complaints filed against him with the Connecticut State Licensing Board. Both from women who said he touched them inappropriately." I paused again waiting for some kind of response, but nothing. I wasn't even sure she was listening anymore. She seemed far away. I continued. "I was recently in touch with a woman who told me Todd tried to kiss her in a therapy session while he was supposedly comforting her."

"Why are you telling me any of this? I don't even know who this guy is," her anger palpable.

"Well that's interesting since I followed Greg last week and guess where he went? It was to an Econo Lodge. And guess who showed up to meet him? I think you know the answer to that one."

Mallory's face turned red. She still didn't say anything.

"Mallory, I'm not judging you. My only concern is finding out who killed Stephanie. She knew you were having an affair with Todd. I think she confronted him with what she found out and threatened to tell his wife everything including the affair. I believe it's possible he killed Stephanie."

"He would never hurt Stephanie," tears streaming down her face. "I know that he's not capable of hurting anyone," she said raising her voice.

"Did you know that he was capable of what he did to those women?"

"I don't believe it. They probably came on to him."

"Why would they do that?"

"Patients form attachments to their therapists."

"Like you did?"

"It just so happens he's leaving his wife to be with me." Mallory was livid.

"Do you really believe that? Do you believe three women, and that's all we know about, would make false accusations?"

"Yes I do," she said emphatically.

I saw there was no way I was going to convince Mallory of anything. She was in too deep with this guy.

As Mallory was getting up to leave, she said, "you're wrong about Greg, you'll see. And don't call me ever again," slamming the door as she left.

I gambled and I was wrong. I thought she would see him as I did, a creep who only cares about himself. I screwed up. I can envision Mallory calling Todd as soon as she left, telling him everything I said. What now?

I called Jack since I wasn't sure what to do next.

"Tracey, what's wrong?"

"I blew it. I spoke to Mallory thinking I could convince her, what a bastard Todd is. You were right. She blamed the other women, not him. Of course she wouldn't believe he would kill Stephanie. What was I thinking?"

"Don't be so hard on yourself. You thought you could get through to her."

"But now she'll go straight to Todd and tell him everything."

"First, you don't know that for sure. Maybe she'll think more about what you said. Doubts might creep into her consciousness. She's in love with the guy so even if she believed you, she wasn't going to admit it."

"I guess you're right. Whether she tells him or not, I have to talk to him."

"Keep your gun with you at all times."

"Will do."

After hanging up I thought about my options which were unfortunately few. Calling Todd wasn't in the plan. I needed to catch him off guard, but where would the best place be? There was always the possibility he might try and come after me first.

I took my gun out of the safe and slid it into my ankle holster. Hopefully it was just precautionary and I wouldn't have to use it. Just the thought of it made me sweat all over.

When I got home I changed into my running clothes. The sun was going down as I exited my apartment building. I jogged over to the park, my eyes darting all around, not wanting any unwelcome surprises. Normally jogging clears my mind but I must be in overload since too many thoughts were coming at me all at once. While I was in the middle of my third loop around I had the same nagging feeling I had told Susie about. I just couldn't grab hold of it. Maybe if I could relax it would come to me.

I went back to my apartment, showered, and heated up leftover Chinese food. I was about to sit down at the kitchen table when I heard my phone ring.

"Hello," not recognizing the number.

"Ms. Marks, it's Mallory."

I was shocked to hear from her.

"Mallory, is everything alright?"

"I don't know. Can I please come over?" sounding very upset.

"Where are you?"

"I'm still in the city."

I was trying to think fast. If she knew where I lived then so would Todd. On the other hand I don't think it would be that difficult to find me anyway.

I gave her my address and told her the doorman would ring me when she arrived. Mallory said she would be here in approximately twenty minutes. I ate fast and pulled on a pair of jeans and a tee shirt. My gun was tucked in my ankle holster. I couldn't imagine what was so urgent.

Thirty minutes later Mallory was standing at my door, her eyes bloodshot. She looked like she had been drinking. I took her coat and I led her into the living room where I directed her to sit on the couch. I sat opposite her on a club chair.

"Are you alright? Can I get you water or a cup of coffee?"

"I'm fine," she said clearly agitated.

"What's going on?" I asked her gently.

She started crying. I got up and brought over a box of tissues and sat down next to her.

"He told me he loved me and that he was getting a divorce. I was stupid enough to believe him. I trusted him," she said in between blowing her nose. "What an idiot I was. I called him right after I spoke with you and told him everything you said. Of course he denied it all and gave excuses, but I knew from the sound of his voice he was lying. I asked him again when he was getting a divorce, and that's when I knew for sure he was never going to leave his wife. He was angry and told me to stop pressuring him. I started screaming at him and he hung up on me." Mallory was sobbing.

I had questions I wanted to ask her but I waited to give her some time. I got up and came back with a glass of water. She drank it in one gulp.

"There was something I was wondering about," I said. "It seemed Stephanie was very upset about your affair. Do you have any idea why?"

"Not really except that she said Greg was taking advantage of me. I told her he wasn't and that I wanted to be with him. She didn't seem to understand."

"Did Stephanie tell you that she had been looking into him?"

"No. I was shocked when you mentioned it."

"So Greg never said that Stephanie confronted him?" I didn't actually know for a fact that she did but I was pretty sure.

"Why would he? Then he would have to admit to me what Stephanie found out."

That made sense I thought to myself.

"I know you told me you didn't think Greg was capable of killing Stephanie. Do you still feel that way?"

"I honestly don't know. I wouldn't have thought that before my conversation with him tonight, but he was so angry when I spoke with him, I don't know what to think anymore."

CHAPTER 55

I called an Uber for Mallory since she was in no condition to take the subway or the Metro North railroad back home.

I was surprised at these turn of events. I knew it didn't necessarily mean that Greg killed Stephanie, but I certainly was going to find out.

I woke up to the pinging sound of rain hitting against my window air conditioner. I wanted to try and get the advantage on Greg Todd so I decided to drive up to his office today and wait for him. I turned on the coffee maker, showered and had a big breakfast since I wasn't sure how long I was going to have to wait for Greg. I was about to strap on my ankle holster when I remembered I couldn't take my gun past the state line.

I took the elevator down to the garage to get my car. As I was opening my car door, I heard footsteps from behind me. I quickly turned around and I was staring into the angry face of Greg Todd.

"How the hell did you get into the garage?" I said startled.

"The question is who the hell do you think you are poking your nose in my business?"

"When someone winds up dead and that person was looking into you! Did Stephanie threaten to tell your wife? Did she threaten to tell Mallory, or both? Did you kill Stephanie to shut her up?" My hands were clenched by my sides and my left foot started to shake.

"I have no idea what the hell you're talking about," he said, his eyes spitting daggers at me.

"Yes you do. You've been lying to your wife and you've been lying to Mallory. And how many of your patients have you tried to take advantage of? Stephanie was going to expose you and everything would have come crashing down on you."

"I may be a lot of things, but I'm not a killer," he said raising his voice.

"Your car was seen sitting outside of Stephanie's house."

"I know how it may look, but I was there once just to talk with her but she never showed."

"What did you want to talk to her about?" I could see the wheels turning in his head.

"Okay, she did threaten me. That's why I went to her house, but to talk, nothing else. I wanted to try and persuade her not to say anything to my wife."

"But she wasn't home so you came back another day, snuck into her house through the garage and killed her when she wouldn't listen to you."

"No, you're wrong. I had nothing to do with her death," he said trying to convince me.

"Tracey, is that you? What's going on here?" my superintendent shouted. "Is everything alright?" he said as he walked over, first looking at Greg and then back to me.

"Everything's fine. He was just leaving."

"I'll show him out. You come back again and I'm calling the cops."

"Thanks John." I said breathing a big sigh of relief.

My foot was still shaking as I took the elevator back to my apartment. When I got inside I threw off my jacket and backpack. I grabbed a bottle of water and parked myself on the couch. My body was trembling. All I could think about was how I never heard his footsteps until he was practically on top of me. He could have killed me before I even had the chance to turn around.

Shit, I heard my phone ringing in my backpack. I let it go to voicemail. Two seconds later it started ringing again. I grabbed my phone and answered.

"We never finished our conversation," Todd said before I had a chance to say hello.

"I believe we did. I'm going to the police with what I found out."

"I'm begging you not to. What do I have to do to convince you I didn't kill Stephanie?"

"I'm not sure there's anything."

"What about my appointment book. If I can show you I was seeing patients when she died, would that change your mind?" he said sounding desperate.

"How do I know you didn't fudge the book? Why would I believe you?"

"Look, my receptionist Lucy handles the appointment book. You can ask her."

I was debating what to do. "I'll get back to you," and hung up. Let him stew for a while.

"Hey Jack, call me."

As soon as I hung up my phone rang. "What's going on?" Jack asked.

"I don't know where to begin." I explained to Jack what transpired with Mallory and with Todd.

"You certainly have been very busy."

"Very funny."

"It turns out talking to Mallory was a good move," Jack said.

"It didn't feel that good when Todd almost scared me to death."

"Well, from what you told me it sounded like you handled it very well."

"Now why did you have to go and flatter me?"

"I thought I would get some brownie points."

"Okay, back to business. I'm trying to figure out my next move."

"What was your gut feeling when you were talking to him?"

"He seemed genuinely upset that I accused him of killing Stephanie."

"Then check out his alleged alibi. From your previous encounter with his receptionist, I don't think she would lie for him, but keep your guard up."

I made some coffee while I was mulling over when to pay a visit to Greg's office. I decided not to give him a head's up when I would be coming and made the decision to go today before he had a chance to do any last minute revisions with his appointment book.

CHAPTER 56

I arrived at Greg's office at one forty-five. I didn't see his car anywhere. Lucy was at her desk.

"Hi Lucy." She looked up with a bewildered expression.

"Hi, I'm sorry I don't remember your name."

"It's Tracey Marks."

"But, but, that's not the name you told me when you came in last week."

"I know. I'm a private investigator," handing her my business card. "I'm sorry I lied to you. I had to find out some information about your boss. I'm here to look at Dr. Todd's appointment book for last December."

"He's not here," she said nervously. "Is he in trouble?"

"No. Can you please call and tell him I'm here."

Lucy's hand was shaking as she dialed the phone. I heard her speaking to Todd. When she hung up she said, "Dr. Todd said because of confidentiality issues I would have to look at the date you're checking and tell you the times he was in session for that day."

I wasn't happy with the arrangement. I would have to trust Lucy she was telling me the truth.

Lucy flipped back to the date in December I gave her.

"Okay, I have it. What do you need to know?"

"I want you to tell me exactly the times of his appointments and any gaps."

"Should I be worried about working for Dr. Todd?"

"Right now I'm just following up on some leads. Do you have any reason to think he did something wrong?"

"Can you tell me what you're investigating?"

"I'm looking into the death of a woman who was murdered in Scarsdale, New York."

"And you think Dr. Todd had something to do with this woman?" Lucy said gasping.

"As I said, I'm following up on all leads. Can you look at the page, please?"

"Sorry," she said looking down at the appointment book. "He had appointments from eleven to two and then from four to seven."

"I know it's a while ago but would you happen to remember anything from that day?"

"Like what?"

"What time Dr. Todd came back for his four o'clock appointment. Did he seem distracted?"

"I don't remember. Would you tell me if you thought Dr. Todd was dangerous?"

"I didn't mean to scare you. I don't think you're in any danger. If you happen to recall anything from that day, please contact me."

When I got back to my car I googled the mileage from Todd's office to Stephanie's house. It listed thirty-seven miles. Could he have driven to Stephanie's place, killed her and gotten back to the office in two hours? It didn't seem likely.

I went back inside Todd's office. Lucy was talking to someone on the phone. She looked up.

"Sorry to interrupt you," I said. I heard Lucy quickly tell the person on the other end of the phone that she would call them back.

"What is it?" Lucy said looking as if she'd been caught doing something wrong.

"If Dr. Todd called you and asked you to cancel his four o'clock appointment or it was canceled for another reason, would there be a record of that?"

"I would have most likely noted it next to the name that was canceled."

"Thanks Lucy, and not to worry."

I decided to drive from Todd's office to Stephanie's house to see for myself how long it would take.

When I arrived at Stephanie's it was three-twenty. It took me fifty minutes. If Todd had left around two at the latest, it wouldn't be easy to drive from his office, kill Stephanie and get back in time for his four o'clock patient. But I guess it could be done. So what now?

I went straight back to my apartment only detouring to pick up salad stuff for dinner.

I changed into a tee shirt and sweats and tried my hand at pasta with spaghetti sauce. How hard can it be? I boiled water, cut up some garlic and sautéed it in olive oil. I sliced cherry tomatoes and threw them in the pan and waited for the tomatoes to soften. In the meantime, I put together a salad. I was very delighted with myself. I opened a bottle of Cabernet Sauvignon and poured myself a glass.

I turned on my little TV I have in the kitchen and sat down to eat. I looked up and there was Randy Stewart on the local channel being interviewed.

"Why did you decide to run for Congress?" the newscaster asked.

I was anxious to hear his answer.

"I've been in politics ever since college. I knew that it was my passion to help people. I was fortunate growing up that I came from an affluent family and had opportunities most people didn't have. My family instilled in me to find ways to give back to society."

I have to say he was pretty impressive when he spoke, and he looked quite handsome in his dark blue suit, white shirt and red and blue striped tie.

Randy Stewart finished his interview telling us what issues he would like to bring forth if he was elected to Congress. If I hadn't known what he did in high school, I would vote for him.

I cleaned up and went to bed with a John LeCarre novel, The Spy Who Came in from the Cold, a great suspense story, just what I needed to take my mind off of everything.

While I was reading I kept thinking that I was missing something on my case. It had been nagging at me for a few weeks but it kept slipping away.

I must have fallen asleep because at some point I woke up with this horrible feeling in my stomach. Oh my God, I remember. It's him, the voice on the other end of the burner phone.

CHAPTER 57

"Jack, wake up. I know who the killer is," unable to contain my excitement.

"What time is it?"

"Who cares, I figured it out. Are you listening?"

"I am," he said sounding half asleep.

"It's the guy who's running for Congress. He lied to me."

"Start from the beginning and talk slowly."

"His voice, I didn't remember it when I interviewed him but ever since we spoke I knew something was bothering me. I just couldn't figure it out. But it was the voice, the same voice on the burner phone. I heard him being interviewed this evening but it still didn't click. I suddenly woke up realizing it was his voice on the burner phone."

"Are you sure?"

"I'm positive." There was a pause. "Jack, are you still there?"

"I'm thinking. My brain doesn't work as fast as yours, especially at three o'clock in the morning."

"Stewart told me he witnessed the rape and didn't do anything to stop it. According to him he apologized numerous times to Maddie. He felt so terrible he was going to devote his time to women's issues. Thinking back on it now, I only had his say so that he watched Joe rape Maddie, but what if he raped Maddie also. Stephanie knew because she witnessed it and never said anything. I think when Stewart announced he was running for Congress, something in Stephanie snapped and she confronted him. If this had come out it probably would have ruined his chances of getting elected."

"If you're right, he's dangerous."

"He might be the one who ran me off the road. Now it all makes sense. That's why Joe and Randy met up. Joe needed to warn Stewart before I saw him."

"We don't know for a fact that he killed Stephanie."

"That's true, but I need to talk with him again. I won't confront him. I'll make up a story why I need to see him. If he suspects anything he's not going to talk with me."

"If he wants to find out what you know he might agree. Just be super careful."

Getting back to sleep was impossible. I turned on the TV hoping it would lull me back to sleep, but no such luck. I got up, put the coffee maker on and washed my face. It was only four o'clock. The sun wouldn't be up for another three hours.

I got back into bed with my coffee and thought about what I would say to Randy Stewart. Nothing inspirational was coming to me.

By nine o'clock I was showered and had finished eating breakfast. I called Stewart at his office at nine-thirty and asked to speak with him, keeping my fingers crossed that he was in. I was informed that he hadn't arrived yet. I asked the receptionist when he was expected. A few seconds later she came back on the line and told me he would be in at one o'clock. I decided not to leave my name.

I went into the office and caught up on bills. Looking through my emails I noticed one of my clients wanted me to run a background check on a prospective employee. While I was running some searches through my databases, my phone rang.

"You must have been reading my mind. I was just about to call you," I said to Susie.

"Oh yeah what's going on?"

"Can you meet for a drink later, say around six?" I said.

"How about at Jake's Tavern?"

"See you there."

At one-thirty I called Stewart. He was in but on the phone. Instead of leaving a message with the receptionist I asked to be connected to his voice mail. I didn't want him to get spooked so I left a vague message telling him I needed his legal expertise on something. I thought that might get him to call me back.

About an hour later my phone rang. "Tracey Marks."

"Ms. Marks this is Randy Stewart. How can I help you?"

"The last time we spoke you mentioned I could call you if I needed some help. I know this is a busy time for you but I was wondering if we can meet."

"Can we do this on the telephone?"

"I really think it would be better in person."

"I'm extremely busy. Between running for Congress and my clients, I have no time to breathe."

"I promise it won't take long." There was a pause.

"I have a meeting outside of the office at four o'clock. I can meet you at the coffee shop where we last spoke at three-fifteen. Please be prompt."

"I'll be there."

Well now that I have the interview I have no idea what to say. I better come up with something quick since it was already two forty-five.

I was waiting inside the coffee shop, when Randy Stewart came in. He saw me and sat down opposite me. I was already holding a cup of coffee in my damp hands. The waitress came over and Stewart said he was good.

"How can I help you?" he said matter-of-factly.

"First, I want to say I saw you last night on the news and you were very impressive," hoping this would put him at ease. "It's the case I'm working on. I think I know who killed Stephanie Harris." His eyes opened wide. "You see the whole time I thought it had something to do with the rape of Maddie Jensen. It turns out Stephanie was seeing a therapist who tried to rape her in his office but she got away before he had a chance. She was going to tell the police but apparently he killed her before that could happen." I stopped talking.

"How do you know all this?"

"I had a computer specialist look into Stephanie's computer. The therapist's name came up on various sites Stephanie was looking at. I confronted him but of course he denied it. I did some digging beforehand and it appears he's had a couple of complaints filed against him, nothing that could get his license revoked since they were he said/she said situations."

"Was there anything else on the computer?" he said

drumming his hands on the table.

Bingo, I said to myself. He was most likely fishing to see if his name came up on anything. "He's still in the process of uncovering information from her computer. At this point I'm focusing on the therapist, but if new evidence is discovered, it may lead me in another direction entirely."

"So how can I help you," he said in a hurried manner.

"Well, I thought since you probably know about criminal law, I wanted your input on how I can prove it's this guy?"

"I think you should let the police handle it."

"I guess I'm reluctant to go to the police. What happens if I'm wrong and it's not him? I may ruin his life and I don't want that to happen."

"I understand, but the police can handle the situation discreetly."

"Can I be liable if I bring it to the police and the person is innocent?"

"No, you don't have to worry about that."

"I was hoping there was another way. This is only my second murder case and I don't have much experience," which is true but I thought that would make my story more believable. I'm not sure I would even buy my own story. Let's hope he does.

"Well, I hope I was of some help. Good luck," he said getting up.

"Thanks. I'll take your advice into consideration."

Instead of going back to the office, I walked around thinking about my conversation with Stewart. I'm not sure I accomplished what I set out to do, which was getting him to think about whether I knew more then I was letting on.

Jake's Tavern was a local neighborhood bar with fairly good food, better than average for a bar. Susie had already staked at a table. Before I even sat down, I said to Susie, "I know who killed Stephanie," in a low voice, not being able to contain myself.

CHAPTER 58

Just at that moment the waitress came over.

"Ladies, what can I get you?"

"I'll have a Cabernet Sauvignon."

"And I'll have a Cosmopolitan. Oh, and an order of Nachos, please," I said.

"Speak, I can hardly wait," Susie said when the waitress left.

"Okay. I was listening to the news last night and Randy Stewart, the guy who's running for Congress was being interviewed. If you recall he's one of the guys who was there when Maddie Jensen was raped. When I originally interviewed him he told me that he witnessed the rape, but just stood by and watched as Connolly raped Maddie."

The waitress came with our drinks and nachos.

"Can I get you gals anything else?"

"No," we both said in unison, practically biting her head off. She left, but not before a look of displeasure crossed her face.

"After I heard his interview last night there was something nagging at me but I couldn't figure it out. I woke up in the middle of the night and I remembered. That was the same voice on the burner phone."

"Are you sure?"

"Yes, absolutely. He was playing me all along. I think he did more than witness the rape. I believe he raped Maddie also, though I have no proof."

"But why did Stephanie wait all this time?"

"I think she buried the memory of what she saw. Don't forget, she was a kid and her friend had been threatened. When she heard that Randy Stewart was running for Congress, all the years of keeping this dark secret to herself was unbearable, and she needed to do the right thing."

"That's a good story. Now you have to prove it."

"I know. I didn't finish yet. I met with Stewart and made up some cockin' bull story which I won't go into, and hopefully he went for the bait. I wanted to put doubt in his mind that Stephanie's computer might have incriminating evidence against him."

"Well, now you've put yourself in a compromising situation. You basically made yourself bait if Stewart is the killer."

"It scares me when you say it like that."

"I'm scared for you. Besides, you have to be at my side when I get married."

"I'll try to stay alive at least until the wedding is over."

"I'm glad you think this is amusing."

"Believe me inside I'm twisted up in knots."

"Make sure your phone is on all the time. Keep your guard up and be aware of your surroundings."

Susie and I hugged outside of the bar. I took an Uber back to my apartment and tried to calm myself knowing I put myself in a dangerous situation. When I got home I threw off my clothes and showered. I was too wound up to cook something for dinner. Instead I had a bowl of Cheerios and milk and stood over the kitchen sink eating. How was I going to prove Stewart killed Stephanie?

I flopped into bed and fell asleep with the TV going. The next thing I knew it was six a.m. I put on my running clothes and went out. I kept my antennas up, not relishing any unforeseen surprises. My gun was tucked in my ankle holster. I had no illusions that Stewart might come after me. But what if I was all wrong? Just because it was him on the burner phone, it's still a leap to murder. Maybe my first instincts were right and it was Greg Todd. After all it was his name that came up on the computer not Randy Stewart's.

When I got back I showered, dressed and walked to my office, stopping along the way for a coffee and cranberry nut muffin. "Hi Anna."

"Tracey, I haven't seen you for a few days. Everything okay?"

"Yeah, I'm fine. Things have been a little hectic. How's everything with you?"

"The same, not much going on, though I did get promoted to

store manager."

"That's great. Does that mean you won't be the one greeting me in the morning?"

"Nah, still me, here you go."

"Thanks and congratulations boss."

I stopped by Cousin Alan's office before going into my office, but it was locked. I realized it was only eight-thirty. Alan and Margaret usually don't get in until nine. I unlocked my door and settled in with the hopes of staying put and catching up with everything I've neglected in the past few weeks. While enjoying my first cup of coffee and biting into my muffin I checked my emails to make sure I wasn't neglecting any clients.

I finished up the background check I had started for my client who was planning on hiring someone for an upper management position at his firm and then sent him a report on my findings. I caught up on answering a slew of emails I had ignored for a few days and started on my report to Christine Harris, updating her on the latest developments. When I looked at my watch it was four o'clock. I went next door. "Hi Margaret, how's everything here?"

"Busy. We got a few new clients Alan's trying to negotiate deals with."

"Always wheeling and dealing. How are the kids?"

"Last time I saw them they were safely on the school bus. Go right in."

"Hey there," I said greeting Alan.

"I'm so glad you stopped by. Any luck with the case?"

"Too complicated to go into now. How's my little man?"

"He was asking for you the other day."

"Really?"

"Well Patty and I were pretty sure it was your name he was saying. He said Trekkie."

"Close enough. I'll take it."

"How's Jack? Why don't you guys come for dinner next time he comes down?"

"Sounds good. Did I tell you Susie's wedding is next month?

She's having it at her parents' house in New Hampshire."

"You mentioned it."

"I see that look in your eyes. Don't even think of asking your next question."

"My lips are sealed."

"I'll have to set up a time with Patty to FaceTime with Michael so he can practice saying my name."

"Good luck with that."

"I'm going out to get a sandwich. You want anything?"

"No. I'm good. Are you staying late?"

"I'm trying to finish up a report for my client and then I'll head out," I said.

"Be safe."

I bought a chicken sandwich at the deli near me with a side of coleslaw and sat at my desk eating while typing up my report to Christine. I sent the report and was packing up when I heard the door knob turn.

CHAPTER 59

"Alan is that you?" No answer. My hands were shaking as I slid my gun into the back of my jeans. I grabbed my cell phone and shoved it into my back pocket. I walked slowly into the reception area where I was staring into the face of Randy Stewart.

"Hi Tracey, I thought we would continue our conversation from yesterday," he said with a mocking smile across his face.

"What did you want to tell me?" Though I was trying not to show any fear my heart was pounding so loud against my chest I was afraid he could hear it from a distance.

"Did you know it was me when you came up with a ploy to see me?"

"I have no idea what you're talking about."

"Don't play with me Tracey. I'm in no mood," he said in a menacing tone. "After our conversation I wasn't sure if you knew I killed Stephanie, but the thing is I can't take the risk. But just out of curiosity, how did you figure it out?" he said inching closer to me.

"It was your voice on the burner phone. I couldn't quite place it until I heard your interview the other day." I could barely get the words out, my mouth was so dry.

"It was Stephanie's fault you know. She wouldn't let it go. I begged her not to say anything, but she wouldn't listen. She was threatening to go to the papers. Even if there was no way for her to prove I raped Maddie my career would be over," he said inching his way a little bit closer.

"How did you get into her house?" I said, trying to keep him talking.

"Oh that was the easy part. She should have made it a little harder to get into her side garage door. When she saw me I could see the frightened look in her eyes. I knew no matter what she said to me, she was never going to leave it alone and I couldn't let that happen. You understand."

I backed up. Sweat dripping down my back. I noticed the black gloves on his hands. Not knowing what else to do, I screamed, hoping someone would hear me.

"Don't waste your breathe. Everyone's gone. We're all alone."

I was shivering. I pulled out my gun and pointed it at him. The gun, shaking in my hands felt like dead weight. I was barely able to hold it up.

"You're not going to kill me so why don't you put the gun down."

"Don't come any closer." I held on to the gun for dear life with my left hand and pulled out my cell phone trying to dial 911. My phone dropped out of my hand, clattering to the floor. As I was looking down on the floor for my phone, Randy rushed towards me. In the next second there was a loud explosion and Randy fell to the floor. For a moment I didn't realize what happened. I looked down and there was blood seeping out of his stomach. I grabbed my phone and dialed for help. I wasn't sure if any words were coming out of my mouth, as my mind was blanking out, trying desperately to remember my address.

"Randy can you hear me?" I grabbed some paper towels and pressed down on his stomach, hoping to stop the bleeding. I watched as his blood soaked my hands. My only thought going through my head was, 'don't die on me.'

The next thing I heard was the sound of an ambulance. "In here," I shouted as the front door opened. Someone was gently pushing me to the side as they took over. I heard someone ask me if I was hurt. I think I shook my head, but I can't remember.

The police came right after the ambulance. After that everything was a blur. They took Randy away and I was left alone with two policemen.

"Are you sure you're alright?" one of the police officers asked me.

I picked up my phone from the floor. "Come to my office right away," I heard myself saying to Susie.

"What's your name?" the officer asked me.

"I think I'm going to be sick," running past him but never making it to the toilet. I went into the bathroom and threw cold water on my face. A minute later I was sitting down at my desk with my head bent over.

"Can you tell us what happened?"

I gave the officer my phone and let him listen to the conversation I recorded between Randy and myself. A few minutes later Susie came rushing into my office.

"Are you alright?" she said hugging me. She turned to the officers and asked what happened.

"Who are you?"

"I'm her friend and her attorney. So please tell me what happened."

"We're not sure. We're waiting to question your friend.

"It's Tracey Marks and she's a private investigator."

I finally spoke. "It was Randy Stewart. He came to the office. I recorded it."

"Don't say anything else."

"She needs to come in for questioning."

"Can it wait till the morning?"

"I'm afraid not. There's a man who has a bullet in his stomach and might not make it."

"Fine, let me know which precinct and we'll follow you out."

"I'm sorry but we can't do that. You can follow us but she needs to come in our car."

"I'm right behind you, don't worry," Susie said squeezing my arm.

Fifteen minutes later we were down at the station. Susie and I were waiting in a room to be questioned.

"I'm Detective Morris and this is Detective Black. Sorry for the inconvenience but we're just following protocol. Why don't you start from the beginning and tell us what happened."

Susie nodded the go ahead. I went through the beginning, starting with the death of Stephanie Harris and ending with what transpired in my office.

"As you probably know already, Ms. Marks has a license for the gun and a permit to carry," Susie said.

Detective Morris played the tape and asked me questions about the struggle between Stewart and me and how the gun went off. I explained the best I could.

"Is Mr. Stewart going to make it?" I asked.

"He's in surgery now."

I was shivering.

"You're free to go now but don't wander too far," Detective Morris said cautioning me.

"I didn't want to kill him. He came at me and the next thing I knew the gun went off," I said, feeling nothing as Susie was driving.

"I know sweetie."

"What's going to happen next?"

"I can't imagine they can charge you. Thank God you recorded it. Why don't you stay with us for tonight?"

"No, I'd rather go home."

"Let's get some take out and we'll go back to your place."

"Shouldn't we call the hospital to see how he's doing?"

"Why don't you wait till the morning?"

I heard Susie talking on the phone but my mind couldn't process what she was saying. When she got off the phone, she said, "I called Mark and told him I was going to stay with you for a few hours. I also called Jack. You shouldn't be alone now."

I fell asleep at some point after Susie forced me to have some Wonton Soup. When I woke up the clock said five-thirty a.m. Susie was already in the kitchen making coffee.

"Everything's going to be fine," Susie said.

"How can you say that? Stewart might be dead."

"And that's not your fault. He's a rapist and a murderer. Don't feel sorry for him."

"Can we call the hospital?"

"They're not going to give you any information. You can call Detective Morris in a few hours. His card is on the table. He can tell you what's going on. Jack's going to be here soon."

"I'm fine. He didn't have to come."

"You're not fine."

The doorbell rang. "I'll get it," Susie said.

Jack walked in and took me in his arms.

SUSIE'S WEDDING

"You look like a princess in your silk wedding dress," I said to Susie as I handed her a small gift wrapped box.

"Do you mind if I open it now?"

"Go ahead."

"It is absolutely lovely," Susie said, trying to hold back the tears as she closed the locket that held a photo of Susie and me as teenagers.

She turned around and I clasped the gold locket around her neck.

As I watched her take her vows, tears were running down my cheeks. I was so happy for her and Mark.

It's been several weeks since I shot Randy Stewart, and I still have trouble sleeping. Although I sometimes wake up in a panic, having been able to tell Christine that I caught her mom's killer helps me to sleep a little bit better. I was grateful that Stewart made a full recovery. His trial would be coming up in a few months and I would have to testify. For the most part I'm coping. Jack's been great, though I wish he wouldn't hover over me so much. Hopefully time will change that.

Mark broke the glass and we all applauded and shouted Mazel Tov. It's official; my best friend is married.

"Did I tell you how beautiful you look," Jack said to me as we made our way to the dance floor.

"Only for the umpteenth time."

"You know, there are some women who would love to hear those words," Jack said smiling.

"Well I guess you just happen to be unlucky since I'm not one of those women."

"I wouldn't call that unlucky," he said with a twinkle in his eye.

As I was eating my way through the hors d'oeuvres, a friend of Susie's approached me.

"I know this may not be the right time, but I was wondering if

I could talk to you alone for a few minutes."

Her name was Joanie, and we walked outside the tent down by the water.

"Susie told me you're a private investigator. I'd like to hire you."

THE END

ACKNOWLEDGMENTS

When I was writing my first mystery novel, Looking for Laura, I had no thoughts of turning it into a series. The main character, Tracey Marks, a private investigator, became a part of my life. Her voice was in my head. While writing the book, my teacher, Eileen Moskowitz-Palma, suggested I create a series depicting the personal and professional evolution of Tracey Marks. I am currently working on my third novel of the Tracey Marks Mystery series.

I have to thank my dear friends for their continued support and encouragement. I would also like to thank my editor, Jennie Rosenblum, for her input and patience. Another thank you goes to my writing teacher, Ines Rodrigues, whose insights were invaluable. And a special thanks to my daughter, Carrie, who is my biggest supporter and is always there for me.

About the Author

Ellen Shapiro is a private investigator and the author of Looking for Laura, a Tracey Marks Mystery. Acting on her passion for writing, she enrolled in the Sarah Lawrence Writing Institute where she took courses in creative writing. Her professional expertise in locating people led her to create the storyline and develop the characters for her novel. She has written articles related to her field for both local and nationwide newspapers. She is a member of Mystery Writers of America. When she is not writing or working, you can find her on the golf course yelling at her golf ball. Ellen resides in Scarsdale, New York.